Paint and Piano

Cover art by Brina Williamson

To order additional copies, please contact us.
BookSurge Publishing
www.booksurge.com
1-866-308-6235
orders@booksurge.com

PAINT & PIANO

2007

KERRI BENNETT WILLIAMSON

Paint and Piano

TABLE OF CONTENTS

1	Twins	1
2	Church Picnic	15
3	On Horseback	29
4	Mr. Lawton	43
5	Outside the Mercantile	57
6	The Libertine	73
7	Mr. Worthington	89
8	At the Dressmaker's	101
9	Grand Plans	115
10	Family Table	131
11	Being Seen	147
12	Dinner Party	159
13	Mr. Gilson	167
14	Off of Men	177
15	Mr. Bentley	185
16	Other Offers	199

ACKNOWLEDGEMENTS:

Special appreciation is due to my darling husband (the wondrous genius of a man who keeps my computer in line and online), my beloved sons and daughters (who are each blessed with far greater writing talent and skill than I could ever hope to possess) and my closest family and friends for their complimentary encouragement and moral support. Many thanks also go out to my online readers around the world for all their generously encouraging and supportive emails and comments at www.bonnetsandaprons.com.

.

DEDICATION:

To my sister, who has long performed better than I
with paint, piano and horses.
To my daughters who have surpassed me in art for quite some time.
To my niece, the horsewoman.

1
Twins

Mrs. Hudson's face was all alit with contented concentration as she leaned forward from her favorite silk damask parlor chair, "*Twins,* my dear! Have you quite forgotten? Mrs. Marsden and I must always remain friends, or at least I must make an exerted effort towards the *appearance* of a sort of fast friendship with her, owing to our having twins in common."

Still leaning back comfortably in his leather wingback, Mr. Hudson's brow settled into a right understanding, "Oh, I did not realize this element of etiquette before. I suppose your finishing schools out east must be responsible for your greater knowledge of such things. So this is why you continually put up with the acquaintance of such a silly woman. I comprehend everything completely and entirely now."

"Only one finishing school, my dear… I've told you many times before, as you well know. You surely must recall: Mrs. Cordelia Hyacinth Ladisleader's Final Finishing School for Young Ladies of High Families."

"My apologies… though, with such a grand and lengthy title as that, surely it could have been two or three schools… and how could you expect a man like me to recall such an endless title… not to mention that I have long thought that the woman's name sounds as if conjured out from an old melodramatic novel. It does not sound real to be sure. Come to ponder on it, neither does the name of the school sound real to me at all."

"I *assure* you that the school was most definitely real, her name was real, and she was quite real… a very fine lady by all accounts. I owe her a debt of gratitude." Mrs. Hudson took another dainty sip of her rapidly cooling tea, slightly rattling her favorite diminutive blue and white porcelain cup against its equally tiny companion saucer as she set it down to rest once again.

"I would venture to guess that you owe your father more than perhaps gratitude for sending you there and paying those high prices for lessons in such as sitting, standing and eating properly… all things you might have learned on your own simply by watching one or two fine ladies at social functions and mimicking their manners."

Mrs. Hudson pondered briefly before supporting her husband's observation, "Well… perhaps you are quite right, my love… and I dare say that our daughters have done very well without being sent to a finishing school out east… though I tried my utmost to convince you that we should send them away to be finished."

"I could not part with them as you well remember… and in my books, they were full young to be sent out into possible dangers of the world." Mr. Hudson spoke with conviction and in all seriousness.

"Too true, my love… the world is a most horribly dangerous place… I have done well teaching the girls myself, have I not?" Mrs. Hudson inquired after a compliment from her husband, as women are often wont to do.

"To look at our twins and their beauties and accomplishments, I cannot fault you for anything. They are true perfection." Mr. Hudson took a generous bite of his heavily buttered and still warm toasted crumpet.

"Perhaps not quite perfect, but very nearly, I dare say." Mrs. Hudson took a cue from her husband and nibbled a little of her own lightly buttered crumpet.

"They put Mrs. Marsden's twins to shame, I fear." Mr. Hudson tried to appear saddened for their neighbor, as he took a generous gulp of his tea.

"Well yes, though her twins are only boys, to be sure." Mrs. Hudson mused.

"Only boys, eh?" Mr. Hudson retorted.

Mrs. Hudson was thoughtful, "They are not anything beyond

the purely ordinary, certainly."

"Oh yes, only quite ordinary… and fairly dull… boys." Mr. Hudson smiled.

"Perhaps not truly dull… I never did say dull." Mrs. Hudson defended.

"No, 'tis true that it was I that claimed them as dull."

"Of course, I admit that boys are something to a man, for a man is wont to have his sons, but a woman… well, a woman must have her daughters, you know."

"Yes, I do see what you mean." Mr. Hudson finished off the rest of his tea.

Mrs. Hudson was reminded of her own remaining tea and hoping that it might still be sufficiently warm, picked up her teacup to take another sip, "Of course, my dear husband… a man always will want his boys and his wife will always want her girls."

"But what of your sons, my dear wife… pray tell me… you do not regret them, surely?" Mr. Hudson inquired sincerely, as he completed consuming his crumpet, before allowing it to begin to turn towards cold.

"Of course not… indeed I do not! You must know full well that once a woman has her sons, she adores them fully as much as she does her daughters!"

"And a man feels the same about his daughters, as well as his sons, you can be assured."

"And our sons are turning out very well too, I dare say." Mrs. Hudson stated rather than quizzed.

"Oh yes, I am prodigiously proud of them. They can throw a rock further than those Marsden twins… and run faster too I would surmise… even though they are so much younger." Mr. Hudson attempted some semblance of seriousness.

Mrs. Hudson pondered the matter as she glanced at her crumpet remains, wondering if she would truly enjoy the last near cold bites of it, "Well, Mrs. Marsden's boys are none too energetic and more prone to spend their days indoors doing who knows what. Neither of them are great readers or musicians or anything that I know of… though they are still young and… well… they may turn out to surprise every one of us… after all… in time, you know."

"Yes, perhaps they will grow into fine young men despite their very persistent ordinary and dull beginnings." Mr. Hudson grinned.

Mrs. Hudson's mind was somewhat distracted in another vein, "Perhaps… but, I have long been relieved that her twins are younger than ours. I would surely not like any speculations about matches between them."

"Indeed not!"

Mrs. Hudson's brow furrowed, "That would distress me greatly. To think that anyone should try to make matches between them, simply by virtue of the fact that they are each twins!"

"Nonsense." Mr. Hudson ardently supported his wife.

"Truly!"

"Our girls do deserve better, I dare say." Mr. Hudson speculated.

Mrs. Hudson emphatically agreed, "To be sure! To match ordinarily dull on all accounts up against great beauty and accomplishments would be beyond folly."

"I think such could be considered akin to sin in some books."

"Yes, to be sure… let the currently dull Marsden twins marry equally yoked ordinary girls… and we will save our extraordinary girls for more deserving young men." Mrs. Hudson reached for her embroidery work which sat next to her on a decoratively carved side table, that she might continue working on it during expected further conversation.

Mr. Hudson queried with a self-satisfying smile, "And just how deserving must these young men be, my dear. I must know what kind of fellows to look for in very great detail if I am to help round up proper prospects for our daughters."

Mrs. Hudson most seriously pontificated, "I declare that my girls are the only truly accomplished young ladies for many miles around. Cadence plays the piano like a true master while Florence paints as a master as well, and both our daughters sing like angels. They embroider, ride sidesaddle upon their horses, speak some French and Italian, and can quote enough Shakespeare to make your head spin! All those other girls seem to do, is to sit at their dressing tables preening and staring at themselves in their looking glasses for hours on end, day after day. All some of them can do is to look fairly well, while my girls do better than that naturally... though some girls cannot achieve any level of beauty even if they spend their entire days working at it."

"I agree that our daughters are truly wonderful creatures through and through and I cannot argue with you on any point to be sure... though, I fear that I must warn you that I have seen Florence riding without her sidesaddle many a time... particularly lately." Mr. Hudson delighted in ruffling his wife's feathers.

Mrs. Hudson sighed exasperatedly, "Well, though she can be a little wild when she wants to and does surely seem to prefer to ride with other than her sidesaddle, Florence knows perfectly well *how* to ride sidesaddle and I think I will insist upon her so doing in the future. We surely paid good money for that special saddle."

"To be sure... I remember the outrageous amount right down to the penny. It pained me greatly to pay for those custom fit saddles for the girls and their horses... and then there was the ridiculously exorbitant added expense of the specialist I was required to hire and bring from afar to train our daughters in the use of those high-bred Eastern contraptions. I can assure you that it takes a good deal of ready money to bring a saddle like that into one's stables out west, and a great deal more to set one's daughters up upon them properly. This is not *England*, you know." Mr. Hudson teased.

Mrs. Hudson began to try to justify her particular extravagant peculiarity, "I know, my dear, but..."

"We are not even in the east, for Heaven's sake. I dare say that I might wonder at a woman in the west needing to impress her neighbors with highfalutin' contrivances... from the east, England or Europe. Of course it is far too late for me to object on that point. My money is long since spent on the extravagance."

"Yes, yes... but... to help justify your expense... can you not encourage Florence to obey my wishes as Cadence does?"

"True that if I want to justify what I have spent in investment towards making my daughters like unto fine English ladies or even rich Eastern females, I must force Florence not to waste my expenditure on her sidesaddle by riding all astraddle. I shall certainly speak to her for you, my dear."

"You well know that she listens to you above me." Mrs. Hudson looked up from her embroidery work.

"What is a father for, but to bellow louder than his wife in order to scare their children into submission now and then… and to make the children mind their manners and their mother." Mr. Hudson smiled boastingly, teasing such as if he were the hidden key to raising their children well.

Mrs. Hudson was oblivious for the most part, being currently obsessed with some rebellious threads in her needlework, "Yes dear."

Mr. Hudson half thought that he might state his case again, perhaps in a more clever way, not having received any proper reaction to such a speech, when he heard quick footsteps and a rustling of silken ruffles at the parlor door.

Florence strode in and was all interruption, "Mother, Father… have you seen my new lace gloves? I thought I left them on that new fancy French side table in the front foyer, but they are not there now. I cannot imagine where else I might have left them."

Mr. Hudson simply shook his head in honest ignorance whilst Mrs. Hudson chastised openly, "What have I told you about leaving your things strewn about? You know how I detest an unruly home!"

Florence countermanded, "I know, I know… but it is most convenient to leave one's gloves near the door when you know you will be going out again soon and you need them there to fetch quickly. Did you put them away, Mother?"

"I told Mary to take them to your room."

"Oh, dash it all, Mother! Now I must run up all the way to my room to find my gloves! How you vex me sometimes!" Florence was gone from the room in one bound.

Mrs. Hudson looked at her husband with a lengthy sidelong glance, casting blame directly at him for their daughter's rebelliousness and rude abruptness, "You truly must speak to her. I am beside myself. I do not know how to manage her. She has been too much for me to rein in for years. She should have been fully under your own dominion long ago."

"Yes, my dear. I will do my duty by you and her, and try to assist you in corralling and civilizing her… at least to some degree." Mr. Hudson could not help smiling as he thought of his impetuous lively daughter. Florence oft reminded him of a high-spirited filly. He was very fond of wild horses and greatly appreciated their strength of spirit. It was always a shame to break a free spirit. He truly did not wish to do it.

"How will I make a good match for her if she does not behave as a fine lady?"

"Well, some men… appreciate some spirit, my dear."

"Perhaps one of your wild western men would appreciate such, but…you full well know that I wish for the very best of men for my daughters… and does not such a… a man of high culture, good breeding and enough money… demand a fine lady for his bride?"

Mr. Hudson was deliberating towards the best answer to his wife's question when Cadence suddenly and silently glided into the room, smiling sweetly at one and then the other of them; as she sought out the book that she had left by the chaise where she had been reading earlier.

Mr. Hudson directed a side-stepped answer to his wife, as he motioned towards Cadence, "At least you know that you have *one* daughter who is a very fine lady… quite capable of catching a most superior gentleman."

Cadence looked at her father questioningly, as she decided to set herself upon the chaise to read.

Mrs. Hudson corrected her husband, "Both our twins are equally capable of making the best of matches… if only you would take the trouble to rein the most spirited one in a little."

"I pledged to do my duty as her father and your husband, my

dear. I assure you, I will begin to bridle, harness and restrain her a little more in the future."

Looking at her husband in inquiry, "That puts me to mind… where was she going anyway?"

Leaning forward and beginning to lift himself up to prepare to leave, Mr. Hudson shook his head and shrugged in ignorance.

Mrs. Hudson inquired after her daughter, "Cadence… where was Florence off to?"

"Riding, perchance?"

"Wearing her new lace gloves for riding? *Impossible!*" Mrs. Hudson was half shock.

"I know it seems quite incredulous for her to wear those lace gloves, but I have known Florence to ride out in the most fanciful of outfits of late, for there is a fairly dashing young man visiting one of our neighbors and Florence hopes to treat him to a few good glimpses of her riding, that he might begin to wish to ask for an introduction to her." Cadence smilingly answered.

"What a fine way to put herself before the young men, eh? She'll be certain to get a good match soon, I dare say, my dear!" Mr. Hudson quipped, sinking back into his chair to settle into a little more entertaining discussion.

"I fear that both our girls need a good deal of help making matches." Mrs. Hudson sighed, as if the work cut out before her was dauntingly colossal.

Cadence pretended to be so very engrossed in her book, that she might appear not to notice or hear a thing that was passing between her parents.

"And you are just the one to do it, my dear." Mr. Hudson smiled.

"Who else but their mother would be better qualified?"

"Indeed, I can think of none."

"But there is so much for me to do to bring good marriages about. I do think I will need some assistance from you, my love."

"Though, what can a father do in the case?"

"Well, I dare say you may happily agree to cover the expenses of many balls, parties, gowns and the like... at least... and also be on the lookout for worthy matches in your day to day business."

"Well, you can be assured that I am quite ready to be on the lookout for worthy young men, but, must there truly be such trouble and expenses in the matter? Can we not simply throw a couple of young men into this parlor in front of the girls? Would that not be sufficient to do the trick?" Mr. Hudson offered, seeming all seriousness.

Though she knew he must be joking, Mrs. Hudson looked at her husband in disgusted astonishment as she instructed him in high-minded guidance, "We must at least throw one sort of coming-out ball, more dances and parties, a few dinners, perhaps a card party or two and there will be many trips to the dressmakers, to be sure."

"Since we are trying to find husbands for twins all at once, and will be offering two for the price of one, thus offering me great savings, I will grant you as many as three parties of differing kinds. I will show my generosity as a loving father by also paying for one new gown each for our daughters' ball. That is my final offer." Mr. Hudson seriously proposed.

Mrs. Hudson was beside herself with shock, "For shame, Mr. Hudson! What a way to put it! We are not selling our daughters! What kind of a business proposition that seems. I must be allowed to plan as many dances and parties as need be to get the job done. And only *one* new gown each? Unheard of!"

"Well, I *am* a business man... and do they not have other gowns? I would think that a new gown for the first dance would be sufficient. We must not overcrowd their wardrobes... or armoires, as you prefer to call them."

"I would think that a new gown for every event would be needful."

"Perhaps out east, in England or in Europe, but here in the west... well... so much less is expected out here in the west." Mr. Hudson winked with a self-satisfying smile.

"What will prospective suitors think if our girls only have one new gown each?"

"Bring out some old gowns and pass them off as new, I'd say. You know that men never notice these things anyway. Do not worry what the womenfolk think or say to each other about it, for the men are truly oblivious. A beautiful woman in any dress will do, for a *man*… and since it is men you are trying to catch… only let yourself worry what men think on the matter."

"Mr. Hudson!" Mrs. Hudson was so exasperated with her husband that she threw down her embroidery work to allow all her attentions to the discussion with him.

"Well, now that I've considered the matter only a little, I do not think that I like your way of making matches. It will be far too costly. Perchance we will leave it all to me. I will find the young men. I will show them our girls. I will offer them a small dowry and we will be done with it. I will pay a far smaller price in that way. As a triumphant businessman, I am sure that I can do the business at a far better bargain."

"Let me remind you that we are quite rich enough to provide plentiful dowries for our daughters, if that were the thing these days… out here… but… the coming-out ball is the thing… and a few parties and such…"

"Why a coming-out ball, I ask you? I am fairly certain that the coming-out-ball is not necessarily the thing out here on the frontier… and besides… our girls have already been *out* in society as you call it, and they seem long since too old to me for such things as a coming-out ball."

Mrs. Hudson was all vexation, "I know I should have given their coming-out balls at least a year or two ago… indeed, I attempted to do so… but do you not recall that you insisted on waiting a while? You did not… feel… like putting out the expense of it, at that earlier time."

"Ah… yes… 'tis too true… I suppose I am to blame for this… this difficulty. Well, dispense with the coming-out ball altogether and simply tell all your friends that your husband is a wild boar and horribly cheap. Will that do?"

Mrs. Hudson sighed a great sigh before shaking her head most vigorously and saying, "Oh, Mr. Hudson… what am I to do with you? You are sometimes more vexatious to me than our four children put together. What good will it do for me to tell a few friends that my husband is so backward as to not pay for a coming-out ball for his only two daughters? Many a father has paid far more, having more daughters. I will still be *scorned* throughout the land."

"I trust that your friends will tell their friends and so on and so forth, until everyone who is anyone from our region of the west all the way out to the east, will all know that all is your wicked husband's fault, and you will be pitied… not scorned, to be sure."

"Even if I receive pity instead of scorn, how will that help my daughters towards good marriages?"

"Leave finding husbands to me." Mr. Hudson seemed all seriousness and Cadence could not help but smile.

"It is not proper." Mrs. Hudson sighed with a frown.

"What could be *more* proper?"

"But, my dear…"

"No, even if I had to pay a dowry… I think perhaps you should leave the thing to me."

Mrs. Hudson began to whimper somewhat, "My love… would you deprive me of a *few* gowns and parties? Would you stop a mother from doing her happy duty and her best for her daughters? Would you deprive your *only* two daughters of their best chances at the best of men?"

Mr. Hudson was entirely thoughtful before answering, "I truly hope and pray that two perfectly eligible and rich young men will take our daughters off of our hands one day soon and that no dowry will be necessary for me to pay them in the bargain. No, I do not wish to pay such if I can get away with it. A good businessman does not pay an extravagant expense unnecessarily, my dear. Though, to throw endless balls and parties… and to pay for endless gowns… well… that endless prospect of expenses I will not quite agree to either…"

Mrs. Hudson could begin to see the limitations of her husband's generosity and quite suddenly chose not to press him too far all at once, at the present, knowing that it is far easier to attain coins here and there over time than to gain a basketful of cash in one try; and so in a smiling and pleasing manner smoothed the matter over, "Well, perhaps we can come to some right understanding together… later… a compromise of sorts… I am sure with our daughters being so very beautiful and accomplished, we will not need to throw too many events to find and make them worthy matches."

"Yes, well… I can see that you are coming over to my way of thinking on the matter… and… thank goodness, because I must be off and away to finally tend to the rest of my business affairs for the day." Mr. Hudson quite suddenly announced as he got up, and first kissed his wife on the cheek and then Cadence on the forehead before fairly abruptly leaving the room.

Mrs. Hudson sighed in slight frustration, looked out the window briefly and then picked up her embroidery work again. Cadence continued reading her book after laboring to find where she had left off when she was pretending to be reading instead of enjoying the lively show of banter between her parents that her ears had fully taken in. Florence soon burst into the room again.

"Mother, you really *must* have a talk with Mary. Do you know that I had to search my room from top to bottom to finally find my gloves? I have been up there all this time! It is as if Mary hid my lace gloves in the last place I might look for them. They were not on my bed nor my dressing table as I might have expected, they could not be found anywhere in my armoire, I looked through every last drawer in my bureau with no success and then the very last drawer I opened in that little pretty piece by my bed, well, that is where they *finally* were hidden! The next time you have Mary put something in my room, could you please ask her to place such things on my bed where I will instantly see them the moment I walk in my room? I have thrown away so very much time trying to find those gloves!" Painter twin expelled exasperatedly.

Mrs. Hudson returned, "If you did not leave your things lying around, I would not have to ask Mary to take anything up to your room and…"

"I know, I know, but that is not the point I wish to make now… just please ask her to put things where I will find them instead of hiding them in the last place I will look."

Pianist twin put her book down and tried to help out with a grin, "I wonder that you didn't choose other gloves to save yourself all that time, sweet sister. Come, come, Florence… in Mary's defense, she is used to putting things away for all of us… and how is she to know where you will first or last look? Of course the place you finally find something is the last place you look for it."

Florence flustered, "Yes, but… oh, hang it all! What help to me are all of you!"

Cadence suspected the source of Florence's frustration, "Do you think you may have missed seeing… that new dashing fellow visiting in the neighborhood?"

"Yes, yes… he has usually been out and about at this time of day and I took so terribly long trying to find my new lace gloves that it is likely too late to go riding and…"

"And be seen by him?" Cadence smiled.

"Well, yes… to be sure."

"Worry not my fair sister… for I heard from Mother that there is a church social tomorrow… and I also heard from Mary that *he* will be there. She had it from that other maid… you know… the Stinham's maid that our Mary is friendly with. So, perhaps you should think about giving Mary a hug for her great news instead of wishing to scold her for her tiny mistake!"

Florence's face lit up, "Oh, what will I wear! All my things are getting to be so old! When do we get new dresses again?"

"Wear your new lace gloves to be sure. Indeed, what you are wearing right now will be just the thing for tomorrow, since he did not see you in them today." Cadence assisted.

Florence kissed her sister with such enthusiasm that she all but knocked Cadence off of the chaise. Florence then grabbed Cadence's hand to whisk her away for a lengthy sisterly chat about the new fellow visiting in the neighborhood. They were gone from the parlor in nearly an instant.

Cadence's book was left strewn on the chaise, though luckily not quite onto the floor; while Mrs. Hudson was left alone to her embroidery and ponderings.

2
Church Picnic

Since it was so very fine out on the day of the church picnic spring social, Mr. Hudson had taken his boys on horseback to hone their young riding skills while the Hudson womenfolk were driving their new buggy which fully protected their dresses from any dirt or dust in the air near the road. Florence was all chatter on the way to the church luncheon as the ladies all rode along together. Mother could hardly get a word or phrase in edgewise and reminded Florence to lower her voice that it might not be heard for miles around. Cadence, at the reins, did not have much of a mind to speak, for she preferred to concentrate her thoughts and energies on driving; nor did she wish to interrupt her sister's hopeful speculations and so she listened rather than join in. Such chattering from Florence was all too entertaining to Cadence for her to wish to suppress or silence any of it, at any rate.

Florence still did not know the tall handsome stranger's name, which vexed her greatly. Sometimes a man's name was everything. If he were to become one's husband, surely his name *was* everything. Mary could not recall it. Father had not as yet bothered finding out for them. Even Mother had not found out either, though Florence would have expected her to do so at earlier than her earliest convenience. Perhaps she had been too distracted by her challenging embroidery of late, or it was more likely that her sons had been far livelier than usual owing to the fine early spring weather and so they had exhausted Mrs. Hudson beyond her ability to cope. The two of them had been in and without the house, so much so that Mary was at her wits end to keep the place clean. Mary's constant complaints about Jake and Hank bringing in dust, dirt and mud, were driving Mrs. Hudson to distraction. Oh, that Mr. Hudson was not gone off working on his business affairs so much! Oh, that he were a fine English gentleman at his leisure to remain at home to whip the boys into shape continually.

By Florence's own rarely humble or unbiased estimations, Mother had fallen down in her duty; for Mrs. Hudson should have known all there was to possibly know about the new fellow visiting in the neighborhood, almost at once since the first day that he had come. Mary could only seem to own that the fellow was handsome, very tall, single to be sure, and there were some speculations that he was excessively rich as well. Thank goodness for Mary. At least she was good for some semblance of information of import this time.

As Mrs. Hudson and her lovely twin daughters rode along under the shining sun, further and further behind Mr. Hudson and his fine young sons who were riding ahead at a fair clip, Mrs. Hudson interrupted her girls' conversation to lament a little.

"Why is your father riding so fast? This is not a race, surely! One of my boys might take a spill at that pace! Oh, why does he push them to become men so much? They are still full young to become and measure up to young men."

Cadence condoled lightheartedly, "I would venture to guess that all men wish their sons to be as men the moment they get off their knees from crawling. A mother must relent and accept a little along the way, I suppose."

"And what of his wife and daughters? Why does he not take care for us? It seems most unkind and ungentlemanly for him to ride ahead of us in that fashion. What would Mrs. Darby think if she saw? What would she say?"

"I suppose we might be truly pitied for at least the day." Cadence lightly teased.

"He should have ridden behind us that he might come to our aid should we need any assistance of any kind, such as a thrown wheel, a lamed horse or some other tragic event of that nature."

"To be sure, Mother, to be sure. His riding behind us rather than ahead would have been better for your nerves." Cadence agreed to some degree.

"Look, look… he is getting so far ahead; he is almost out of sight! And he does not seem to ever look back to check on us. Does he not care what becomes of us?" Mrs. Hudson was becoming all agitation.

Cadence attempted to soothe her mother, "But it is such a very fine day and we are traveling at an easy pace on a good road. I am an exceptionally dependable driver whether on a carriage, a buggy, a wagon or whatever wheeled contraption a horse may be hitched up to, as you well know. Father must feel assured that we will be completely safe along the entire way. This buggy is brand shiny new, as you well know… in the newest tip-top shape. He would not ride ahead so far if he imagined that we might be in any semblance of danger."

Mrs. Hudson nodded outwardly while still worrying inwardly.

As she tidied and pulled on her new lace gloves, Florence took full advantage of the moment of silence and conjectured at an energetic pace regarding who would be wearing what and who might be matched up with whom by the end of the day. She glowed with happy speculations. She claimed that the new fellow would be hers by the end of the day, to be certain.

As Cadence guided their buggy into the picnic grounds, Mr. Hudson was there to greet his wife and daughters and to help them out and onto the rapidly greening grass. Each looked a pretty spring picture in their fine newly trimmed bonnets, though Mrs. Hudson feared that their dresses from the spring or summer past would appear to seem so very old to onlookers. Mrs. Darby, wearing a new grand hat trimmed full of at least large colorful feathers, was soon by Mrs. Hudson's side. Mr. Hudson took such opportunity to seek out some business acquaintance or other to try to talk of anything other than business, in keeping with the church picnic spirit and the fine spring day off and away from work related matters. Jake and Hank were off and long gone with friends. Florence swiftly pulled Cadence towards the first group of young people she spotted.

Mrs. Darby began with concern written plainly on her brow, "I notice your husband left you females in his dust today. Not a very fine thing for a man to do to his wife, I would say. If you do not speak to him, perhaps I will. I do believe that he needs a good talking-to. What was he about?"

Mrs. Hudson attempted to defend or some such thing, "Well, he was teaching the boys to ride a little faster, the buggy is so safely sound and new, and my husband knew that Cadence was at the reins. He trusts in her powers of driving implicitly, you know. He did not worry one whit for us on such a fine day. The road was very dry and…"

"But you must have been nervous, all the same. What if something dire had happened? Truly, your husband must be put to notice on these sorts of things. Men must be men to their ladies, as you well know."

Mrs. Hudson did not like to admit it to any degree, but she was in Mrs. Darby's powers as usual, "Yes, of course, I was fretting to the girls somewhat along the way, though Cadence tried to reassure me."

"Such a lovely girl, Cadence is. Oh, but what a wife she will make some very fortunate young man. You know I wish I had a son left for her. If only my sons had been younger. I am keeping an eye out for a good match for her, I assure you, my dear."

"Thank you. I am indebted to you."

"Well, you owe me nothing if I produce nothing."

"But trying is almost everything."

"True… too true." Mrs. Darby shifted her parasol to shade her face completely from the sun as they sauntered along, arm in arm, towards a group of ladies they were inclined to always visit with.

"I have been talking to Mr. Hudson about hosting some events at our house in the next while."

"Yes, well, that is a splendidly good idea, my dear, for you should not put it off much longer. Your girls are fully old enough to marry."

"True, but, this past winter seemed such a long one and I did not have much of a mind to think on such things when my thoughts were all about keeping the house warm… and there is spring cleaning to do… Mary cannot do it all very quickly… especially with Jake and Hank running in and out, tracking mud in and all… and I have been looking for another girl to help out… though Mr. Hudson is loathe to part with any more money on another maid."

"Yes, well, spring is finally here and the birds are singing and it is a perfect season for making matches… so get your house in order and host a ball or some such event."

"To be sure."

Mrs. Darby leaned in close and whispered in her low voice, despite none in earshot as yet, "Have you heard anything of that new young man?"

"A very little."

"Well, his name is Mr. Lawton… a Mr. Oscar Lawton, if you please, and he is all things charming. That is a very nice name, is it not?"

"Yes, very nice."

"He is single, from the east… and rich they say."

"From the east? Rich?"

"Yes, my dear."

"Have you met him as yet, then?"

"Yes, as handsome as everything. Oh, there he is! Wave your girls over to you and I will go fetch and bring him to introduce to you all." Mrs. Darby was off, bustling towards Mr. Lawton.

Mrs. Hudson anxiously tried to catch her daughters' eyes until Cadence finally looked over, and thus she promptly hauled Florence with her to go to their mother. Florence jibbed somewhat, but Cadence was firm and finally triumphed. By the time they reached their mother, they were each a little out of breath, more from Cadence pulling forward and Florence retreating backward, than the length of the walk itself. They were half giggles owing to the tugging between them.

Still giggling a little, Cadence spoke first, "Yes, Mother?"

"Mrs. Darby is bringing that new fellow over to meet us. His name is Mr. Oscar Lawton. Is that not a nice sounding name?"

Florence informed, "Yes, Mother. We know all that by now. He is the talk of all the young ladies. Each thinks herself to be his eventual captor."

Cadence added, "It seems there is nothing we do not know of him already… and Florence is still certain that he will be hers by day's end."

Florence clarified, "Well… I could not help but see him staring at me all the while we were over there, so, it is clear that he likes my looks very much already… and I do like his looks… and his name is surely nothing to frown at. Florence Lawton would do very well for me, indeed."

Mrs. Hudson jittered, "Oh! Here he comes! Here they come! Turn away and pinch your cheeks, girls!"

"Mother… just look at Florence's cheeks… they are quite fully flushed already. On a day such as today, the sun and warmth has done its work for us to be sure… and quite as likely, our faces are too reddened all over already." Cadence corrected.

Florence laughed, "*Au contraire*, my dearest sister… the pinkish hue of our cheeks is truly perfect, I assure you! Worry not, Mamma!"

Mrs. Hudson calmed herself somewhat, "Well, I suppose you do not need to pinch your cheeks after all… and, no… I do not think your faces too red, although, they might have been a tad too ruddy, directly after your silly behavior on your way over here. What were you each thinking, tugging and pulling to and fro like that? What must people think of you two? I declare, you are quite beyond the age of such a spectacle. What must I do or say to bring you to a proper level of decorum?"

Florence explained in a lively spirit, "I did not wish to come, Mother, for I did not know the reason why you were motioning us over to you. Had I known I was to be introduced to the handsome and famous Mr. Lawton, I surely would have cooperated with Cadence in coming promptly."

"Perhaps that will teach you to be more obedient, Florence. You just never know what good may come of doing as you are told." Cadence counseled with a smile.

"Hush, girls, hush… they are nearly here." Mrs. Hudson thrilled and scolded all at once.

Florence side-glanced briefly towards Mrs. Darby and her prize, and then turned to her sister with a lowered yet still delighted tone of voice, "He looks better and better the nearer he gets."

"To be sure… unusually handsome young man that he is… indeed, I do finally see what all the fuss is about." Cadence concurred, amusedly.

Mrs. Hudson hushed her girls again as Mrs. Darby brought Mr. Lawton closer to them. Cadence and Florence half pretended to talk to each other in a fashion that deemed them ignorant of the coming suitor. Mrs. Hudson knew not quite what to do with herself, whether to look here or there, whether to talk to her girls or to pretend to talk to her girls, whether to smile at the venerable Mrs. Darby and the tall handsome companion who was escorting her friend towards them, or whether to pretend to be on the lookout for her husband or their boys. All seemed a kind of awkwardness. The waiting was a sort of torture to at least Mrs. Hudson. Finally Mrs. Darby and Mr. Lawton were near enough for somebody to say something as a first communication between the two parties.

Mrs. Hudson nervously ventured, "Hello there."

Mrs. Darby returned, "Well, here we are… here we are."

Cadence and Florence could pretend not to notice any longer, and thus they looked over and nodded with two degrees of joviality. Florence tried to play coy, wanting at first to seem more like her sister in this way, a shy form that was certainly more natural to Cadence. As always, the clothing and bonnet that Cadence had chosen unmistakably spoke of her tendency towards constancy and quiet. Florence was covered in colorfully luminescent garb that loudly pronounced her inborn flair and delightful clamor that could seldom be ignored by anyone in her vicinity.

Mrs. Darby introduced as she orchestrated official waves of her hand, "Mrs. Hudson, Cadence and Florence, this is Mr. Lawton.

He is friends with and has been staying with all our neighbors, the Stinhams."

Heads slightly bowed politely all around.

Mr. Lawton graciously offered, "It is so very nice to meet you all. I have heard so much about you. The neighborhood is replete with the beauties and accomplishments of you and your daughters, Mrs. Hudson."

"You are too kind, sir." Mrs. Hudson answered while her daughters smiled demurely, Florence still containing her instinct to put herself forward.

Jake and Hank suddenly ran up to the small party, all laughter and red-faced full of energy. Their hair was wet with perspiration due to running about constantly since their arrival to the picnic. Jake grabbed Florence's dress a little in passing, discomposing her somewhat. Cadence quickly stole herself slightly aside to chastise her little brothers in whispers about propriety and manners before she sent them towards their father for some maturely masculine guidance. All others in the little group were not distressed in the least, indeed, beyond Florence's minor notice; they all seemed oblivious to the recent transpiring of boyhood shenanigans.

Mr. Lawton continued his charismatic attentions to the ladies, "I noticed that you and your daughters have not yet sampled from any of the refreshment tables. May I escort you all to take part in the delicious fare?"

They all nodded in unison and Mrs. Darby's face shone with great satisfaction as she spoke to Mr. Lawton almost as if his attentions were for her alone, "You are all things charming, dear sir."

Mrs. Hudson shared with all there but more particularly focused towards Mr. Lawton, "Now that you mention such, it reminds me that I am truly quite famished. Yes, let us proceed towards the refreshments. Are you not very hungry by now, my dear daughters?"

Florence finally spoke to the man she had been admiring from afar for some many days, as she had been most desirous to do long since prior, "It has been many hours since I partook of any nourishment. I am in need of something to be sure. What delights might I expect to be able to choose from, Mr. Lawton?"

Mr. Lawton was only too happy to begin to describe what he considered the most favorable of all samplings available. As they all strolled towards well laid out tables of delectable offerings of sustenance, Mr. Lawton easily charmed each one of them, but his attentions soon turned markedly towards Florence and her own charms.

After having eaten their fill, Mrs. Darby soon took Mrs. Hudson by the arm off and away for a private chat. The two settled on chairs at a table under a tree with their chosen desserts, before Mrs. Darby really got going, "Well now, my dear… it is better for us to leave the young people to themselves for a bit, do you not think? Let them have their little secrets, you know. There is no harm in giving them private moments in public places, I always say. What could be wrong about that? So… what a satisfying thing for you… look at them! That most charming Mr. Lawton is fixed for your daughter Florence, to be sure. I predict a wedding before summer is come and through! What an easy thing for you! No excessive expense of parties or balls and dinners to get one daughter off of your hands!"

"Well, I…"

"Though every single young woman in the town and beyond it has already been vigorously throwing herself at the famous Mr. Lawton, he seems now to have his eyes firmly set upon none but your Florence. And why not?! What a beauty she has turned into… and still full young enough. Always so stylish and colorful! And so very tall, too! A womanly woman, that is for certain. You must feel so very proud of her… and of Cadence too, of course. Yes, Florence is a true beauty and unmistakably full of feminine charms. I would hardly have thought that your Florence would turn out so excessively feminine years ago when she was running about with the boys… it only seems like yesterday, you know… your Florence running wildly about… climbing trees… winning races against boys… looking like one of them to be sure… you know… at Church picnics of old. I remember full well how I would stare at her tomfoolery and monkeyshines, and wonder at her wild behavior. I confess, my dear Mrs. Hudson, that I truly pitied you back then. Oh, how you must have suffered with embarrassment!"

Mrs. Hudson tried to defend herself a little, feeling increasingly mortified, "Well… yes… Florence was always full of energy… but I did *try* to teach her proper manners…"

"Ah, well… that is all past. She has turned out to be a lovely young woman… such a beauty. Though, if you don't mind my saying… she is still a wee bit of a wild western woman, to be sure. Between you and me, I blame that folly in her on your husband… husbands are supposed to rein these young people in when they get to a certain age. What can we women do when the children grow taller, stronger and so much faster than we are? How can we manage them? The men must step in. Surely older children are more the men's domain than our own? Well… nonetheless, Florence is a true beauty, despite her wild ways… I suppose artists are wont to be a little wild or unruly… at least willful, anyway… and what an artist she is too. I wonder if Mr. Lawton has heard of Florence's talents in painting. Well, I wager that he likes a little wild west in his women. Some men do, you know. Likely as not that Florence's galloping about impressed him as, well, very… different than the… well… calmer, more prim and proper women he has likely been used to out east… you know… more like Cadence. Perhaps he finds Florence exotic… in a way… a sort of wild way… wild and beautiful, I dare say."

Mrs. Hudson did not know what to say other than, "I tell her not to gallop… I insisted on walking horses… and she does not prefer her sidesaddle…"

"Well, out here, who expects a sidesaddle anyway? That was a very grand effort of yours to order up sidesaddles for your daughters and quite gallant of your husband to pay for them, but surely it was an unnecessary expense and bother? What do we need with sidesaddles out here in the west? The wilds of the frontier do not warrant sidesaddles, to be sure. I did not trouble with such useless finery for my own daughters… though… they were not allowed to gallop, I can tell you. My husband would have put a stop to it if they had but tried. I made certain that it was clear to he and they that I would not stand for any galloping about… not my daughters at any rate. I would have taken their horses away from them altogether if they had tried galloping on them. I thought such a rule and guidance enough, out here in the west… where sidesaddles would have never been seen… but for you, my dear."

As was often the case when she was around her older, richer and so formidably persuasive friend, Mrs. Hudson became more humble and quiet than usual. She remained silently paused in the sort of awe that she was so very used to, when Mrs. Darby was near to her.

"Well, well… all your worries about Florence flitting about on her filly will be soon past. Her sidesaddle will be neither here nor there. Mark my words… she will be married to Mr. Lawton in a matter of months… her galloping days will be behind us all… thank the heavens above… and then instead of driving you mad, she will be driving a buggy like the rest of us."

Mrs. Hudson hesitated and then offered, "Of course I would like to see both of my girls married off soon."

"And Mr. Lawton is just the one for Florence. We will have to keep on the lookout for a beau for Cadence, now that Florence is all but betrothed."

Mrs. Hudson worried, "Florence is easily thrown in the way of a man because of her passionate spirit and romantic heart, but Cadence makes me wonder. What kind of man could satisfy Cadence?"

"Perhaps Cadence will be easier to please than Florence, though? All she needs and wants is a steady sort like herself. I am quite certain of it."

"Perhaps."

"I know of quite a few young men that we could toss next to Cadence to see what may happen between them."

"Oh, thank you kindly… could you then?"

"Oh, yes… I can send for them from miles around… and we two should begin planning some parties and dances."

Mrs. Hudson only nodded. Mrs. Darby leaned back as much as she could in the chair she was sitting on, sighed as she looked around to see anything of interest to her that there might be to be seen, and then "Oh, there is Mrs. Marsden... did you hear about her lads?"

Mrs. Hudson perked up at the thought of their conversation turning upon somebody else instead of making her own self uneasy, "No... what?"

"Well... you know how her twins are such quiet boys, never running around getting into mischief like your sons tend to do sometimes?"

Mrs. Hudson disappointedly cringed and halted, as she reluctantly nodded ever so slightly and waited in obedient anticipation.

"Well... it seems that their minds are more active than their bodies... more active than anyone might have thought, to be certain... they set a part of the house on fire in one of their strange scientific experiments! Mr. Marsden barely had the fire out before it might have begun to consume their entire house, and indeed, perhaps their entire set of properties!"

"No!"

"Yes! And now the law has been laid down hard upon them both. Mr. Marsden will not let them out of his sight and is making them busy with much work. Thank heavens my own boys are grown and I do not have to worry about such things. Well, like too many boys, they were left to their own devices too many hours in a day, week upon week, month after month, and as the good book says, you know... the Bible says something like... a child left to himself will bring his mother to shame... or her house to ruin... or some such thing. Let that be a lesson to you, my dear. Your own boys are still young enough to wreak great havoc. You had better put them under your husband's wing far more since you cannot be expected to keep up with them... or if he is too busy to mind them... well, you know, since he is gone on his business matters so very much of the time... have your stable master or ranch hand or some man about the place take greater charge of them."

Mrs. Hudson felt most uncomfortable and was all silence once more, though she nodded compliantly in a repentant humility.

Mrs. Darby took pity on her protégé by spotting the Hudson

twins, "Oh, look there... there are your beautiful daughters and all their young friends. What a happy party on such a fine day! Love is in the air, my dear! Spring is in the air!"

The two ladies continued in their afternoon chatter, well shaded under the tree they had chosen for that very purpose.

By the end of the church picnic that day, it was clear to all folks with eyes to see that Mr. Lawton had his own eyes fully transfixed upon Florence Hudson. Cadence was reservedly happy for her sister, though all other young ladies of marriageable age and demeanor at the springtime event felt some level of envy that one of the Hudson twins had captured the imagination of he who was considered to be the most eligible bachelor currently residing in the area and round about it.

3
On Horseback

O h, there you are… I have found you… but, where is Florence?" inquired Mrs. Hudson of her steady twin, at the lovely lass's bedroom door.

Cadence promptly answered from her settee, where she had been reading, "I am quite certain that she went out riding. She is out on her horse, Sunset."

"Did you notice if she was riding sidesaddle… or… I dread to ask… like a man, all a-straddle?"

"Oh, I would assume that her special side-saddle is still hanging up in the barn or the stables… somewhere. I fear to inform you, my poor dear mother, that Florence's especial expensive high society riding device has long since become a home for spiders."

"Why must she persist in riding in such a wild manner?" Mrs. Hudson expressed in distress.

"Well…" Cadence began to try some explanation for her sister.

"She knows what is expected of her. I am certain that your father spoke to her on the matter recently, as I had instructed him and he had agreed to do. I know that Florence seldom pays attention to me, but will she not even listen to her own father and abide by *his* counsel?"

"You know how willful she is, Mother, and so very inclined to do as she wishes… we all know that she has long been oft inclined to gallop… and surely… it is far and away a better thing for her to ride astride. Sidesaddle feels none too safe when such speed is attempted. I can attest to that fact, to be sure."

Mrs. Hudson was all agitation, "Oh dear me, why can your sister not behave as a fine English lady?"

"Perhaps you should remind her that some day soon she may meet with a fine English gentleman while out riding, and that to behave far more like an English lady, would be more to her benefit in achieving the attentions of such a gentleman."

"Perhaps, yes… and perhaps you might mention such to her also."

"I dare say she might mend her ways for the sake of a chance at love and a worthy match."

"Yes… that is the way to convince her to listen and mind our counsel… indeed it is… she will do anything… almost anything… to please the young men." Mrs. Hudson was intensely thoughtful.

"Perhaps with the most eligible Mr. Lawton roaming around in the neighborhood, Florence can be convinced to dust off her sidesaddle and slow down to properly impress and then to fully catch the new fellow." Cadence smiled with a wink.

"I dare say… yes… perhaps you can convince her to slow down so that she can safely sit sidesaddle. You do. I can depend on *you* in that regard."

"Mother, you very well know that I savor safety as assuredly as she hungers for excitement… and you can depend on me for many things."

"Yes, yes. Why can your sister not be more like you? It is so distressing to worry over such a daughter!"

"But Mother, surely you recall that only yesterday you were lamenting that I was not more like my sister and that I might end up a spinster because I will not make any effort to put myself forward and in the path of any eligible man."

"Well, of course you could take a lesson or two from your sister on that count."

"Can you not see, Mother… how very different she and I are? She is all passion and I am content to remain calm."

"Oh, why can you not each learn from the other?"

"Perhaps, by and by… we will."

"At least try to convince her to make use of the sidesaddle…

for my sake. I paid a pretty penny for those custom saddles, to be sure."

"If she will not walk her horse as I do mine, and she must gallop, surely it is better for her to sit squarely on her horse rather than to be tossed off to her death or at least some serious injury. Since you do not ride, you know not that to sit sidesaddle is barely to sit on the horse at all. One seems almost more off than on, when sitting upon such a saddle. It is no wonder that I fear to proceed faster than walking. Indeed, since you indentured me to that sidesaddle, I have been riding less than ever before… and I never venture beyond walking now." Cadence near lamented.

"Yes, well… mercy me… why will she not slow down… I purposely requested of your Father to purchase walking horses for you both and so he did… much good that a walking horse has done in your sister's case. I was under the misapprehension that a walking horse was a walking horse… and that it would not but walk. Why did she ever insist on teaching her walking horse to run in the first place?"

"I do not know… but that such as running is in her very nature… and since she needs must gallop, we can not wish her only half on her horse, about to be tossed off her sidesaddle at any moment."

"Oh my, but can there be any twin daughters who look so very alike, who are so extremely divergent in thought and passions?"

"I think not."

"Since you were tiny girls, and nobody but me could tell you apart…"

"You did dress us identically… it is hardly any wonder that only you knew Florence from me."

"But you *were* identical. In the beginning, I had difficulty knowing you two apart myself… but in such short order, Florence's willful spirit was near always apparent and that became the surest way to distinguish between the two of you." Mrs. Hudson sighed.

Cadence began to reminisce, "I dare say we enjoyed tricking others when we were younger. Florence always wanted to pretend to be me and forced me to play as her… that we might fool everyone…"

"But nowadays… you two are so very different…"

"We are not really *that* divergent, Mother…"

"Yes… yes, you are."

"Perhaps only in spirit or temperament… we differ slightly?"

"In dress, in manner, in all facets of behavior…"

"In some behavior and of course our attire, yes…"

"Of course you two could fool us all if you exchanged dress and mannerisms, but…"

"You would not have us exactly the same, surely?" Cadence sincerely inquired of her mother.

"I suppose not."

"I think I feel a sudden and strong urge to go riding. Perhaps I will go out and find Florence and speak to her about sidesaddles for you. Trust me to convince her to ride sidesaddle with me for a while." Cadence offered.

"Yes, yes… that would be most helpful if you would… if you could convince your sister…"

"I am determined to convince her to ride sidesaddle as a mode of transportation towards making a perfect marriage. Perhaps she will promise to ride sidesaddle until she marries… and then once she is married, perhaps her husband will hold sway over her to keep her from galloping forevermore." Cadence smiled to proffer such an iron-clad plan.

Mrs. Hudson's furrowed brow relaxed a good deal, "Yes… yes and… I dare say that once she begins having children, her galloping days will be done…"

"Very likely, Mother… very likely." She embraced her mother gently before leaving her to her motherly ponderings.

Cadence was promptly off and away towards the stables after a few moments spent readying herself, and some more moments spent fetching a light snack in the kitchen. Upon arriving amid the corrals, she found the stable master.

"Tex… would you mind saddling up Ivory for me?"

"Only too happy to fetch your horse for you, Miss."

"I suppose you had better put the sidesaddle on her."

"Yes, Miss Hudson. It's a fine day for a ride, Miss."

"Yes, very much so… thank you, Tex."

"It's nice to see you getting back on your horse finally, since you haven't been riding in so very long."

"Yes, I know… I've been cooped up inside all winter and I thought that on such a fine, dry spring day, I should make sure I remember how to ride. You wouldn't happen to know which way my sister rode out, would you?"

"That-a-way… westward, Ma'am." Tex pointed as he answered Cadence's query.

"And would you happen to know where she was to be riding today?"

"Said something 'bout a ride 'round the Stinham's properties."

"Of course… yes… and, she hasn't been back this way yet?"

"No, Miss."

"All right then, I will ride that way and if Florence returns, tell her where I've ridden to… and please do send her out to retrieve me."

"Yes, Miss. Will do, Miss."

Cadence fairly patiently waited for Tex to bring Ivory complete with sidesaddle and bridle. He was prompt as always. Cadence felt a good deal awkward as she mounted Ivory, even with Tex's assistance. She thought to herself that it had been far too long since she had been up on her horse. It was good to have an excuse to do so this day. She was not as yet ready to become a buggy, wagon or carriage lady, exclusively. She preferred to stay horsewoman to some degree, though never quite the energetic rider that her sister was. If only she wasn't so prone to obey. The sidesaddle did tend to limit her enthusiasm for riding. Oh, for the good old regular saddle days… before she was playing the fine young lady for her mother. Perhaps sometime she should choose to follow Florence's example and ride the old western way. Indeed, she did not wish to forget how to gallop altogether, after all!

Cadence rode out westward towards the Stinham's place. She

and Florence spotted each other almost simultaneously along a common road and hailed each other with cheerful smiles from afar. Cadence continued walking her horse towards her sister, though Florence chose to canter enthusiastically to meet up with Cadence more speedily.

Florence first spoke, "What brings you out here?"

"You." Cadence grinned.

"Me?" Florence was curious.

"I decided to ride out to find you."

"And now that you have found me, what do you want of me?"

"I wish to ride with you… and speak with you."

Florence motioned which direction they should ride together and then proceeded to continue their conversation as their horses calmly walked side by side, "It is nice to see you finally riding after all this time. I've missed our rides together. But, what do you wish to speak with me about. You have me at a sudden loss and all curiosity."

"I told Mother that I would counsel you." Cadence smiled broadly.

"Counsel me… for Mother… oh no, not that!" Florence laughed.

"Oh, yes… and you are well used to it."

"Yes, yes… of course I am accustomed to excessive counsel from all sides, and more particularly your own counsel and fine example, oh wise and most obedient sister… you put me to shame, as always."

"Oh, you know that we are simply of differing temperaments… and that I do not always obey either."

"Well, you've always seemed to me to be the steady and obedient daughter whilst I've long been the willfully rebellious one."

"I do not truly think that at all. You are passion, I ponder. You feel, I think. We are simply as if two sides of the same coin."

"True… too true. You have proven yourself the thinker."

"And can you guess what I have been thinking on my way here?"

"I have no idea, truly."

"Do you know how Mother frets about you galloping all astraddle?"

"Oh, not that! Leave me be, to my horse-riding joy!"

"Yes… well, I do understand that you love to gallop, but you would please Mother so very much if you could walk your horse and use your sidesaddle at least sometimes, or perhaps just for a little while… you know… until she is fretting more about something else." Cadence grinned.

"Father did speak to me a little on the matter. Mother has more than hinted here and there. I do keep planning on walking with my sidesaddle… but then… I always seem to feel like going for a gallop."

"You have proven that you follow your feelings." Cadence smiled.

"Yes, yes I do."

"Well, much expense was laid out for our sidesaddles and so forth, and we were given *walking* horses that were especially purchased for us… we should comply with our parents' wishes… at least some of the time."

"I do not believe that Father truly cares if I…"

"He *does* care about the wasted expense."

Florence pondered briefly, "I suppose he does."

"Mother cares a great deal. She worries what people think and say about her daughter riding wildly about the countryside. She wishes for us to be as fine English ladies." Cadence reminded.

"You know that I do not care what people think or say." Florence tossed her head defiantly.

"Well… my dear sister… to appear the fine lady, is to catch a better man…" Cadence winked half teasingly.

"Errant nonsense… I will not relent on that count. I do not believe it." Florence smugly announced with a winkish smile.

"Mother thinks that a fine English gentleman would prefer a fine lady, the kind who would only ride sidesaddle… though since there are no English gentlemen to be had in these parts for the time being, perhaps you should consider what a man like… Mr. Lawton,

35

let us say… would think of a fine lady riding sidesaddle compared to a wild woman riding in the western style."

"Oh, I am certain that he would not care either way."

"Well, ladies riding sidesaddle are few and far between out here on the wild western frontier… and such would set you apart from all others to be sure." Cadence tried.

"I tend to believe that my high spirited style has already set me apart." Florence laughed.

"You are determined to stay as you are?"

"You know that I always tend to do what I wish." Florence was emphatic.

"Perhaps you could at least ride sidesaddle a little near home from time to time… simply to please Mother and to allow Father the satisfaction in thinking that his money paid to set you and your horse up was not all in vain." Cadence attempted.

"Perhaps." Florence finally complied.

The sisters each looked especially lovely that fine spring day. There was a perfect mix of clouds and true blue sky, and the sun danced in and out from behind the silvery clouds, beams and shards of light shining upon the twins and their handsome mounts. Cadence did truly appear as a fine English lady, sitting sidesaddle, as Florence was every bit a superior western riding woman. Both young ladies sat straight and tall in their saddles, their horses seeming proud to display them to the world.

A man's voice was suddenly heard from behind them, "Whoa! Ladies!"

The young ladies turned to see that it was young Mr. Stinham riding up to them. At any other time prior, Florence would have been loath to speak to him and might have found some hurried excuse to gallop away, leaving Cadence to politely converse with him before finding her own pretext to part company, for the thoroughly frumpy, somewhat stupid and especially self-important Mr. Vincent Stinham was no young man most self-respecting young ladies would enjoy spending any time with. However, it was a very different matter now, for the especially agreeable Mr. Lawton was a guest resident at the

Stinham family home and thus speaking to this Stinham fellow could perchance advance any young lady's chances with Lawton. Florence instantly determined that she could exercise some patience with Stinham, on the likely chance that Lawton might ride up or that Stinham may later put in a good word for Florence with Lawton due to her friendliness and appeal on this occasion. Cadence and Florence both nodded hellos to the young man as Stinham approached.

After Stinham came nearer to them, in no especially mannered or pleasant way, he jubilantly shouted fairly loudly, "Well, well… ladies! What a fine day for a ride, yes? And after such a long winter, too, as you well know. Spring has finally come! How now to see you so close to my property! It is almost as if you were looking for me… and now here I am in all my glory! Are you not pleased to meet up with me? I suppose you missed me at the church picnic, but, alas… I could not be spared from some business duties, poor fellow that I am. Well, well… I am delighted to see my lovely neighbors. We never see enough of each other, to be sure. We must find excuses to see each other more often!"

Florence had wondered when he would draw breath and pause that she or her sister might say something, and thus she took the first opportunity to take pains to be pleasant, "Hello, Mr. Stinham. It is a fine day and we are pleased to meet you."

Stinham answered, switching his momentary gaze from Florence to fixating on Cadence, "Yes, yes… well… you both look lovely today… Oh, what a fine horsewoman you must be, Miss Cadence Hudson! Look at you on your sidesaddle! I can't recall the last time I ever saw any woman in these western parts riding sidesaddle… well, it must have been you last year, I would think. What a circus woman you could be the way you balance on that contraption! I do not know how ladies do it, indeed I do not. I would be thrown from my horse or slip off to my death for certain if I ever attempted such a feat!"

Cadence thanked him for the compliment, while Florence wondered how to bring Mr. Lawton into the conversation without being insulting or appearing desperately obvious in her desire to become attached to him and he to her.

Stinham continued, "Yes, Miss Cadence… you know that you remind me greatly of fine ladies out east or in Europe. It has been a while since I have been to Europe. I do wish to go again. Yes, indeed, I must plan an extended trip or tour soon. Now, neither of you young ladies has ever been over the ocean, have you?"

Cadence and Florence both shook their heads against the affirmative, and indeed, they both wondered if they would be treated to a lengthily boring dissertation on the delights of Europe by this young boastfully dull and undeservedly wretchedly rich young man.

Just as Stinham seemed to be fully taking in excessive breath to continue with his prideful bragging, another manly hale was heard by them all. Florence was first to match voice to personage, and her face was most suddenly all alight to recognize Mr. Lawton riding towards them. She waved her hand in the air especially energetically, not trying one jot to mask her excitement in seeing him.

"Hello, sir!" Florence called out first, while her sister composedly nodded with a polite smile from beside her. Mr. Stinham also smiled to see his friend.

Mr. Lawton hurried his horse a little to lessen the distance between them before haling back again, "Hello! What a delight to find you all here."

The Hudson girls and Stinham all did nod, but Florence's enthusiasm at seeing Lawton could not be mistaken by anyone there.

"I was seeking out my friend, but what a greater find to see him with you both." Mr. Lawton continued as he glanced at Cadence and then his gaze firmly settled upon Florence.

"We are so very delighted to see you." Florence spoke for both herself and her sister, her eyes fixedly meeting most happily with Lawton's.

"What a treat this beautiful day is and beautiful ladies surely can be an even greater treat for the eyes." Lawton flattered most generously.

Florence blushed near considering the compliment entirely her own.

Lawton glanced at Cadence once more and discovered, "Sidesaddle! You are most obviously a skilled horsewoman. Not many women dare to travel sidesaddle, especially out in the west where it is not so admired as in the east or in Europe. Bravo to you, I say."

Cadence could not resist smiling over to her sister in a measure of teasing vindication before fairly defending Florence with a generous accolade, "My dear sister rides sidesaddle equally well, if not far better to be sure, Mr. Lawton, though she tends towards galloping, and we all must know how ill advisedly unwise and truly dangerous riding at such a fast clip could be on a sidesaddle. Surely it would be errant folly in such a case? I love to walk my horse, but since Florence loves to gallop, it is an especially good thing that she rides in the western way most days."

Both men nodded vigorously, saying such things as, "Too true." and "To be sure".

Florence was all delight at the pleasingly praising attention.

As their horses each swatted flies away with their tails and shimmied their skins for the same purpose, the four riders traded pleasantries for a short time before Florence began hinting to her sister with her eyes and movements, that she wished for Cadence to distract Stinham and even move him away somewhat, that she herself could fully focus on Lawton, and in so doing, obtain Lawton's complete and doting attention upon herself. Cadence knew what Florence was about and chose to pretend otherwise in feigned ignorance for a time, as she had not determined within herself if leaving her sister alone in such a way with this man was entirely within perfect propriety, but more especially did she wish *not* to have Stinham all to herself (oh what sheer torture that could be!) for whatever length of time Florence would surely wish to dote upon Lawton. No, propriety or not, Florence would have to suffer with the company of Mr. Vincent Stinham just as Cadence must, for Cadence truly did not wish to become a target of affection for the young Mr. Stinham.

Since Florence's attempts at subtly persuading Cadence to take

Stinham away somewhat had failed miserably, she took the matter into her own hands, "Well, Mr. Lawton, as you so admire a lady on a sidesaddle, let me demonstrate to you why I must ride in the western way instead. Let me challenge you to race me back to my home."

Lawton accepted and thus they were both off and away galloping, leaving Cadence to patiently walk her horse home in the dire company of the horridly rich Mr. Vincent Stinham. She would *thank* her dear sister with much scolding later on, for the opposite of a pleasurable experience at present.

Once Cadence and her irritatingly verbose escort arrived back at her home, she found that Florence and Lawton had been enjoying a private tête-à-tête sitting together in the garden. Cadence was forced to invite Stinham to join her, as she joined Florence and companion, for Cadence was not desirous of being left alone any longer with her annoying neighbor, nor did she fathom quite how to encourage him to take himself homewards.

Mrs. Hudson soon spied the pretty little party in the garden and had refreshments brought out to them, along with convincing her husband to join in with her on an impromptu visit with the young people. Mrs. Hudson could not be more delighted while her husband was summarily bored and he resisted most vehemently as his wife hinted towards bringing the young men in for dinner. No, Mr. Hudson found ways and means to put a stop to that direction of arrangement in his wife's mind, for he dearly desired a private dinner that evening with only his dear family, after having suffered a long and tiring day's work.

Soon the young men were riding away from the Hudson property. Florence was in raptures over Lawton, Cadence was contemplative about the new young man in relation to her dear sister, Mr. Hudson was satisfied to be looking forward to his nearly served meal and Mrs. Hudson was all disappointment that the company of one particular young eligible man was not to be added to their dinner party that night. However, plans were set firmly in motion in her mind for a dinner party including Lawton very, very soon.

Well after sundown that night, Florence visited Cadence in

her room to swoon over Lawton. When Cadence began to tire of her sister's endless ecstatic ramblings, Florence pounced in a good humored jibe, "Stinham is enamored with you!"

"What?!" Cadence jolted.

"Mr. Vincent Stinham is half mad in *love* with you!"

"Are *you* mad?!"

"No, no, no… he is *passionately* in love with you!"

"Twaddle, I tell you!"

"Are you *blind*? He swoons over you constantly." Florence laughed.

"Nonsense. He is like that with most every young woman round these parts. I have seen him myself."

"No, no… I do believe that he reserves special attentions for you."

"Oh, please… *do* be serious…"

"If you do not like him…"

"You know that I would never…"

"Then you must stop being so very nice to him… for you are encouraging him… he will give you an offer very soon if you are not very careful and you do not change your tone with him."

Cadence attempted protesting her innocence in the matter, "But I never have… I do not…"

"You dare not allow him to continue to fall for you… you must spurn him somehow…"

"I rarely ever speak to him as it is!"

"I dare say that *today* was the cincher. He has fallen completely over for you." Florence shook her head reproachfully.

"Well… I assure you that if he fell for me today, such was *your* fault for leaving me to ride home with him! And that puts me to mind that I owe you a scolding for galloping off and leaving me with Stinham like that! How could you… you selfish, unfeeling girl!"

"Oh, dear… of course I was being selfish… wanting to get away from Stinham… and keep Lawton to myself… but you would not choose to follow my hints…"

"Of course not… I did not wish to be left *alone* with Stinham!"

41

4
Mr. Lawton

Mrs. Hudson's little dinner especially designed to bring Mr. Lawton into the family by forever attaching him to Florence was unfortunately severely marred by the presence of Mr. Vincent Stinham, for Mrs. Hudson, loving mother that she was, could seem to find no way to invite the desirable former young man without inviting the undesirable latter. Though she attempted to form any creative power of thought towards a perfect solution on the matter, it seemed that the fates were surely against her on this point and the annoying fellow came along with the dashing young man.

A day before the dinner, Mrs. Hudson found her studious daughter reading in the parlor and interrupted Cadence's book to enlighten her whilst about to go begging for her assistance in the upcoming affair, "Cadence my dear… Mr. Lawton will be joining us for dinner tomorrow night! Is that not grand for your sister? Indeed, I know that you would agree with me that it is a wondrous thing for Florence! Every girl in town and beyond it is already wild with envy that Florence has near got the man as her very own! Mrs. Darby told me all kinds of things pertaining to what everyone is saying regarding Lawton and his being in raptures over Florence. You would not believe what all the young ladies and their mothers are already saying! Speculations for a magnificent match are already abounding! I could not be more delighted, as you can well imagine. Now… though… there is one discomfort… for you, my poor dear… and I do regret to inform you that I could not find a civil way to bring your sister's prospective fiancé here to dine with us without also inviting that odious young Mr. Stinham into our intimate family party… So, do you think that you could be a distraction to him… you know… so as to leave Florence free to visit more attentively with her dear Mr. Oscar Lawton?"

Cadence was all vexation, "Oh… dear no… not that! Mother! How could you ask *that* of me? You know how we all loathe the man and… well…"

"Oh, please… can you not be patient with our youthful neighbor for Florence's sake?"

Cadence was all determination and counsel as she enlightened her mother with some news, "Mother… Florence has informed me that she is very certain that… that Mr. Vincent Stinham… has taken an interest… in me. You would not wish to gain him as my *own* fiancé would you? If I converse with Stinham to distract him, I may receive an offer from him… before Florence does from Lawton!"

Mrs. Hudson became all thoughtfulness, "Oh, no… that could not be… surely that is not so… perhaps it is only Florence's fancy… her overactive imagination… she is such a creator of stories… or she is simply teasing you… you know how she so likes to tease… so much like her father in that way… Cadence, you have not noticed any preferred attentions from him… have you?"

Likely more a defensive posturing rather than a purely factual and entirely honest answer, Cadence began to go against her more humble nature and expressed, "Well, I am not inclined to notice any such possible attentions my way… though… once Florence informed me of her observations in the matter… of young Mr. Stinham and his attentions towards me… in retrospect, I could see that such might be so. Florence has counseled me most vigorously to avoid all interactions with Mr. Stinham… unless I wish for a proposal from him. I do think that she is right in this, Mamma."

Mrs. Hudson lost her mind momentarily as her imagination soared wildly in strange places, "Well… as sole heir to the Stinham family fortune and properties, he will be horribly rich to be sure… he is very eligible… not unkind… if you could tolerate being his wife…"

PAINT & PIANO

"Mother!" Cadence was all horror.

Mrs. Hudson returned to relative reason, "Yes, yes… forgive me… he is detestable to be sure… of course you could not be so very mercenary as to… someone like you could not… I suppose it is beyond a possibility for you to… oh dear, it is so sad that so much money should go to such a young man. What a waste. Of course he will have to find himself some other young lady… a very stupid or a very mercenary woman… and any woman who could overlook his… many… follies… will be very well taken care of it is certain. Sometimes one wonders at heaven and the universe and all these sorts of things. Why are some of the most stupid people so very rich? And why must some women trade love for money in marriage? I pity the girl who marries Mr. Vincent Stinham, to be sure… though she will be so very rich. Alas, I…"

"Enough about him and marriage with anyone, Mother… what are we to do with him while he is here for dinner? Can not you or Father keep him busy, that I will not be required to?"

"Yes, yes… to save you, I suppose we must. Oh dear me, but your father will be so very distressed. I fear he might be quite angry with me. He was loathe to suffer a dinner with company to begin with… you don't know what lengths I had to go to, to bring the scheme about… and then he was truly thoroughly put out to hear that young Mr. Stinham was a part of the package… you know… just to get Lawton here for Florence… and now… to know that you can not keep the repulsive young man occupied for your sister's sake… that your father and I must do it… oh, that will do your poor papa in for certain. How will he digest his meal properly? It will surely ruin his entire evening… and it will be the devil to pay for me! What am I to say to your father?"

Cadence felt a stroke of genius come upon her, "What about the boys? Jake and Hank might love to be assigned to keep our loathsome visitor distracted! This would be just the sort of game that they would love to play! Do not necessarily tell them the reasons why, but simply say that they may tease, taunt and bore Mr. Vincent Stinham as much as they may like. Ordinarily, they are banned from such enterprises

45

and thus they may delight all the more in their taunting, picking at, and babbling towards the man. What do you think? They could be of some assistance in this regard, could they not?"

Cadence felt a little prick of guilt for her inventive idea as Mrs. Hudson lit up, "Oh, yes… very decent thought, my dear girl. My energetic boys could be convinced to bother young Mr. Stinham the evening through! I will solicit your father's help in this. He will know exactly what to say to his boys to create the best and most effective result during dinner and afterwards. Such will give him so very much comfort to know that he and I will be able to share the responsibility of distracting Mr. Stinham with our boys, since you can not be expected to do so. Jake and Hank will surely take over and enjoy having a grand time of the task in the process! Your father and I will be spared any trouble with young Stinham all evening long and the perturbing fellow will be thwarted from any designs he might have upon winning you… yes, rest assured… your brothers will be kept busy keeping Stinham busy. Oh, this is a pretty plan of pure genius, my dear! Your father will be so very proud of the two of us for coming up with such a plan!"

By the next evening, just prior to her finely planned dinner, Mrs. Hudson was flitting about making certain that every little thing was perfect for their honored guest, Mr. Oscar Lawton. She felt assured that her husband had primed their boys sufficiently to do a very fine job halting any attentions that Mr. Stinham might wish to pay Cadence, and also to prevent the annoying young man from interfering with his friend's attentions towards Florence. Though the plan of soliciting such tireless help of the boys was initially concocted to protect Cadence from Stinham while also saving Mr. and Mrs. Hudson from bothering with the man, it was soon strikingly remembered by Mrs. Hudson that distracting Stinham was first vigorously considered to protect Florence, that she and her young man could be left to themselves as much as could be considered possible in an intimate family dinner party such as was to be. All must be done to keep Stinham from interfering with Lawton's attempts towards Florence. Yes, that was the material point of it all.

Mary had been kept horridly busy all the day long and had already long since run out of energy, though she still had a grand meal to put on. She had begun to make hints of complaining but was promptly reminded by Mrs. Hudson that she had always had it very easy in the Hudson household since such fancy formal dinners or parties of any kind had forever been such a very rare thing here, being that Mr. Hudson usually preferred a simple meal and always desired a quiet evening without company (owing to his regular need to recover through peaceful rest, from his day's work of business). Mrs. Hudson helped Mary to determine that she was lucky indeed to only be required to work so very hard on such exceptionally rare occasions. Mary was cajoled into repentance, happy acceptance and a renewal of strength and energies that could carry her throughout the evening. Mary also partook of some quickly gulped food with attendant strong coffee, which also would entirely aid the young maid to fulfill her many laborious duties with full vigor and energy until evening's end, whereupon she would finally retire to her bed beyond fully exhausted (though joyful to know that the next day would surely go easier on her).

Mr. Lawton was everything pleasing upon his entry into the Hudson home. Indeed, Mr. Lawton was in every way as pleasing as Mr. Stinham was unpleasant. For every pleasant word that Lawton spoke, Stinham contrasted with at least three dull, boastful or annoying words. Lawton was handsome and charming. Stinham was slothfully irritating. Lawton was thoroughly attentive to Florence. Stinham attempted attentions towards Cadence. Throughout dinner and conversational visiting afterwards all evening through, Mr. and Mrs. Hudson did all in their power to steer Stinham away from Cadence, as she ignored the man to her utmost abilities. Jake and Hank delighted in their especially assigned duties and were as if nimble wolves nipping at a lumbering moose, sitting either side of young Stinham at dinner and staying so very close to his sides afterwards, as if flies on a dirtied cow. Stinham tried to escape the boys but it was of no use. The more the abhorrent young man tried to avoid them, the more they delighted in pestering him, tiring Stinham with questions of every strange variety, and torturing him with outlandish tales from their young boyishly energetic imaginations. What an exceptional pair of partners in crime the young lads were. Their father had known that they surely had such innate abilities and potential within them, but even he was somewhat surprised at their high levels of instinctive skill in the worthy enterprise.

Stinham was forced to exercise patience with the boys in order to keep up his appearance of good temper and kindness, all the while that he could not help but recall his former gleeful anticipation at the thought of getting closer to Cadence that evening. He had not given thought to how close he would find himself forced to be to her younger brothers. In point of fact, Jake and Hank did so very well at exasperating Stinham; that even Mr. Hudson was brought all the way to a little repentant pity, and said father did feel the need to step in now and then simply to make certain that things were not taken too far by his sons. As loath as he was to feel a great deal of compassion for the young Stinham, Mr. Hudson did think that he might need to keep some semblance of neighborly friendship with the Stinham family as a whole, at least. He, his wife and Cadence had been spared so much of Stinham and his general annoyances due to such amazing raw and budding talents of the boyish youngsters, and so, Mr. Hudson thought he could and should do a good turn by sparing Stinham if only a little here and there. Even with such kind and caring interferences of Mr. Hudson, by the time Mr. Vincent Stinham left the Hudson home late that evening, he was delightedly and decidedly happy to get himself out of there and to go home for respite's sake. Though he had not given up entirely on Cadence, he had determined that the Hudson household, particularly when the dauntingly intimidating younger brothers were about, was not the best place to entertain attempts at attentive intentions towards a young lady. No, he firmly determined that he should try his hopes and luck again with Cadence elsewhere. Courting around the forebodingly impressive likes of Jake and Hank Hudson was decidedly impossible!

As much as Stinham had failed to find a closer and surer footing towards Cadence, his friend Lawton had contrarily succeeded with Florence. Mrs. Hudson and her flamboyant daughter were both in a fine way towards planning a wedding. Cadence watched and waited. Mr. Hudson was more reflective than responsive towards the idea as yet. Jake and Hank had barely noticed the impressive gentleman in Mr. Lawton and his successes with their colorfully beautiful older sister; for they had been far too busy veraciously torturing the pitiable Mr. Stinham with all manner of vexations that they could dream up for one event.

Because Mr. Stinham had suffered an unpleasant evening dining with the Hudson family, Mrs. Hudson had been easily able to manage an invite for luncheon the next day to only Mr. Lawton. What a delight! What a mercy! Some excuse or other had been made on both sides: Mr. Stinham having suddenly claimed excessively important business affairs to attend to on his father's behalf and Mrs. Hudson manufacturing a need for the most eligible Mr. Lawton to keep her lovely Florence entertained for a time; that she would not become lonely during her midday meal. All this apparent social deficiency within the Hudson family circle that following day was supposedly owing to all other persons in the household having other pressing matters to perform, and not being able to stay a full hour or more to keep Florence company whilst she ate daintily and ever so slowly (as Lawton was made to believe was Florence's especially feminine way of eating all her meals). Mrs. Hudson always enjoyed painting a pretty picture, especially of her daughters, when a most eligible young man was in audience to her speech.

The story that Mrs. Hudson had manufactured and told (not to outright lie in unrighteousness but to justifiably deceive only just a little for the sake of a good marriage) to the most eligible and amiable Lawton was that all in the entire family but Florence would be forced to gulp down their food, perhaps even within the utilitarian and somewhat barbaric regions of the kitchen, so that they may promptly retreat to what was only described as varying sorts of *elsewhere*. Mrs. Hudson thought herself innocent of any wrong-doing by fabricating such a story relating to accomplishing the feat, good-humoredly considering herself within the bounds of saintly duties and the work of angels on earth, smiled upon by heaven itself. Matches must be made by mothers, and sometimes somewhat shady means might be needed for worthy ends. All heaven and angels would be thorough in understanding.

When Mr. Hudson realized that his noonday meal was to be interrupted and spoiled in such a disruptive manner for the sake of the romancing of one of his daughters, he determined to plan a business luncheon away from the house that he might eat at his leisure and avoid indigestion. His plans were easily successful and he avoided the event entirely. Mrs. Hudson and Cadence loyally consumed their lunch in hiding, in the kitchen with Mary, who performed her usual dance between a few bites here and serving things there, from the kitchen to the dining table and back again, over and over until the meal was entirely served. Jake and Hank were given a picnic lunch to take with them to their tree-house, a haystack, any upper regions of the barn, somewhere in the summer kitchen, an obliging field or anywhere that suited their fancy. The boys could have not been more delighted with the arrangement, and hoped that many such romantic daytime meals would be prepared for either of their sisters' benefit so that they themselves would be often free to eat wherever they so chose and with as ill manners as they always delighted in expressing, but seldom were allowed to exhibit (most certainly not at the family table nor in public eating events). Their only hope to eat freely in a wild and free manner was off by themselves where they would not be seen by any who more usually would be scolding them to behave properly. Oh, that the summer long would be filled with courting luncheons, thus forcing the Hudson boys into the wild to gorge themselves wildly with their very own private boxed lunches.

Mr. Oscar Lawton was everything wonderful in Florence's eyes during their fairly private meal, and her young man could not have felt more fortunate in his luck to have come so close to being able to consider bending down upon one knee to ask a most particular question of such a breathtakingly beautiful and preciously chaste and pure young lady.

With Cadence's assistance, Mrs. Hudson did her utmost to keep herself to the kitchen; though such a loving, dutiful and caring mother could not help herself but to slip out to listen in on the young couple's luncheon conversation at least a few times (and all done masterfully without their notice, for she was hid well enough from behind the door). Mrs. Hudson was prematurely hoping that her most careful machinations would result in a proposal that day, for, with so much privacy, could not the young Lawton manage it? Mrs. Hudson was sure of her colorful daughter's answer.

"Oh, what a thrill of thrills… I sense an offer coming on, indeed I do!" Mother whispered to companion daughter whilst Mary was briefly out of the kitchen doing her lunchtime duties.

Cadence answered back in a whisper, "Surely not! It would be all too sudden, I would think. Too soon, I feel. Has Lawton as yet consulted with Father?"

"No, no… but I feel it in the air. I am assured that Lawton wishes to ask… and Florence wishes to answer. They wish to be engaged to one another."

"But propriety would dictate that Lawton should speak to Father first, would it not? And should there not be a more lengthy time in the courting phase? Would not people expect that?"

"Well, in the old days to be sure, but nowadays… well, these days and out here… you know… in the west… certain formalities are not so necessary as they once were or may still be elsewhere."

"But, she barely knows him… we barely know him… would not Father object to giving his permission so soon?"

"No… I think not… your father will approve… I am certain of it."

Mary came in again and Cadence's conversation with her mother was cut short for privacy's sake.

The two lovebirds continued their lovely luncheon for quite some time, before finally strolling out into the garden for further and seemingly more removed privacy. Such an eventual ending to the meal was all too late for Mary, for she had been becoming increasingly anxious about putting all things away and lamented in many whispers to Mrs. Hudson and Cadence in the kitchen, that the remaining food would needs be fed to the dogs, having been left out so very long. Cadence had wondered for propriety's sake what they should do if Florence and her man continued at lunch much longer than what had seemed to lengthen to a few hours. Mrs. Hudson wondered if Lawton's courage was gradually rising enough to meet the task of coming-out with the awaited question. Surely he had been given enough time to speak of what was on his mind and in his heart?

Mrs. Hudson stole Cadence away and up into a room above the garden where they (or at least she) could clandestinely spy upon the couple below. Cadence was torn between the intrusive folly of peeking at the couple and the possible impropriety of leaving them entirely alone for so very long.

In hushed tones, Mrs. Hudson was all elation, "Well, my dear... I do believe *this* will be it! At any moment, Lawton will make Florence an offer and she will *accept* him!"

Mrs. Hudson thrilled so excitedly so, that to not know better, one might think it was *she* who was the young maiden about to be made an offer to. Cadence could but nod in gentle agreement.

Mrs. Hudson was shaking and shivering with excitement, "Ooh... I wish I could hear what they are *saying*... though, more especially... I do wish to know what *he* is saying! Perhaps I should open the window just a crack and try to listen in a little..."

"Mother! No! Do *not*..." Cadence barked in a hushed whisper.

"Oh, tosh... they will not know..." Mrs. Hudson very quickly, carefully and quietly opened the window in ignoring defiance of her daughter's counter command (as if she had always been in the habit of spying upon people and knew exactly how to open any window in amazingly swift silence), while Cadence recoiled back in a horror of sorts. Thankfully for the upstairs matronly spy, spring air had already caused windows to be opened often, since having been shut up for all the winter weather. There was nothing to fear of a stuck or noisy window by having to be forced open with any difficulty.

Cadence stood afar off, near the door, wishing that she had or could get permission to leave, all the while knowing that her mother would insist upon her staying as interloping companion to take part in this most invigorating covert activity. Such spying was always more delightful when there was more than one person in the party, for thrilling words and rousing glances could be exchanged and the spirit of the thing was all the more exhilarating. Mrs. Hudson stood as near the window as she thought she could get away with, wrenching herself to attempt to hear anything, finally gaining the courage to continue peeking into and through the window from time to time.

"They are sitting very closely together." Mrs. Hudson expressed in a kind of motherly ecstasy, calling out in a measured whisper, sending the communication over her shoulder to reach her colluding daughter.

In relative distance away from the window and a kind of comfort remaining close by the door, Cadence counseled, half to end the shared surreptitious activity with her mother, "Do you think it wise to allow that, Mother? Shall we permit such intimacy to occur between them, alone like that? Should I not find my way into the garden to force them to part company at least a little? They seem too much at ease for two who are not yet married, or at least not yet betrothed. Perhaps we should join them to save Florence from impropriety?"

"Stay where you are! If we interrupt them, how will the young man get his offer out? Lawton wishes to propose, Florence wishes to accept and we must let him gather his courage and allow them to take their time to get through it. The thing can be accomplished *today* if only we but *stay* out of the way. To be sure, we *dare* not interrupt them or *all* will be lost for today! I may not sleep again tonight if there is no offer today! I was terribly short for sleep last night due to my anticipations for the excitement today, as you well know."

"Must we really watch and listen, though, Mother?"

Mrs. Hudson considered and offered a convenient reply, "For proprieties sake, yes, we must watch and listen, my dear. Shh… he's saying something… I must try to hear. Ooh… I wish he would speak more loudly. Why must he talk in such quieted tones… especially being a man… his deep voice should carry further…"

Cadence hung back all the more, clinging to the doorway. She felt a certain shame in being there to take part in such an activity. What would or could she say to her sister to justify herself if Florence came to know about this? Would Florence understand the compelling power of their mother upon herself? Would Florence refuse to take part in such goings-on if it were she, herself, who was down in the garden with a young man?

Mrs. Hudson thoroughly enjoyed her afternoon entertainment and it seemed her personal highlight of the year. Though she saw nor heard very little of pertinence or importance; and felt some frustration that the distance, her position of spying and the quietness of the conversation below thwarted her ability to ascertain the full scope of the events transpiring beneath her; Mrs. Hudson was beside herself with joy that she at least was in some way a part of the secret event between two lovebirds of which her own daughter was a part in the pair. Ah, young love. The thrill of it all!

Mr. Lawton was obviously loathe to leave Florence that day as was Florence distressed to let him go, and so the pair took comfort in planning their next meeting, before departing in a sort of mutual sorrow whilst parting in truest bliss.

Mrs. Hudson was all frustration and shock to find out that no offer had occurred and been accepted. How would she sleep well at all that night? How would she rest easy however many days and nights as she awaited the eventful announcement? What were the young people about? Why the need to wait? Was Lawton only playing? Where was his courage to forge ahead with promptness! Had she and her own husband been so tardy in their own betrothal so long ago? Indeed not! She could not at present take the pains to recall the particulars, but was thoroughly certain that they had done things in a timely manner. They had not made her own mother wait in such agony of suspense! How could this Lawton drag his feet and make her wait to see her daughter accept him? What infamous and villainous dawdling! Indeed and to be sure!

Mrs. Hudson would simply have to wait. Patience was a virtue, after all. Many rendezvous days occurred between the pair of lovebirds and though few neighbors round about saw much of the courting activities (for most of such happened on private Hudson properties, with Mrs. Hudson doing her duty by her daughter in her extraordinary efforts to hear and see something of the transpirations), much was heard beyond because of the loosed tongues of Mrs. Hudson and more especially even Mary (who herself happened to also see and hear a thing or two of Florence and her Lawton). Mrs. Hudson divulged near all to Mrs. Darby and beyond while Mary spoke to every maid and resemblance of friend she could grasp and hold the ears of. Every maid in the territory passed any tidbit of news to any maid or any person who had ears to hear. The lively buzz about the town and surrounding countryside hummed a merry tune, dancing in the days' spring breezes and floating on the night winds. Busybodies, chatterers, prattlers, gossips, informants, tattle-tales and all such of the like, had near their fill of it: Florence and Lawton were the thing. Grand speculations of the newly up and coming Mr. and Mrs. Oscar and Florence Lawton were the talk, indeed, almost the only talk, of the newly settled in spring season. The subject of Florence and her beau was as if the only color to wear. People, or more especially, the ladies, young and old, could not get enough of the talk of it. Speeches abounded about the pair so much so that husbands, fathers, brothers, sons and beaux were bothered to such a thoroughly tiresome degree that all men and boys about the town and beyond were full of complaints, having heard far more than enough of the newly new but fast becoming old subject. Many men were heard to say such as, 'when would the pair finally be hitched so that women would stop talking of it?'!

Everything came to the point one quiet evening under the stars.

"Florence, my love?"

"Yes, my dear sweet Lawton?" Florence was in resplendent raptures in knowing anticipation.

"Oh… I do not quite know how to phrase it…" Lawton was all hesitations.

"Feel free, my darling man…"

"I wish to make a certain kind of speech…" Lawton's voice was shaky.

"Just speak it!" Florence's tone was pointed towards almost shrill.

"Dare I get down on one knee?"

"Of course you should… you silly thing!"

"Then I will… then I will!"

"Do… please do!"

Lawton's courage rose up enough to take him with steady strength down upon his one most important knee, and his voice deepened in equal strength of conviction and courage, "Will you… will you marry me?"

Florence squealed in delighted laughter, out aloud enough to have wakened the moon above, "Finally! I thought you would never get around to it! What took you so very long! Why did your courage not equal my passionate desire to answer you with affirmations? Yes! Yes! A thousand times, yes!"

Florence's outward bursting and thrills of loudly vocal verbosity were enough to bring Mrs. Hudson out of her bed (the comfortable place that she had retired to early on account of a headache due to having been over-heated that day) to dash to her bedroom window where she strained to see what the lovebirds (of whom she had wondered if she should give up hope upon, for the engagement completion seemed to be taking so very long to transpire) were doing and saying. Mrs. Hudson strained and stretched and was entirely enthralled to see the young couple embrace. Oh, where was Mr. Hudson?! Was he still reading that infernal book in his own personal library at the back of the house? Why had he not as yet retired? Did he intend to finish the book in its entirety this very night? Or, perhaps he had fallen asleep, reading in his great chair or upon his grand lounging couch. Would she need to go find her husband? Did she need to seek out her own husband to bring him to her? She wished to share this grand moment with her husband, the father of the eventual bride!

5
Outside the Mercantile

Mrs. Darby breathed out deeply as she shifted her weight for the sake of her feet, "Well now… with Florence engaged, we really must hurry things up and along for the sake of Cadence… 'tis surely time *now* to find a husband for her! What do you say to a ball? How soon could you possibly manage such an event?"

Mrs. Hudson's brow furrowed a little, "To be certain I must think and plan for Cadence now… but, I do believe that I will have to finish up with Florence's wedding plans and expenses first… Mr. Hudson will not…"

"Yes, of course… to save expenses to please your husband, you can start to showcase Cadence to all the young men around and about, you know… at dinners and parties relating to Florence's engagement and wedding. That is most assuredly the way to do the thing. I have long heard that while you are in the business of marrying off one daughter, you will likely find a pretty partner for another amid the process! I practically did the same with my own. That is the easiest way. Do you not think?"

"To be sure… yes, of course."

"You will use the excuse of Florence's wedding to spend the money that is needed to get Cadence a husband as well… and your husband will not know what you are about… he will pay for everything thinking that he is simply doing his duty by Florence… and all the while you will be sparing no expense on behalf of Cadence and doing your own duty by her!"

"Yes, you are quite right… indeed, that is what I will be doing.

I will do right by both my daughters. I will get Cadence a husband while getting Florence joined to hers."

"Yes, yes… only one event can be used as if it were two, in the bargain."

"I shall manage to get my husband to agree to pay for all events associated with Florence's wedding…" Mrs. Hudson was all thoughtfully hopeful.

"Of course… of course it will. You will manage him, to be sure." Mrs. Darby agreed in encouragement.

"Surely easier than convincing him to allow me to host anything else, even for the sake of seeking and finding eligible young men for Cadence to choose from."

"Too true… very sadly true… your husband is a vast deal more challenging than mine, I dare say. I do pity you, my dear. Your work is indeed cut out before you." Mrs. Darby shifted her weight again, for her feet were calling out little pains up to her.

Mrs. Hudson let out a great sigh, "Mr. Hudson is a true rock when it comes to guarding his money… though there is enough and to spare of it. I wonder that he does not find joy being a little more liberal with his money by me."

"You will find a way to do what must be done, my dear. For the sake of her children, a mother can do most anything, if she has a mind to… and oft times she must lead her husband in these and many other things."

"Yes, Florence's good fortune will turn into equal good fortune for Cadence through my diligence as their mother… even perhaps in spite of my husband to some degree."

"What we wives must *go* through to trick our husbands into submission! 'Tis a very good thing that women are so much more clever than men, I dare say." Mrs. Darby boasted.

"And my husband will be none the wiser through it all… though… still… I am saving him money, to be sure… and if I were to consult him fully on all pertaining matters, he would agree that all in all I was being prudent, *after* all." Mrs. Hudson considered due diligence in relevance to due obedience to one's husband, particularly her own.

Mrs. Darby was all instructive warning, "Oh, no… do not consult him… no, no… that will not do. Consulting one's husband on such details is *always* folly, my dear."

"To be sure, to be sure. You are quite right." Mrs. Hudson nodded obediently.

"Well, you know that I will be helping you every step of the way, my dear friend. As my own daughters and sons are all married off, what else have I to do? I must help my friends in marrying off their children. If I cannot help the entire world marry off their children, surely I can help my *dearest* friends!"

"You are most kind."

"Not at all, my dear…. it is the duty of a friend. You would do the same for me, I am quite certain." Mrs. Darby shifted her weight yet again. It was a wonder that she did not think to suggest sitting down nearby, considering the discomforts of her feet in standing at length, but her mind was so actively engaged elsewhere that she had no truly conscious thought for the pains of her feet.

"Truly… indeed I would."

Mrs. Darby changed course a little, "I wonder… did you know… that your Mary told my Betsy that Florence went and got herself engaged to Lawton prior to your husband's consent? Is this true?"

Mrs. Hudson was thinking on preparing what to say when Mrs. Darby took a deep breath and saved her friend a turn to talk as she continued, "Well, since they are to be married soon enough, I suppose that there is no harm done… and you can be assured of my silence on the matter, though I cannot vouch for such with my Betsy… silly girl that she can be. She is as good a worker as ever I've had… and that is truly why I keep her… all things considered… but, the girl has a loose tongue, to be sure. I always do my utmost to keep everything from her…. else the whole world will know everything. Perhaps you can silence Mary in these things? Your husband must have been vexed at not being consulted properly, I would guess? Though, they did seek his permission once they agreed to the match I suppose? They did not keep it a secret long I presume?"

"Yes, well…"

Mrs. Darby characteristically interrupted, "Well, well… what's done is done anyway… and all will be forgotten once they are married… means to an end… means to an end, I dare say… near any means to a proper end. Yes."

Mrs. Hudson was wondering what her side of the conversation should be when Mrs. Darby turned her head and spotted someone from across the way and called out loudly, "Mrs. Ledner! Mrs. Ledner! Come over here!"

With that, Mrs. Darby waved her hand rapidly, wildly motioning towards herself and Mrs. Hudson, where they stood in front of the town's mercantile shop. During their discussion, people had been coming and going, in and out of, and to and fro in front of the shop, though Mrs. Hudson and Mrs. Darby were standing off to one side (in front of the window where all manner of seasonal items were prominently and proudly displayed to entice all who passed by to not forget to enter therein to partake), where the two women enjoyed some semblance of conversational privacy amid their own public display.

Mrs. Darby quickly turned back towards Mrs. Hudson, "I'll wager that she has a pretty piece of news for us, for I had it from my maid Betsy, who had it from Mrs. Ledner's maid that Mr. Ledner caught a young man red-handed… well… red-faced, I dare say… trying to kiss their daughter on their front porch! Did you ever *hear* of such a thing? Who left them *alone* on the front porch like that in the first place, I ask you? My husband would have brought out his guns and they would have been blazing, before the fellow half had the corrupted idea or notion in his silly mind, I tell you! No, all the young men who courted my daughters knew what was what. We made certain of *that*, I assure you. I dare say that a young man was as likely to lose a hand as not, if he tried to lay it on one of our girls! Everyone knew *that* was as good as a fact, I can tell you."

Mrs. Hudson tried to look as shocked as might be expected and Mrs. Darby continued with a tone of concern, lowering her voice a great deal, for Mrs. Ledner was making her way closer now, "I had it from my Betsy that your Mary claimed that you left Florence alone with Lawton for *quite* some time in your garden? Is that true? Did you, my dear?"

Mrs. Hudson answered in a necessary whisper as Mrs. Ledner approached them, "Oh, no! Not at all, I assure you. Mary did not know that Cadence and I were spying over the garden the entire time from a window above. We saw and heard *everything*, my dear. Everything was done very properly... do not worry your mind in the slightest on that count."

Mrs. Darby satisfactorily whispered very lightly, "Good. Good. I did not think that you would have been so unwise. *You* know what to do for your daughter's sake."

Mrs. Hudson nodded in agreement briefly to Mrs. Darby before nodding a polite hello to the advancing Mrs. Ledner, who was just about to arrive to stand before the two of them.

"Hello, Mrs. Ledner!" Mrs. Darby haled noisily as her other friend drew so very near.

"Hello, my dears." Mrs. Ledner expelled upon her official bustling arrival.

As was her usual way, Mrs. Darby took the reins, "Well, well... what a fine day to come to town. I fancy that everyone we know is here, or thereabouts! I dare say the winter had us all cooped up like frustrated clucking chickens with few others to cackle to, and now we will find any excuse at all to come to town to talk to and fro! Add to that all the new things to be seen... and bought! Our husband's funds will be drained for certain!"

Mrs. Ledner attempted to stroke her friend's pride, "Well, I cannot imagine that *you* could drain your own husband's funds for *all* your attempts... not in *our* town, to be sure! Would not you have to spend many years in *Europe* to spend your husband's ready funds?"

"I dare say I would! I cannot imagine that even *I* could do it! I talk a great deal too much to allow for enough time to spend anywhere *near* my entire husband's ready money! Yes, my husband should be thankful for my wagging tongue for it saves him a great deal of money after all!" Mrs. Darby laughed, for she was not truly unrighteously proud of her wealth nor was she ashamed of being so rich, due to her husband's many years of hard work and attendant good fortune.

Mrs. Ledner smiled at Mrs. Darby and then also towards Mrs. Hudson. Mrs. Hudson smiled back, though she was not entirely fond of Mrs. Ledner, for she did not know the woman well at all nor did she care to get to know her better, despite the fact that she could not point to an exact reason for this sentiment within herself and such thoughts in her own mind, but in her heart, she did not feel up to expending energies and time upon furthering the acquaintance. Mrs. Darby and Mrs. Ledner continued conversing while Mrs. Hudson stood idly by, looking about and beyond them and herself, hoping to appear entertained or amused in some form or fashion, whether or not she was or could be diverted to any degree for the time being.

Vying for information (itching to tug this way and that, as if in the mood for a molasses taffy pull), Mrs. Darby leaned in towards Mrs. Ledner in her lowest though still very audible whisper, "So… my dear… tell me all about your daughter and… and… that rascal! Tell me all that I might not have heard as yet! You must have *so* much to tell me."

Mrs. Ledner confessed, "What is there to say? The stupid fellow behaved as a libertine and my husband nearly whipped him within an inch of his life for his attempt. He was chased off, is never to return, and that is the end of it."

"Well, I fear that the end of *talk* is not quite yet."

"Let people talk. I care not. What more is to be said, anyway?"

"Well… you know that your daughter's *reputation* is tarnished for it. Perhaps you *should* care. People *will* talk, my dear." Mrs. Darby's face had a look of serious discipline about it.

Mrs. Ledner did not attend to Mrs. Darby's stern looks, "It will soon blow over. My daughter is not at all at fault for the devilish thoughts or actions of any young man."

"*Some* say that you and your husband are… are somewhat at fault for leaving them alone."

"*Nonsense.*" Mrs. Ledner's tone was truly annoyance.

"But, you will take care in the future with *other* fellows?"

"I suppose we may watch more closely now… though I do not claim any responsibility for the sins of some lad."

"Well… you just *never* know with these young men. Some will seem all gentlemanly like and then… then, they turn into *wolves*, I dare say."

"Yes."

"We must guard our daughters against them." Mrs. Darby tried to rouse Mrs. Ledner to a proper height of decorum and honor.

"Of course."

"It is our *duty* to our daughters."

"I dare say."

"All things should be kept firmly within the realm of modesty and decorum; I always say… you know… for the *safety* of our daughters."

"To be sure." Mrs. Ledner gave Mrs. Darby a quick, sharp look that strongly hinted of annoyance and then fussed with her bonnet, trying to straighten it, having disheveled it after tucking some stray hairs inside the rather ugly thing.

"Well… well… it is a lovely day." Mrs. Darby looked about her, glanced at Mrs. Hudson, who was still looking elsewhere while listening intently, and then spied into the store through the window. Mrs. Darby was rapidly tiring of Mrs. Ledner.

Mrs. Ledner had grown equally tired of Mrs. Darby and so spoke her final words before leaving the two other women to be by themselves once more, "I understand that there are some new cameos inside and I think that I must have one of them today. Well, I am off to drain a little of my husband's funds."

Mrs. Darby and Mrs. Hudson nodded their requisite polite farewells, but the moment that Mrs. Ledner was inside the store, Mrs. Darby burst in a suppressed whispering eruption, "Oh, I despise that woman! There is just quite simply something about her that I cannot describe… but I do not like her!"

Mrs. Hudson was most thoroughly and terribly delighted to nod vigorously in agreement. The two women found new common ground together which more firmly cemented their friendship as they enjoyed exchanging un-pleasantries regarding the nondescriptly disagreeable Mrs. Ledner, each woman outside the shop window taking turns glancing at such said woman through said window as Mrs. Ledner scoured the new cameos inside. After a time, the conversational exchanges against Mrs. Ledner slowed and speculations about the cameos took precedence.

As was usual, Mrs. Darby took charge by beginning, "I dare say that I have an itch for a new cameo myself. I have half a mind to go in there right this minute to get myself the pick of the lot, whether or not Mrs. Ledner has set eyes on whatever I may set my own upon!"

Mrs. Hudson chuckled, "I dare say!"

Just then Mrs. Darby spied Mrs. Hudson's twins advancing towards them from across the street, "There are your beautiful girls! Here they come to you! I shall have to stay to congratulate Florence and then perhaps I should go grab myself at least one new cameo! I suppose I can leave you to your dear daughters?"

"Yes, yes of course. They will wait with me while I watch for my husband and sons. I dare say that at least one of them will wait with me, anyhow."

"Cadence, I dare say."

"Yes, my good old steady Cadence. She can always be depended upon."

"Perhaps I will steal your flamboyant Florence away with me into the shop! I will buy her a cameo as an engagement gift, I wager! That will give me a chance to give her some old wise advice while I am at it, do you not think?"

"Yes, of course, to be sure. Please do feel free. I always appreciate your kindnesses, advice and help for my dear daughters. I am so very obliged to you, as always."

Mrs. Darby set out towards the Hudson twins, intercepting their approach. She grasped Florence's arm as she swept her into the mercantile shop, her mouth in hasty action of verbosity as her purse was readying itself for lively business inside. Cadence took her cue and took herself to her mother.

"Mother, your feet must be so very tired! How long have you been standing out here? Let us sit you down on that bench just over there so that you may rest your feet. Has Father not come yet? I thought he would have surely come by now. What is he about? Does he not know that you are awaiting his return? Where could he be?"

"He took the lads to look at some new horses."

"Oh… that does explain everything." Cadence smilingly teased.

"Well, you know how your father can go on and on about horses."

"But did you wish to stand or even sit out here all the while you wait for him? I would have thought that you would like to mull about in the mercantile or… perhaps visit your dressmaker, or…"

"The day is lovely, there is a gentle refreshing breeze and I am quite comfortable in the shade here. I did go into the Mercantile shop earlier… to spy out some new cameos there… though I ended up fancying a new pair of amethyst earrings that I thought perhaps I should ask your father about before obtaining them for myself… I *did* have them put aside for now."

Cadence mothered her own mother, "We know that Father will not likely purchase the amethysts for you… you know how he has an aversion to jewels and laces and such… and he so loves to tease you that he will not likely give you permission to treat yourself to them without a good deal of coaxing and scolding from you… you know… until you are so very greatly vexed that the enjoyment of buying the earrings would be all gone out of you… so, therefore… let me go in and buy them for you. I have so very much allowance from Father that I have not spent as yet."

"Oh, my goodness me… thank you, my dearest girl!"

"I will also retrieve Florence from Mrs. Darby while I am inside. I suspect that my sister will soon like to be released from her generous master."

"Do not forget to look at the new cameos. You may fancy one of those for yourself. I dare say you could afford one."

With Cadence gone into the shop, Mrs. Hudson was left to herself outside. She was content to be so. Closing her eyes for a spell, she as if took a little respite from the day, shutting out light and sights around her; though the volume of sounds without her seemed to heighten, for with one sense dimmed, others became more intense. Still, she was able to settle all her senses and shut out the entire world for a time, resting herself as she rested on the bench. Time seemed to stand still. She did truly not know how much time had elapsed before her daughters were at her side.

Florence awoke her mother from the sort of wakeful slumber, "Mother! Look at what Mrs. Darby purchased for me as my engagement gift! Is not this cameo lovely? I have never seen such a pretty face on a cameo as this one. The artists who carve these miniature masterpieces are of true and thorough genius!"

Mrs. Hudson was blinking, trying to focus her vision upon the piece of jewelry, the light seeming to blind her sight, in a prolonged though temporary way. She could finally see again and enjoyed Mrs. Darby's gift to her daughter.

"It is very fine, Florence. Truly, it is exceedingly beautiful. And to think that after so many women have perused past the new cameos, something so very perfect as this particular one was still there for you to choose for yourself."

"Yes, it was as if saved for me."

Mrs. Hudson quite abruptly halted her thoughts and asked, "Did you *thank* Mrs. Darby profusely? I hope you paid her especial gratitude for her generosity towards you?"

"Oh, yes, of course Mother! What do you take me for: an ungrateful simpleton?"

"No, no… I simply wish to be certain that Mrs. Darby knows that you are grateful to her for her kindness towards you. And what of you, Cadence, did you choose a cameo for yourself?"

Cadence roused herself, "Oh, yes, Mother… I near forgot about your amethyst earrings! They are so beautiful! How wonderful for me that you were so short of your own allowance that I was able to share of mine and buy them as a gift for you!"

Mrs. Hudson was so very thrilled to receive her gift from her daughter that she promptly lifted herself up off of the bench to embrace Cadence for her generous offering.

Florence pouted a little, "Cadence never seems to be able to spend all her money on herself while you and I are just the opposite, Mother. Forgive me for having nothing left to treat you to something with as well."

Mrs. Hudson embraced her Florence nonetheless, "Both of you are a gift from heaven above, my dear daughters… regardless of any gifts you ever give me. What could a mother want for more than to have two such beautiful and wonderful daughters?"

Mother sat herself down in the middle of her bench and patted either side of it that her daughters would join her. They each complied. Despite not wearing any purple that day, and thoroughly disregarding any seeming need for a color match or coordination, with Cadence's help, Mrs. Hudson worked at putting on her new marvelously lovely amethyst earrings. Her old pair of whatever she was wearing could certainly go into the bag until arriving home again. Continually fairly oblivious to the entire active flurry around about them, mother and daughters continued in their visiting.

Mrs. Hudson began in another direction, "Where is your young man, Florence?"

"Oh, he had this and that thing that he wished to do… though I left him in the saloon earlier and what do I know… he may even still be there now."

"The *saloon*! Oh, no! You were *not* in the saloon!" Mrs. Hudson was beside herself in shock at her rebellious daughter's casually admitted behavior.

"I only had a *sarsaparilla*, Mother!"

"Even *still*… the saloon?!" their mother was still all shock.

Cadence put in support for their mother, "I told her not to go in."

Mrs. Hudson looked at Cadence, "*You* did not go in?"

"Of course not."

Mrs. Hudson turned to Florence, "You went in… *alone*… with Lawton?"

Florence corrected, "*Stinham* was with us… chaperoning, I

suppose you could say… and then there were all sorts of other folks there, you know… so of course you certainly could not say that we were alone."

"Oh, my good *gracious*! If you could not *stop* Florence from going in, perhaps you should have gone in *with* them, Cadence? You know… to prevent your sister from being alone with Lawton in a public place like that… particularly a… saloon." Mrs. Hudson did not even attempt to hide her mortification.

Cadence answered in her own defense, "*Stinham* was with them."

"But even *still*…" Mrs. Hudson's tone was full of lament.

Florence clarified, "Stinham was with us, Mother. You *know* how Cadence is trying to steer clear of Stinham. It is all she can do to keep him from proposing to her… especially ever since I had my own offer from his friend Lawton! Stinham is *obviously* continually seeking just the right moment to rest upon one knee for Cadence… my poor, poor Cadence…"

Mrs. Hudson was now all lamentations, "Oh… mercy me… what am I to do… what will people think and say… my own daughter in the saloon… like a common dancing girl… oh, the horror of it… what a *scolding* I will get from Mrs. Darby when she finds out…"

Florence could not restrain herself, "Oh, snobbery, tosh and nonsense… what do I care what she might say or think…"

Mrs. Hudson severely scolded Florence, "You should care! She has been most generous to you today… and you do not care about her *opinion* of such things? What sort of a *daughter* have I been raising?"

Florence moderated her message somewhat and tried to help her mother to see her own view of things related, "I just thought that people in general make too much of a 'to do' about such things… I did not dance nor did I partake of any spirits. I enjoyed one innocent sarsaparilla and was on my fiancé's arm the *entire* time. I was under the *protection* of my beau. I did not think it so very *wrong*. You and some of your friends can be so terribly prudish sometimes."

Mrs. Hudson only shook her head and looked down. Cadence

smiled at both of her bench companions, while she tried to comfort and calm their mother with an arm about her. Just then, a noise in the street before them alerted the three ladies.

Mrs. Hudson was all agog with surprise to see her sons running down the street chasing a dog, in plain view before her own eyes. As she leaned forward, one of her arms raised, her first finger pointing towards Jake and Hank, and her mouth moving, well opened, as if to say or shout something. Though, as if in a bad dream, no sounds would come out to escape her lips, for her or anyone else's ears to hear. Neither Mrs. Hudson's mind nor voice did work enough for the moment, to get out any words relating to a question posed to her daughters as to why her sons should be displaying themselves before the townsfolk in such an untoward manner, nor to call out to the boys to bring them unto repentance that would result in halting their speeding rascality in the midst of all things moving upon the road.

Upon closer inspection, it was apparent to the three Hudson women that the dog held something in its mouth, which was obviously of great import to the boys. As the shaggy critter traversed along, weaving in and out between anything and anyone in its path, Jake and Hank were laughing and shouting whilst running close on its heels. While the boys were pursuing the wild little beast, all persons in the town within hearing and sight of the spectacle could not but be compelled to notice the Hudson boys racing along after their target. Many townspeople began to also notice Mrs. Hudson in particular, as she continued sitting in front of the mercantile shop, in horrified dismay. Oh, but what a humiliation the entire event was to her. Cadence tried to calm and soothe her mother by grasping one of her mother's hands into her own two hands, as she was saying such things as 'there, there' and the like.

"Where is your father?" was all Mrs. Hudson finally managed to get out in a horrified whisper whilst she wished to disappear from the center of town and into oblivion.

Cadence offered, "They came from the direction of the livery stables. No doubt Father is still deeply involved in some discussion of some horse or another."

"No doubt… but *why* did he not stop the boys and *where* are they going?" the twins' mother lamented, having begun to find, awake and compose her mind to better offer speech.

"Likely as not Father has not noticed them missing as yet and they are simply following where the dog may lead them. If Father does not stop them soon, they will be halfway to California or even the moon before they or the dog slows down." Cadence joked.

Florence laughed at Cadence's unexpected remark.

Mrs. Hudson slapped Florence's leg and rebuked her, "This is *no* laughing matter!"

Still in giggles, Florence defended, "But Cadence's joke was…"

"You and your brothers will be the *early* death of me!" Mrs. Hudson was approaching anger, unlike her usual tendencies.

"Oh, *Mother*… do not be so…"

Due to feeling overwhelmingly embarrassed, Mrs. Hudson lashed out somewhat, "Why must you be so rebellious in nature, Florence?"

"What of Cadence? It was she who…"

Feeling especially for her mother, Cadence repented quickly and offered aid to her sister, "I'm truly sorry Mother, I should not have joked so. Do not fault Florence, for it was surely all my fault for causing her to laugh."

"Thank heavens Mrs. Darby is *still* in the shop."

With the commotion of the Hudson boys and their object of prey gone down the street and around a corner, Mrs. Hudson could finally breathe a miniscule sigh of relief, though she feared that the entire town was still staring at her in disdain.

A voice came from aside the three of them, which turned out to belong to a smiling Mrs. Darby, "Deary dear… my husband will reproach me with a *fiery* fury! I fear that I have bought up *half* of the shop today!"

Mrs. Hudson's head whipped around to see her friend juggling packages, Mrs. Darby's face flushed with the exercise of hanging on to all of them at once. Mrs. Hudson wondered if her own face was flushed with mortification. She wondered if Mrs. Darby had seen anything of the spectacle that Jake and Hank had just displayed before everyone on the main street of town, from inside the shop.

Cadence offered a kindly suggestion, "Mrs. Darby, let Florence and I help you to your buggy with all those. You have very nearly dropped something and are quite likely to drop near everything very soon without our help."

"Yes, yes… my dear… that is *most* generous of you. I certainly do need some assistance. Thank you very kindly."

Cadence and Florence left their mother briefly to aid Mrs. Darby in getting all her things to her buggy down the street. Beyond helping an older woman carry her packages towards her destination, it was Cadence's secondary design to hopefully keep the kafuffle of the Hudson boys' just recent display from reaching Mrs. Darby's ears and mind just a while (if only a few hours, realistically), as if this exercise might give a little respite relief to her own mother's heart by keeping pertinent gossip down to a minimum. By the time the girls arrived back to their mother, who was sitting quietly and somewhat dazed in a sort of confusion, Florence spotted their father approaching them. Painter daughter pointed her advancing father out to her mother, hoping to offer calm or comfort of any kind. Mrs. Hudson looked up but did not seem fully cognizant as yet. As soon as Mr. Hudson stepped in front of them, his wife laid into him.

"Why were you not watching our *boys*?! Do you know what they have *done* before the entire town? I am so *horribly* ashamed! This will take a good deal of time to overcome, I *must* say. What will people think and say of me." Mrs. Hudson was visibly agitated.

Mr. Hudson did not know quite what to make of his wife's questioning but did answer her as best he could, "I saw them playing with a dog. It snatched something away from them and then away they both went after the mongrel."

Truth be told, Mr. Hudson was secretly amused at what he had seen of his sons' shenanigans, though he knew that he must rouse himself to feel completely chastened by his wife, in order to work towards full and righteous repentance.

Mrs. Hudson hinted of tears for her shame, "Why did you not

stop them from chasing the beast?"

Mr. Hudson had not yet noticed his wife's eyes welling up with salty water, "I was speaking with Mr. Dodge and could not break away that instant."

"Well, they made a *raucous* exhibition of themselves in front of *everyone* and now they are lost somewhere around that corner down there." Mrs. Hudson explained and then finished with pointing to where she had last seen their sons round a corner.

"I wonder that you did not go after them when you *saw* them… or send one or both of the girls to chase them down."

Mrs. Hudson was rising in a slight approach towards anger, "*Ladies* do not chase boys down."

Mr. Hudson felt an urge of teasing overcome him, "Oh, and *gentlemen* do then?"

"You were *supposed* to be watching them!"

"I *was*… they were with me… until they ran off… and I could not chase them just then."

Mrs. Hudson was flabbergasted with her husband, "Well, can you not go and look for them *now*?"

Cadence tried to bring some peace or at least calm to the situation, "We will help you, Father. I am certain that they could not have gone too far as yet."

As the girls rounded the corner with their father, the boys were in the midst of their return and thus all was well again, or at least some semblance of well being with the Hudson family, who returned home together in the way in which they had come to town that day.

6
The Libertine

M r. Hudson had not been any too pleased with the way in which Mr. Lawton had engaged himself to Florence. Was not a man to be consulted *before* an offer was made to his own daughter? Lawton was from out east. He knew the way these things were done. Or at least, he should have been aware of the proper way of bringing such a thing about. Mr. Hudson was supremely vexed that he had not been approached by the young man before the engagement was entered into, but, more than that, Florence's father felt as if he was near the *last* to know. Why had not Florence told him right away? Why had not his wife told him? And now he was expected to pay dearly for every expense of the match. All he seemed to be considered *good* for was to put down the cash for the event. What sort of new tradition was this? A father was the father after all! He could say yea or nay. Mr. Hudson had half a mind to say nay on the occasion.

Florence had told Cadence and her mother about her engagement to Lawton before Mr. Hudson knew anything of the affair. Even Mary the maid had wind of it and had spread it far and wide before the father of the prospective bride knew a single thing. To be fair, perhaps it was true that speculations had been strewn about on the breezes long before the actual engagement had finally taken place, and perchance Mr. Hudson was not truly the last in the region to know for certain once the thing was finally done, but he did feel a stinging sense of having been left out in the cold on this extremely important point. He had always pictured such an event unfolding very differently. An especially respectful young man would come to him and beg for the hand of his daughter. Perchance as father, he might take days, weeks or even months to decide on the matter. The whole thing was under his command. The yes or the no was based upon his own whim. He could allow his daughter to be wed or he could refuse altogether. All would bow and be subjected unto him and his authority. His wife could do all the matchmaking she pleased if she liked, but when it came down to the point, the moment wherein there must needs be a decision on the matter, his own word was every whit of the law and he, and only he, could choose to bring the thing about, or to end it forever before it had any chance to have begun.

Being that Mr. Hudson was so especially fond of his own fair Florence, particularly appreciating her free spirit and untamed will, he was all the more perturbed that any young man should sneak in and try to steal his fair daughter away out from under his nose without so much as a 'by your leave'. In the man's mind, this thing was akin to but far worse than horse thievery for pity and heaven's sake. Were not horse thieves routinely hung at least out west?! Could a young fellow steal a father's daughter from him with so much more impunity than if he had taken a horse? What sort of blasphemous business was this? Should a father suffer and submit to such treatment from those around him? It was all he could do to calm himself. As a man not normally given to such passions, this point was strangely a thorn in his side. Mr. Hudson had truly fancied in the past that perchance he, himself, would be fortunate enough to select the perfect young man for each of his daughters. He did not take kindly to being told by his daughter or even his wife, that this or that young man was now betrothed to one of his daughters, and that he, the father, was expected to simply comply to and then pay for each and every one of the arrangements. Some sort of sacrilege or irreverence it all seemed, to be sure.

On the other hand, Mrs. Hudson was simply so elated to have a still young daughter engaged to be married to a most eligible gentleman, that she did not seem to have a care for what manner in which the thing was secured. Florence was engaged and Mrs.

Hudson was gleefully joyful to begin to plan all the arrangements. What more was there to consider? Why worry over the manner in which the pleasing matter was hatched? Yes, Florence had come and told her mother first, but what daughter would not tell her mother first? And beyond and besides all that, was not the father in the case hidden and asleep off and away where Florence may not have known where to find him even if she had desired to speak to him first? It was quite true that Florence was full fond of her father, to be sure, and perhaps she might have sought him out in an instant if she had known his whereabouts. Florence had simply happened to find her mother earliest (for Mrs. Hudson had intercepted her daughters approach in the heat of the moment) and knowing that Mrs. Hudson was the kind of woman and wife to tell her husband everything straight away, there was no foreseen possibility that Mr. Hudson would not know everything promptly after his wife had been acquainted with all facts. Mrs. Hudson thought herself to have behaved fully and truly within protocol and propriety, for she had gone to tell her husband right off, but the dear exhausted man was fast asleep in his library late that night. Candle in hand, she had stood over her darling man, looking at him fast asleep, wondering if she should dare to wake him to tell him the happy news that she was bursting with. She near leant over to shake him, but, her love for him intervened as she saw him almost as if a sleeping babe, nestled into his comfortable couch, covered by one of her own shawls. No, she could not bring herself to wake him. The matter could wait until morning. What harm could there be in waiting until the first light of the next day to apprise her husband of every little thing that she herself now knew?

Was it her own fault, as mother of the bride-to-be, that Mary had just happened to overhear Florence and Cadence talking either that night or early the next morn and was so full of the news that she ran over to a neighbor's maid to be *first* to spread the news among that class and in that quarter? Was it Mrs. Hudson's *error* that Mr. Hudson had arisen so very early and had gone out on pressing morning business without having seen any of his household first? What had he even breakfasted on? What could have been so very important and where could he have taken himself to in such a hurry? Indeed, Mrs. Hudson had not slept in as late as was her usual practice due to the pressing news of import that she firmly wished to pass on to her husband as soon as may be possible, and had gone all over the house looking for him to share her joy of the engagement news. She had become so terribly distraught at not finding her husband instantly and then protractedly, that she had even gone out and around the surrounding Hudson properties trying to find the uninformed father of the bride-to-be. Oh, mercy and pity be! *Where* could the man be?! No, it was not Mrs. Hudson's blunder that Mr. Hudson seemed in hiding on such a significant morning. She had missed her *own* breakfast trying to find him to inform him of every thing that she herself knew. She had finally given up and had gone in for some food before fainting away altogether. Her husband would be told when he finally appeared. It was only *circumstance* that Mary's having spread the word round about set such wheels of chatter in motion prior to the all-important man in the case having heard any thing of it.

Perhaps Lawton having sometime that night told young Mr. Stinham, who then told his family and friends the next morning, who subsequently told everyone they knew early that day, was also a major factor in the case. Perchance as well, Mrs. Hudson should not have told Mrs. Darby such news when she happened by before Mr. Hudson had happened to finally come home and be told such himself: for 'twas too true that Mrs. Darby was keen to get herself up and gone promptly so as to tell everyone she knew of the secured affair. Yes, it was true that much of the town and even perhaps the entire territorial area was aware of the fact of the latest betrothal news before Mr. Hudson was, despite all such news having been properly pertaining so much to him proprietarily, but, was it also not true that Mrs. Hudson had continually speculated to her husband of the likely impending engagement? Was it even a surprise to him after all? No, it was truly an expected event and proper piece of news, and if Mr. Hudson had been listening to his wife and all which she had communicated to him in all this great length of time, he would have seen the thing coming at any rate. No, Mr. Hudson was making a big 'to do' out of nothing. So Mrs. Hudson thought.

Owing to the fact that Mr. Hudson felt slighted in a grand way by all around him, his mulling and thoughts over Lawton and the said young man's worthiness were more protracted and intense than they more than likely may have otherwise been. Mr. Hudson could not but feel a good deal offended by the young man who had not properly sought a father's permission for his daughter's hand honorably, and father's sense that son-in-law to be might not be everything Florence deserved propelled him to begin to think more and more regarding the matter. Mr. Hudson found himself slightly out of character when he sought out and spoke with old Mr. Stinham in reference to learning more about Mr. Lawton, the Stinham family guest. Not having discovered anything that he seemed to be looking for, Mr. Hudson sent inquiries to his many business contacts eastward. Mr. Hudson wished to know more about this Mr. Oscar Lawton. Mr. Hudson had determined that if this said Mr. Lawton was not all that he represented himself to be, a father could always put a stop to a marriage with his own daughter at any point along the path until the business was finally done. If this Lawton fellow was not worthy of Florence, Mr. Hudson would make certain that Lawton did not marry Florence.

Mr. Hudson's displeasure with Mr. Lawton's way in betrothing himself to Florence was so very pronounced that he did happen to mention his sentiments abroad in occasional quips and gibes here and there, so much so that word of Mr. Hudson's prejudices against Lawton were fast becoming the talk of the town and beyond into even the furthest regions of their entire territory. Husbands and sons told wives and mothers. Womenfolk fanned the flames of the news. The wildfire spread. Such a kafuffle it all had become! What an entertainment! It was not enough to speak of the news that the handsome and rich Mr. Lawton was engaged to the beautiful and accomplished Florence Hudson, for Mr. Hudson did not seem to like the betrothal as a whole and all neighbors near, far and wide delighted in chewing on the unpleasant business. What a delightful piece of gossip to dance amongst during the shining days of spring!

One fine day whilst Mr. Hudson was out on business, Mrs. Darby showed up on the Hudson doorstep to invite herself in for a cup of anything with Mrs. Hudson.

"Oh dear, my dear… what will you do?"

Mrs. Hudson was wordless, sitting in her own fine parlor with her revered friend.

Mrs. Darby was not fazed, "With your husband so very dead set against the match, how will you pull it all off despite his objections?"

Mrs. Hudson attempted, "I shall not admit to him being *dead* set against…"

"But, *everyone* is talking of it. Your husband is dropping hints and such *everywhere*. He has said so very much against the poor young fellow, that even the *men* are all agog with the chatter of it!"

Mrs. Hudson truly did not like to be talked of in such a way by the townsfolk and did nervously laugh falsely as she tried to lighten the reality of her feelings, "My husband does like to joke and tease…"

"Well, in some regards, I do not blame him… you know… since he was not consulted in the case prior to the business being done and so much of it was as much as set in stone before he caught wind of it."

"Well, he did have half a mind to say no when he was first informed."

"He is surely blameless on that count, to be sure." Mrs. Darby sipped from her cup.

"Regrettably, he did take some personal offense."

"I dare say."

Though no listening ears were likely anywhere near, Mrs. Hudson leaned forward and virtually whispered, "He would have appreciated Lawton's humble entreaty."

"But of course! What goodly father would not *expect* it?"

"Yes, well… I did try to smooth it all over."

"Difficult for you, to be certain…" Mrs. Darby sipped once

more.

"I had hoped that Lawton might attempt to smooth things over himself."

"Did he *not*?!"

"You know… an apology or *something*…"

"*Truly*! One would have thought that he would have attempted… something."

"Perchance an application *after* the fact…"

"Yes, yes… it makes one *wonder* about the young fellow."

"Or at least an *explanation*…"

"Yes, surely…"

"Mr. Hudson is quite usually a *very* agreeable man and could be reasoned with… you know… *appealed* to…"

"Lawton *should* have done something… to be sure." Mrs. Darby was all compassion for Mrs. Hudson's plight.

"As it was, all the applications for understanding and such were a good deal left to myself to orchestrate on the engaged pair's behalf." Mrs. Hudson sighed a great sigh.

Mrs. Darby was all disgust and deep feeling for what her friend had been required to suffer due to Lawton's laziness in the betrothal business. In keeping with profound compassion, she did not bother mentioning Florence's possible weakness in managing the affair to save her own mother from such attempts at aiding the said situation, for that would have been far too much for her friend to bear about her newly engaged daughter at this time.

Not especially long after Mrs. Darby was on her way (her buggy's wheels and her horse's hooves taking her to her next personally appointed place to chatter, though not to spread rumors, but only to clarify them), Mr. Hudson arrived home to partake of some luncheon with his dear family before setting off on further business. He tenderly kissed his wife's cheek before sweetly kissing the cheeks of both his daughters. He gently patted the heads of his two young sons. He tried to appear light-hearted throughout the meal, though his heart was beginning to feel a trifle heavy. Mr. Hudson was not all jovial jesting as per his usual self. He sensed satisfactorily that none of his family could see his concern for his Florence, written on his own personage. Cadence did notice something amiss and did wonder within herself, however, though she did chock up what she saw and sensed as relative to what had already passed regarding the engagement, rather than anything up and coming. Being a man of active business and generous means, Mr. Hudson's vast inquiries regarding Lawton sent out eastward, had gradually, though fairly quickly begun to yield a basketful of unpleasant fruit. As husband and father, he was not yet ready to share the picture that was being painted of Florence's new fiancé. He would wait a while longer. He would gather more information. He would be certain of the facts and see as clear a picture as could be fashioned before showing it to his womenfolk. He could barely fathom what he was finding. How could he burden his wife and daughters with such? He must know *all* before telling anyone *any* thing.

Having lifted himself up upon his horse and ridden away from his beloved home and family, as Mr. Hudson strode along, his thoughts rapidly mulled over every fact that had been sent to and placed before him by his most trusted and tremendously reliable sources. What was being painted of Lawton was a terribly ugly picture of the man. Quite assuredly a recent widower, the death of his young rich wife (of only a matter of what seemed to be months) was speculated to have been suspicious. Those who were close to the situation and the parties who knew the couple well, truly wondered over the sudden and untimely death of a healthy young woman, the tragic event which the new and young husband did not seem the least distressed over beyond worrying about people's opinions of him. Could Lawton have had anything to do with the death of his wife? Could he possibly have married and murdered her for money? The thought seemed to make reason stare, though; many murders had been hatched in history to full fruition for far less cash. Add to his cloudy widowhood and accompanying generous inheritance, Lawton had even more recently broken with and run from a subsequent hurried engagement with a young and also rich woman, who later was found to be with child, and had reported with firmly professed

PAINT & PIANO

conviction that the child was most definitely Lawton's own. Word also was that Lawton had run from numerous debts here and there, as well as from challenges to duels over many points of honor. He had squandered and gambled away much money, appeared to have tainted the reputations of many a young woman over some time, and had generally become considered a blight of a man throughout much of the eastern parts where he was known. Where Lawton was very well known, he was not in the least well respected long since. Had the man come west to escape a ruined life and reputation out east?

As some little time passed, most neighborly happy thoughts and plans of the upcoming sacred union betwixt Florence Hudson and her Oscar Lawton, which had overshadowed town and countryside chatter about Mr. Hudson's not having fully approved of his daughter's fiancé and the manner in which she was obtained by the young man in their mutually binding betrothal; were but a thorn or a prickle to Mr. Hudson in light of his weightier concerns. His mind was more disagreeably engaged. How on earth was he to inform his dear family of the burdensomely horrid news that he had honorably obtained in the protective efforts of a father over his daughter? More news had come to him. Mr. Hudson was thus armed with more facts, more details, more proof and more damning evidence against the infamous Mr. Oscar Lawton. True duties must be performed. A man must forsake his fears and execute just laws oft times. One especially chosen and prepared late evening time, when Mary had been given the night thoroughly off (and thus she was safely away out of earshot), after the boys were put securely to bed; Mr. Hudson brought his wife and daughters into his library for a very quietly serious closed-door pronouncement. The most difficult task of his life thus far, Mr. Hudson proceeded with clarity and brevity, though without omitting any pertinent proven fact; and ended with a declaration of Mr. Lawton, the libertine and blackguard, having been banned from the Hudson house, all surrounding properties and more imperatively, being barred from ever seeing, speaking with or communicating to Florence again.

All the Hudson women were pure shock. Mrs. Hudson was replete with convulsive shakes and a mighty thundering confusion. Cadence was complete accepting somberness. Florence was all tears, horror and impassioned disbelief as she swiftly took herself to her own room, locking everyone out of it, even her trusted and most beloved twin sister. Tex and all other hired hands around about the place had been set on secret guard outside that night by Mr. Hudson. They had each been given strict man-to-man instructions to prevent Florence from escaping, should she attempt to do so. No person on the Hudson estate slept a wink of rest that night, beyond Jake and Hank, and eventually Mary who finally brought herself home and to bed after all difficulties had been done without her knowledge.

By the next day and night, many hired men were still taking guard duty turns around the Hudson home, Mary had slipped out, beyond (to begin the spreading of the news) and back, Mrs. Hudson (who now kept to her bed with a certain sort of sorrowful sickness and a headache malady for the time being) had been given thorough information from her husband (and permission and indeed even *requests* from him) to feel free to tell Mrs. Darby (or anyone else that she pleased), everything that she had been made aware of about Lawton the libertine. Mrs. Hudson was not yet ready to face Mrs. Darby, for her own mind was mulling over dreary details such as the best way in which to offer back Florence's engagement cameo gift to her friend. Mr. Hudson wished his wife would rouse herself up and get to the serious female business of gossiping against the evil man who had toyed with their fair daughter's heart. After all that had transpired, Mr. Hudson longed for tattlers to spread the truth like wildfire around the town and beyond. What good were gossips if they did not do their duty when valid information fully warranted such? Why were women seemingly made by nature and divinely designed to chatter, if they did not wag their tongues when crucial events demanded the spreading of such pertinent and serious news? Mr. Hudson thought it a real kind of ironic blasphemy against heaven that tongues were not unleashed at the *most* relevant and worthy times. Did not hearsay, rumors, conjecture, speculations and all such prattle run about on women's lips when such was *not* backed by truth? Why then could not such talents and desires exercise their full power when times and conditions cried out for justice of this sort? Why were women possessed of such nonsensical natures? Where was the sense in these creatures? Mr. Hudson felt an urge to wag his *own* tongue against Lawton from the rooftops of town. Was he alone *required* to do such? If the women would not do their duty by his damsel daughter, he would strike out and proclaim the words that were still lying unjustifiably silent as the grave.

On a second or perhaps third night whilst all horrid news was still very fresh, Florence could still not believe the facts before her and announced to Cadence, whom she had finally allowed into her bedchambers, "I will elope if need be, I tell you! I will run away if I must!"

"Think what you are *saying*! You do not truly mean that. You only speak so… but would *never* do such."

"But I am a grown woman. I am no longer a child. I am not a little girl anymore. I can do what I like. I can go *away* with him." Florence was all defiance.

"That would be errant *folly* and you well know it."

"No, no… I do not *know* such to be folly."

"Come to your senses. *Think*!" Cadence commanded.

"Oh… how can I think… what I feel is… this is *such* a horror! How could this happen… to *me*!"

"It is better that all these things came to light… *before* the marriage took place."

"I will not allow vicious rumors or lies to keep us apart. I do not believe *any* of it. If Father and Mother try to prevent me…"

"But, it is *proven* that he was formerly married."

"Well… so, he had a wife. She likely died of some infectious fever… and now he is free to marry again. He loved before… does he not deserve to love *again*?"

"But why was his manner so deceptive in the case? Why not admit openly from the start that he was a widower? Why hide the truth from even you?"

"Perhaps he feared that I would turn away from him… reject him… He might have feared me a believer in only *one* true love. He knows me passionate enough to choose not to forgive him for loving elsewhere enough to have been married before."

"Even if I allow you *that*… though I suspect…"

"*What* do you suspect him of?"

"I hardly know, though… there has been some speculation…"

"*Speculations!*"

"Well, her death was suspicious…"

"You think him a *murderer*?! You think that I could love a man who could murder his *wife*?!"

"There was a great deal of money in the case… he gained great wealth due to her death…"

"You think him capable of killing his wife for her *money*?!"

"Many men have killed for less…"

"How could you think such *villainy* of him?!"

"I do not *truly* think such… but… it is all too strange…"

"My own sister, my only truest friend… could *believe*…"

"But, what of the… *other*… news… facts…"

"Do not even *speak* of them!"

"But I *must* speak to force you to think of such things. Could you consider marrying a man who… who… fathered a child, and deserted the child and the mother as has been reported?"

"Reported… I can not… I do not believe such falsehoods… such must be fabrications on that woman's part. It could be nothing but a *lie!*"

"But Father researched the case and there seems to be some generous proof of it…"

"No… I do not believe…"

"Well then… what of the gambling… and the embezzlements of those funds… Father found full proof of *that*. You could not possibly consider marrying him now."

"Yes, yes I *could!*"

"Florence… I do believe that he wished to marry you for convenience sake… to try to get hold of some of Father's money…

or at least to find respectability and income out here in the west where nobody knows of him and what he has done in the east."

"How can you say that?!"

"I do not think that he *truly* loves you and... you can love *again*."

"No! He is the *only* man for me! I will not love again if I cannot have my Lawton!"

"I am certain that you will heal from this. All will be well... in time... I assure you."

"No! It will not! You are without feeling! You have no heart! You have not loved! You do not know anything of my heart and pain now!" Florence threw herself onto her bed, fully watering her pillow with her tears. Cadence stayed to comfort her sister by softly stroking her back even as Florence tried to motion her away.

In time, that very night, Cadence was able to bring Florence to a semblance of sanity and calm. Cadence's reasoning with her sister was far more fruitful than even she thought was possible in so short a time. Miraculously, Cadence even brought Florence to a little laughter relating to the tragedy. Though Florence would most likely have been inclined to pay all due respect to her sorrows by remaining in a kind of mourning for at least a lengthy period of time, Cadence's especially exertive effort to bring her sister back to her former common state of happiness, did promptly hold sway and enact power to convince Florence to more quietly let go of her grieving for her loss of Lawton, despite her general fondness for an outpouring of tears on any such especially sad occasion.

In the coming days, Cadence helped Florence to possibly begin to see any little folly in her trusting ways and careless heart. Cadence begged Florence to learn to think a little more, even as the painter sister insisted that she had great difficulty in trying to feel a little less.

Very soon, Mr. Hudson's impatient hopes for all women in the region to convict the criminal and vindicate the victim in every conversation near and far, began to be gradually granted. The news (including wild speculations that went even far *beyond* the facts that he had gathered against Lawton), was not kept silent excessively long. Mr. Hudson could begin to comfortably sleep nights again. Tongues were finally wagging on the side of truth. Soon, all people of good or even any conscience at all, harbored intense disdain towards and about Mr. Lawton, so much so, that the Stinham family cast the spurned man out from amongst them. Old Mr. Stinham and his wife did not wish to be considered guilty or filthy by association. What or who was this Lawton fellow to them anyway or anyhow? He was only a sort of friend, mistakenly made by young Mr. Vincent Stinham on a trip out east. Lawton could go back to whence he came or to the devil for all they cared. Old Mr. Stinham was so wretchedly vexed by the entire affair and his family's association with the now proven libertine, that he instructed his dutiful wife to make herself strenuously busy running and gabbing about, to make certain that they, the noble Stinham clan, truly was not held or considered responsible in any way or form, for the likes of the outcast of whom they had now most thoroughly washed their hands of. Mr. Lawton and his character were resoundingly denounced by every last Stinham. Even young Mr. Vincent Stinham turned his back fully against his former friend, for he fully well knew that to remain friends with such a man was no way to get himself his own proper bride. In secret swiftness, Lawton slithered away in shame and where he went, nobody knew.

Luckily for Mr. Hudson, he did not hear of any wagging tongues that faulted Florence to some degree, for trusting Lawton enough to engage herself to him in the improper way that all claimed she professedly had done. Plenty of pity was bandied about for Mr. Hudson, though he knew not about it. Mrs. Hudson was pitied as well. Even still, Mr. and Mrs. Hudson were faulted for not reining Florence in more than they heretofore had done.

When Mr. Hudson thought that the time was right, and when he finally thought up the right way to do it (and somewhat sometime after his boys already had heard all from any source within their own hearing), father told his sons of the end of the engagement of their sister to Lawton. Shortly thereafter, from the depths of the cellar and basement, and the heights of the loft in the barn, the alcove in the summer kitchen, the play place of the attic and the consecrated territory of their very own beloved tree-house, Jake and Hank did delight in never-endingly whispering their latest, though not terribly creative chant, "The rotten Mr. Lawton."

Mr. Hudson had heard his sons' new favorite phrase early on in their days of chanting against the horrid interloper, and had advised them earnestly and with the most morbid of threats against their bodies, that they should not breathe such words within the hearing distance of their poor wailing and grieving sister. Though, one still starry night when Florence thankfully had just barely begun to near entirely overcome her distressed and distraught spirit regarding the wretched libertine that had wormed his way into her innocent heart through such treacherous means, the Hudson brothers could be heard, even by her, shouting with attendant laughter from the tallest top of their tree-house, "Mr. Lawton turned out to be rotten!"

Even Florence had to laugh upon hearing the seeming song. Oh, but she loved her dear sweet young brothers, and more especially, she adored her dear protective father, which specific affection for the males in her immediate family sphere, was all the more a contrast to her newly found hate of young men in general.

7
Mr. Worthington

Soon you will be married and I will persist towards being an old maid." Florence sighed in a sorrowful swoon, throwing herself onto her red velvet chaise.

"Me? Married? What errant nonsense do you speak of? To *whom*, I pray?!"

"Do you need *ask*?"

"What silly suitor has Mother found for me? I fear to ask!" Cadence laughed.

Florence continued revealing her thoughts in her mysterious manner, "Mother has not found him, but in a sense, Father has helped to bring him to you."

"Of whom could you possibly be speaking?""

"Mr. Worthington, of course!"

"Mr. Worthington? Mr. Connor Worthington?" Cadence was all astonishment.

"What other Mr. Worthington could I possibly mean?"

"Has Mother... or Father..."

"Nothing as yet... nothing that I know of..."

"Oh... then why... why did you mention him in reference to me?" Cadence curiously posed.

"Well... he is in the territory again... and Father has invited him over for dinner tonight and..."

"And?"

"And perhaps he will rally his courage to ask you to become *his*, this time!"

"Florence... what has put this idea into your pretty head?"

"Surely you know that he is ardently in love with you?" Florence advised in query.

"Surely you jest!" Cadence returned in utter amazement.

"Why is he always here, at our house… when he comes… I ask you?"

"His business with Father brings him often."

"Then why so much time spent walking with you?"

"He has no sister. I suppose I fill that role for him."

"Oh, so he is only in want of a *sister*? That is so very kind of you to be as his sister." Florence giggled good-naturedly.

"We are friends… also."

"Ah… friends also. So he was in want of a friend as well and thus you are friend to him."

"We are good friends." Cadence protested gently.

"But you only like him as your friend. Nothing more could *ever* blossom from the association?"

"I… I think not. We are only good friends… like brother and sister."

"Could you not ever feel *more* for Mr. Worthington?"

"I have not considered that."

"*Consider* it."

"No, I do not think so. I am content to be friends."

"Well, he is quite obviously not content to only have you for friend and sister. His affections have blossomed so much more than to be your brotherly friend, to be sure. You must be living in a foggy dreamland of sleep, my silly one."

"No… you must be mistaken." Cadence shook her head, inadvertently bobbing her bun somewhat.

"Have you no eyes to see, my dear sister? Can you not see how he *looks* at you? How he *speaks* to you? His passions towards you are plain for all to see!"

"You are imagining romance, Florence! Mr. Worthington only ever thought himself a friend… he looks on me quite as a brother would… truly." Cadence was unwavering.

"Oh, I am quite convinced that, in *that*, my darling oblivious sister, you are entirely mistaken!"

"No, you are wrong. I am certain of it." Cadence was firmly adamant.

"You had better prepare... *beware*, my dearest!" Florence warned.

"Beware?" Cadence raised an eyebrow.

"For his proposal."

"Proposal?! I see nothing of the sort... Connor has no intention..."

"*Connor*! You are on first name basis with him... in secret! I knew it!" Florence elated.

Cadence instinctively put on her most serious tone for added impressive emphasis, "Mr. Worthington... has not thought anything of the sort. I promise you he does not intend to propose to me any time soon, nor in the future..."

"Of course he does! Mr. Worthington's marriage proposal is *imminent*!"

"We are only good friends, I assure you."

"He means to make a lifelong and most dear friend of you."

"I still cannot see why you have manufactured this silly notion!"

"Are you blind?!"

"Whatever are you speaking of?"

"His lengthy gazes... his little sighs..."

"Florence! Again I say, you imagine things... you imagine what you *wish* to see... what you *hope* to be true."

"Oh, no, Cadence. I would imagine and conjure up someone *far* more dashing for you. No, I see clearly. I see clearly whereas you are blinded in a fog."

"*More* dashing?!"

"Yes! I find him quite... dull."

"Dull! Dare not say that! He is perfectly interesting and witty."

"Ah-ha! You find him perfectly interesting and witty!" Florence laughed aloud.

"Mr. Worthington is a perfectly good fellow... but..."

"*But?*"

"Well, I suppose that… I do imagine… loftier…" Cadence was purely thoughtful.

"Loftier? Yet he is perfectly good, as you said…"

"He is a perfect friend… a very good person… an equal… but should not a husband be a man that a woman can… look up to… more?"

"Even *more* wealthy?"

"No! I had not thought of money!"

"Well, do not be too quick to discount money, my dear. You are the practical one of us two. It never hurts to marry a rich man. Even *I* can see that."

"I meant… wiser…"

"Older?"

"Perhaps."

"Well, I suppose if you fancy an older man, you will find plenty of offers, I dare say."

"I do not fancy an older man… I just…"

"You want someone less like a brother… more like… a father?"

"Oh, no… no… I just wonder if a woman needs to find her husband in… high esteem…"

"You do not highly esteem Mr. Worthington?"

"I do esteem him. I highly regard him. He is a good and true friend…"

"As you said… but?"

"I worry that I could not… learn from him."

"So, you desire some sort of… *scholar*, then?"

"No… no… simply someone with greater… grander… knowledge than I possess myself."

"But, Mr. Worthington is well educated, surely?!"

"Yes, of course… but there is… something… wanting, I think."

Florence half joked, "He is *too* amiable, perhaps."

Cadence paused and then concurred, "Perhaps… yes…" and

then she almost seemed annoyed, "He dotes on my every word or whim."

"Oh, this is too much, sister! You recoil at such?! His doting is *proof* of his love, to be sure! And what woman does not wish to be doted on, I ask you!"

"I fear he... worships me."

"He dotes! He *worships*! I like him better and better! He is truly the man for you! Why do you *resist* him?!"

"But, does a woman wish to marry a man who... is something like... a perfectly loyal servant... or pet?"

"A servant! A pet! Oh dear! Poor Mr. Worthington! If he only knew you thought such of him. His heart would break into a million pieces!"

"Dare not share what I have just said! I am only thinking aloud as you well know! Do not repeat any of my speech in reference to..."

"No, no... of course I would never... I will not divulge a thing... to anyone... worry not, my sweet sister."

"Dare not."

"I will not. I promise! As solemnly as the grave!"

"Good then."

Florence's eyes lit up brightly, "Ah! I see what you are saying! You wish for a mysterious man! Someone who puzzles you... and perhaps ignores you... an aloof creature... who could possibly have it in him to mistreat you... but chooses not to. Some sort of man's man. Some women crave that sort of..."

"No, not at all! I simply wonder at a man who... the way Mr. Worthington hangs on my every word... and would say yes to everything that I would wish. I think..."

"You think too much... as always!"

"No I..."

"And you do not think he is in love with you! Oh, you are as an infant in matters of love! You need me to teach you what is what, pertaining to all things of the heart!" Florence fell off of her chaise laughing.

After some hesitation to recover from her slight annoyance with her sister, Cadence helped Florence off of the floor and back onto her chaise, where Florence set about completely composing herself and straightening her dress.

"I cannot let Mother find me in such a position!" Florence giggled.

"Indeed not. You would suffer lengthy lessons in etiquette in the least. Mother's vast and extensive education would be brought down hard upon you as in our schooling days past."

"But, back to lessons of love that I must teach you…"

"Yes, yes, we all know that you have acquired some special knowledge and experience where love is concerned. I admit myself a child in that realm." Cadence conceded as she checked herself and hoped not to have upset her sister's heart at all.

Florence was unfazed and all seriousness, "Perhaps I simply pay more attention than you to such things… that is all."

"Perchance it is that you care more for matters of love. You wish to marry. It could simply be that I do not wish such for myself."

"You do not wish to marry?"

"At present I still feel full young to contemplate it… and who is to say that I will ever feel inclined towards marriage?"

"Tish tosh! You will want to marry when the right fellow comes along to talk you in to it!"

"Mr. Worthington could be as right as any man. I can find little if any fault in him. I like him as much as I think I would any man. It could only be that… well, perhaps it is that I am not right for marriage."

"Oh, do not say such a thing."

"Well, I do not feel… *ready*… to consider any marriage."

"You and I are still young enough… we have time, to be sure. I have always been more inclined to marry early… and perhaps you will likely marry later."

"Perhaps… I would really rather not think of marriage as yet… though do not confess such openly to Mother… as it would distress her… and thereby distress me… due to her scoldings and lectures."

"Yes, stay a spinster a little longer if you please. And no matter what Mother, her friends or the prattlers tattle around, neither you nor I are old maids as yet!"

That evening, Cadence tried to forget all Florence and she had spoken of, whilst Florence's mind could not sway from every word that had passed between the two of them earlier that day. Florence tried not to stare, as she could not help but watch Mr. Worthington as he persisted in staring at Cadence. Cadence seemed all but oblivious to Worthington's almost mooning over her. Florence was now more certain than ever that the poor fellow would ask for Cadence's hand in marriage very soon. Tonight or perhaps tomorrow, she thought. Florence hoped upon hope that Cadence would comply and make the worthy fellow the happiest of men, for Florence firmly believed that Worthington could make her sister very happy indeed. Cadence's doubting thoughts aside, Florence felt such a fondness and warmth for Worthington.

The very next day, after the Hudson family luncheon, to which Mr. Worthington had been most cordially invited by Mr. Hudson, Mr. Worthington paid special attention to Cadence.

"It is very fine out." Mr. Worthington announced.

"Indeed, it is." Cadence smiled up at him.

"Would you like to take a turn outside around the gardens with me, then?"

"Certainly… I would." Cadence nodded with another smile, not truly suspecting anything beyond their former comfortable conversations, until she began to sense her friend's nervousness. While Cadence had thought herself adequately prepared or at least forewarned, when Mr. Worthington eventually earnestly requested her hand in marriage quite suddenly by some roses (the location of which seemed an almost romantic plan or gesture in itself), she did not respond as perfectly well and kindly as she would have liked to. Her mind could not seem to arise to the occasion.

"I am honored… truly honored by your proposal, but I… I… have generally thought that perhaps I shall never marry… or at least… I have not thought myself… inclined to marry… in the near future. I consider you a dear friend… quite like a brother… to me…"

Mr. Worthington was perceptibly stunned and clearly appeared working towards becoming composed before he could bring himself to speak. Cadence saw his obvious discomfiture and wondered how she might have done better to soften the blow. She did not wish to lose his friendship. He was very dear to her. Worthington eventually managed a reply which was surely not the best he might have hoped to offer.

"Ah… dear friend… quite like a brother… I comprehend your meaning. You… you wait for a… more pleasing offer."

"No… to be sure… you are quite pleasing enough… I only… do not think to marry."

"But… the right offer… would be accepted."

"No… no… I think not. At present, I cannot imagine an offer that… a man… whom I would accept."

Mr. Worthington thought that he understood Cadence better than she did herself. He quickly became thoroughly convinced that his offer was beneath her dreams of a perfect husband. Mr. Worthington surmised that had he been a richer, handsomer and more interestingly witty fellow, his deeply felt offer would not have failed with this beautiful young woman that he had come to so greatly admire and love.

Cadence could see some of what Mr. Worthington was feeling but could not imagine how to adequately protest in order to convince him otherwise. She felt a truly warm affection for him but dared not speak anything of it, particularly for fear of encouraging him to hope and try for her acceptance at some later date in the early future. Cadence considered her response far from warm enough, but did not know how to remedy what had passed her lips already between them. Her feelings of friendship for Mr. Worthington were so very dear to her; yet, she did not feel a need to become his wife. How could she communicate clearly regarding the place in-between where she felt such admiration for him and yet did not wish to cross the bridge into matrimony with him? If she were inclined to marry anyone, it could surely be him. She believed that Mr. Worthington must feel all confusion, for she felt it keenly herself.

The days that followed held much discomfort for Cadence and Worthington alike, for his and her father's close business relationship and warm friendship brought the young man over to the Hudson house many times. Cadence had not dared to tell Florence of what had transpired in the garden. She would not surreptitiously, symbolically or otherwise wound Worthington by divulging his heart's desire to even Florence. No, Cadence wished for this secret garden event to remain an undisclosed thing. She determined that neither her parents nor her sister should know of it. Florence's continued hints and teasing about Worthington to Cadence here and there were rebuffed by Cadence with gentle fury. Florence was all the more convinced that Worthington was working his passionate magic upon her sister. Painter believed that pianist would fall to the young man's charms in due time. Each day that went by, Florence seemed to see Worthington as all the more handsome and dashing, than she had heretofore ever believed her own mind capable of. The more she saw her sister and the young fellow together or even apart, they seemed a perfect fit for marriage to her. Florence's romantic heart now danced at the thought of Cadence marrying Worthington.

Quite suddenly, it surely seemed to Florence, that Worthington was gone from their parts and she thought that she had heard him say to her father that he was to be gone for an extended length of time. Florence was not quite certain, but she had thought she may have overheard Worthington say that he might even take a trip to Europe! What was the man about?! She could not believe he had been over so many times and had not tried for Cadence. Florence could not believe that she could possibly be wrong about the fellow's intentions towards her fair sister. What could have gone wrong with Worthington?

Cadence felt Worthington's broken heart intensely and was very sorry for it. She wished that she could go back to the garden and try again. Perhaps she could have gently dissuaded her friend from wishing for marriage with her without breaking his heart so severely.

Cadence could see that their dear friendship had been harmed horribly. Worthington was deeply injured and his great difficulty in managing such pains around Cadence was palpable. She could see no way to comfort him without cheering him to try again towards further matrimonial attentions her way. How could she possibly comfort him without encouraging him? Florence's confused vocal musings and curiosities to Cadence about Worthington pained Cadence to hear. Of course she knew what Worthington must be feeling and why he was planning not to return anytime near as soon as he would usually have done. Worthington's planned extended leave of and from Hudson territory was painfully obvious to Cadence.

The day after Worthington was gone eastward, Mrs. Hudson abruptly commandeered Cadence in to Mr. Hudson's library for a conference. Cadence instantly knew what might be coming. Mrs. Hudson closed the door behind them after they entered the manly retreat. Mr. Hudson had obviously been waiting there for their arrival.

Mr. Hudson spoke to Cadence in an uncharacteristically serious tone, "You quite surprise me, Cadence. I cannot think why you have rejected Mr. Worthington. He is well set up, comes from good family, has been a close business associate of mine for quite some time… and I thought of you and he as fast friends."

Mrs. Hudson put in, "What were you about, saying no to the good fellow?"

Cadence looked down, not knowing what to say in response. Her mother continued, "Indeed, he is as handsome and rich as anybody. Your father and I are beside ourselves in confusion."

Cadence's father added, "You know how highly I regard him. I would have been so pleased to call him son. I thought… we thought… that you liked him…"

Mrs. Hudson clarified, "Indeed, we thought you might be in love with him. That is why your father encouraged him to try for you. You and he have been… have seemed… so very amiable together… such good friends… and now…"

Mr. Hudson lamented a little, "I suppose I should have had

your mother inquire of you first... but you appeared so... well, from my vantage point, I would have thought that you were in fact encouraging him yourself."

His wife agreed, "Yes, we both were certain that you would say yes to him."

Mr. Hudson began to elaborate somewhat, "He did everything right and proper by me, coming to speak to me about his feelings for and attentions about you first... before he approached you at all... unlike the wicked Mr. Lawton... and..."

Mrs. Hudson helped, "Now he is gone away... for nearly forever, if you please..."

Cadence looked up, sadly, "Gone away... *forever*?"

Mrs. Hudson grieved, "Yes, broken-hearted... he has gone off to try to forget you... who knows *when* he may return again."

8
At the Dressmaker's

Spring was well in the air and Easter still being amid the season; it was always a good excuse to order up new dresses. Mr. Hudson had been easily convinced to approve of the expenditure. New spring dresses would be quickly fashioned for the Hudson women just in time for Easter Sunday. Mrs. Hudson was all things cheerful as she and her daughters made their way to her dressmaker, for the ordering of dresses and gowns or any such feminine purchase was always a sure way to bring great happiness to a woman like her.

As Mrs. Hudson and her girls were entering Miss Tinsdale's shop, a certain Mrs. Felter was leaving, but as was always her way, she had to stop to inform anyone in her path of any current rumors that she had become aware of, most particularly, any unpleasant news that pertained to anyone before her.

Mrs. Felter began, "You and your girls are the talk of the town, you know."

Mrs. Hudson dreaded what was to come but stayed composed as the girls observed all, "How so?"

Mrs. Felter glanced briefly over at Florence and then looked back at her main target as she dug in, "Well, of course I'm sorry for the mess you all have had to suffer with Mr. Lawton, and I do not fault Florence in the least over the matter, though some do and there has been a great deal of talk regarding all that. People do not approve of all that went on, on Florence's side, you understand, though I primarily blame that Mr. Lawton, you see... but that is not all... people begin to say that you will not be able to marry your daughters off... that this bad start has tainted them in the eyes of others...

and, well, you know that Cadence hasn't had any offers and she does not put herself forward at all, indeed, she sits back and few notice her…"

Mrs. Hudson contained her anger and remained pleasant on the surface, keeping the veneer of society well intact, while she defended, "Well, Mr. Lawton was proved a libertine and a blackguard to all… and everyone knows that my Florence was an innocent throughout… even the entire Stinham family have banished the criminal from their property forevermore. That should be proof enough, I dare say."

"Speaking of the Stinhams, I did hear that young Mr. Stinham, Mr. Vincent Stinham, has long since taken a liking to Cadence… I'm sure you must have heard by now, or at least suspected it… and that… well… that Cadence is playing coy with him… but, I am certain that will come to nothing… since he is so unpleasant to look at… no mother with any feeling would force a marriage of that kind… well, especially with your daughters being so very lovely themselves and not really wanting for money in any respect… not a soul would expect you to encourage such a match simply for mercenary reasons of money." Mrs. Felter paused her speech for want of breath.

Cadence looked somewhat shocked at the news of Mr. Stinham pertaining to herself, while still resisting her anger at Mrs. Felter for discomfiting her sister by her speech about the horrid Mr. Lawton. Florence could not hide that she was not at all surprised that Mr. Stinham should like her sister, even as she was continually doing her utmost to pretend that she did not care one whit about Mr. Lawton, nor what anyone might say against her regarding him and what had so recently transpired between them.

Mrs. Hudson was all frustration but continued in calmness to set the record quite straight once and for all, for she was not all too fond of any of the Stinham family, "I'm sure that Mr. Vincent Stinham is a goodly fellow, and he is worthy by all accounts, but I desire that my girls should marry for love, and there has not ever been one hint on either of their sides regarding Mr. Stinham, even though we all have been neighbors these many years and they know him quite well enough… though I do truly wish him all the best in finding… some other… lovely young lady to marry."

"Yes, well…" Mrs. Felter added, "Speculations abound that you cannot or will not be able to get your daughters married any time soon, if ever at all."

Mrs. Hudson was at a loss for words and was trying to formulate something worthwhile, when Florence put herself forward for her mother's sake, "Cadence and I may or may not be inclined to marry after all, but I assure you, if we so choose, we will be very able to choose well. We are surely in no hurry, after all, since we are barely old enough to consider the matter anyway."

Mrs. Felter did not really wish to speak to Florence at all and so looked at and directed her answer to Mrs. Hudson, "A spinster in the making is a spinster before you know it. I am only giving you kindly advice, my dear. All I am saying is that from what I hear, if you do not mind the season and harvest whilst you can, men about the territory will think your girls beyond worth catching in the very near while."

Mrs. Hudson was truly aghast at such a speech and could hardly keep an agreeable countenance amid her measured reply, "I assure you that my daughters are still full young enough to bide their time for the best, rather than to settle badly quickly. I am a mother who cares for her daughters more than enough to do right by them as I see fit… in keeping with my husband's guidance, of course."

"Of course." acquiesced Mrs. Felter and then she continued to torture Mrs. Hudson with some expansive news to do with other people around about (most of the speech unpleasant hearsay), before the busybody was off and on her way.

Mrs. Hudson gave her girls a long exasperated look of disapproving disgust as she rolled her eyes and swayed her head in the direction of the retreating Mrs. Felter, an unspoken communication from mother to daughters, meant to tell all that she was feeling to her girls without saying a word about it, since their dressmaker was well within earshot, though Miss Tinsdale's back was turned to them slightly. Mother guided daughters towards the inner realms of the shop.

A spinster herself, Miss Tinsdale, was likely still young enough in appearance for her years, looking somewhere around thirty years of age or thereabouts, though her number of years since born was in actuality long forgotten (since her true age had been her own very great secret), for she had not revealed how old she was to a single person in many a year. Tending to feel a little beneath every one of her clients, she was always somewhat inclined to put on airs to try to raise herself up in importance. With her face lifted high, she waved Mrs. Hudson and her girls into the shop.

With a slight nod that seemed nearly a bow, Miss Tinsdale began, "We have the latest fabrics and colors from Europe... everything that is all the rage there... all these colors I have here for you to survey."

Still worn out from her distasteful discussion with Mrs. Felter, Mrs. Hudson only fairly attempted to half-heartedly agree, "Yes... lovely."

Miss Tinsdale motioned her hands over a multitude of choices and then continued her presentation, "We have silks and muslins, and linens and cottons. Please do feel free to handle any and all that I have here for you. I am certain that you will soon have your heads full of plans for dresses and gowns to take you through the all important upcoming seasons."

"Yes, to be sure." Mrs. Hudson managed. Cadence and Florence smiled and nodded in unison.

"Just look at all the colors we have for you to choose from. Are they not all lovely colors for Easter? Now... if you cannot decide upon one color each, we could certainly make up dresses with more than one color in each dress, if that would be to your liking... if you fancy that sort of colorful thing... but, better still, why not order up more than one dress each if you cannot settle upon only one color?" Miss Tinsdale paused for much needed breath.

Ordinarily, Mrs. Hudson would have jumped at the chance to find any excuse to order more than one dress each in one offing, but, she was still reeling from her run in with Mrs. Felter. All her high spirits had been temporarily dampened by the disagreeable encounter.

Cadence smilingly tried to aid in the matter, "Father would not likely approve of that. We have permission to order one dress each this time... for Easter... you know."

Mrs. Hudson rallied herself, "Yes, I suppose I must pars a little at a time... my husband is a very generous man, Miss Tinsdale, but sometimes he takes a frugal turn of mood, as you must understand... and thus I then must order up things one at a time, that he will not notice the expense all at once, you see."

"Well, if you find that you would like to order two dresses each, I could sew up the second dresses a little later... you know... one dress now... and a dress in the wings." Miss Tinsdale tried to be helpful to Mrs. Hudson and her girls even as she was attempting to help herself to a little more business.

Mrs. Hudson's spirits lifted and she was all cheerfulness once more, "Yes, what a capital idea! We will need summer dresses just around the corner, my dears!"

Cadence and Florence both smiled and were comforted to see their mother in higher spirits once more, for they did not like to see her sadly affected by town tattle and silliness. They each instinctively joined in with heightened excitement about all their choices and the opportunity to possibly order two dresses each.

Mrs. Hudson thrilled, "Look girls! Here is some very lovely silk in a most delightful pale blue. Would it not look grand on me? My blue eyes beg for such a color, would you not both agree?"

Both girls nodded happily to see their mother's enchantment over a bolt of fabric. Miss Tinsdale echoed Mrs. Hudson's sentiments about the blue silk and how well it would look with her blue eyes.

Florence joined in, "And here is some beautiful deep rich green silk for me, that would enhance my own eye color."

Mrs. Hudson and Cadence nodded in blissful unison. Miss Tinsdale also nodded smilingly.

Mrs. Hudson thrilled, "Oh, I truly do adore silk! Indeed, I truly do prefer it."

Miss Tinsdale assisted, "You cannot do better than silk, to be sure."

Mrs. Hudson added in answer, "And though silk can be so very expensive, especially out here in the west where it can be considered such a luxury, I do not pretend to boast when I admit that my husband is quite rich enough to pay for it, I assure you, Miss Tinsdale."

"I presume you will all be choosing silk, for both spring and summer dresses each, then?" Miss Tinsdale happily inquired of all three Hudson ladies.

Still thinking slightly of her father's often frugal tendencies, Cadence complied somewhat, though in another direction, "I do like this lovely brown cotton. I do tend to prefer cotton anyway."

Miss Tinsdale put in encouragingly, "Silk is always a luxurious choice, although cotton is very nice as well."

Mrs. Hudson disagreed in half astonishment, "Cotton? Oh, no… silk is the thing. How could you prefer cotton, Cadence?"

Miss Tinsdale tried to keep the peace between them, "Silk is surely the thing nowadays, but cotton is enjoyed by many as well."

"I do not know, Mother, but I do prefer cotton to silk… indeed, I think that I always have." Cadence replied, not yet knowing what other added explanation to offer.

Florence defended her mother, "I do not like to go against you in any thing, my dear sister… you know that I never wish to disagree with you, but Mother is right and you are quite wrong. Cotton can never compare to silk."

Cadence offered, "I suppose I enjoy the simple beauty of cotton. It truly does seem to suit me. I suppose that I am cotton and you are silk, Florence. I am not so fanciful as you, my effervescent sister. Our difference in this matter should not come as such a surprise, surely, for we differ in so many things."

Florence simply harrumphed.

Miss Tinsdale did not know how to help at present and stood aside, looking on.

Cadence pondered aloud, "But would not Father be pleased if we could each be satisfied with cotton? Silk is so much more expensive…"

"Your father has agreed to pay for dresses, and he did not stipulate any particular sum. Why choose cotton when he will pay for silk? Settling for cotton, with silk at our fingertips would quite simply be silliness and folly." Mrs. Hudson stared at her practical daughter in disbelief.

Miss Tinsdale began to busy herself off to the side, straightening out some fabric and laces, pretending not to listen to the animated discussion further, for the moment.

Cadence furthered her attempt, "Since we were speaking of possibly ordering two dresses each, I simply thought that if we were to choose cotton for our dresses, we would be more able to justify such to Father and therefore he could more likely be persuaded to pay for two dresses apiece for us."

Mrs. Hudson and Florence stood staring at Cadence. Neither knew quite what to say or even think. Miss Tinsdale played oblivious and away. Mrs. Hudson finally articulated her mindset on the matter, "I was not particularly thinking of telling your father about the second dress until later… when he would be more amiable to the idea. He has agreed to pay for spring dresses and so we will have spring dresses… in silk if we like. If we order summer dresses today, I will convince your father to pay for summer dresses a little later… and then we will come and get our summer dresses… in silk or even cotton if we so choose. Mr. Hudson will be none the wiser."

Cadence was not prepared to countermand her mother on the point, though she thought her Mother's form of secrecy errant. There was a momentary air of discomfort.

Florence grasped another bolt of silk fabric if almost to clear the air, as she fanned out the end of the fabric piece, "What of this red silk. Would I not look splendid in this strikingly scarlet color? I would wager that it would match some of my favorite jewelry exactly!"

"Indeed!" exclaimed Mrs. Hudson.

Florence picked up another bolt of silk fabric and displayed the end of it flamboyantly, "Oh, this purple is divine. I must have this.

Can you not just see me in this? I could not be ignored in this."

Cadence could not resist her sister's charms, "You will look splendid in either and you can never be ignored. You are always quite divine, my dear sister."

Florence looked to Miss Tinsdale, "Which should be my spring dress and which for summer?"

Mrs. Hudson looked to Miss Tinsdale equally for the expected advice. Miss Tinsdale could not seem to decide whether the purple suited spring or summer more, nor could she advise any better on the red.

Without any firm advice or instruction from either her mother or Miss Tinsdale, Florence simply followed her own impulses, "I will have purple for Easter and red for summer. Is that settled, Mother?"

"Oh yes, why not? You will look beautiful in both, as your sister so rightly stated." Mrs. Hudson beamed.

As Mrs. Hudson labored over her own choices of two fabrics with Miss Tinsdale's assistance, Florence played with lace and advised Cadence as she mulled over this and that piece of cotton. Cadence finally settled on a lovely pale green cotton fabric, for she oft chose green to enhance the color of her eyes.

Florence finally insisted, "Cadence, if you must persist with cotton for your spring dress, please do indulge at least me and choose a silk for the summer, I beg you. You must see the finer qualities of silk... or at least you must be able to feel it! Feel this silk... it feels so very creamy... almost alive or some such thing. Please choose a silk... if only for your dearest sister. Will you not make me happy on this point?"

Cadence was cajoled into enjoying the tactile sensation of silk but was not yet persuaded to settle on any color of silk for herself, let alone a second choice of fabric. Cadence was resisting for the sake of her father.

Florence persisted in trying to wheedle her sister, "What about this deep rich green that I was considering for myself earlier? Since it would look so good on me and with my eyes, we both know that you would look equally good in it. If you like, think of it this way: choose it for yourself with the sure knowledge that I will borrow it from you… and then you only need feel half guilt in the matter, since it will end up as much mine as yours."

Cadence could not allow her sister's last idea to escape her notice, "But you well know that even if I choose a fabric and color that you adore, my simple style is not your own… come, come, my sister… you would never be happy in a dress of mine… without all the puffs, ruffles and lace… all the adornments that I so usually pass on… you know you would not wear my dress… you never have wanted to wear a thing of mine since we were so much younger…"

Florence laughed, "There is far too much truth in what you say… but… your speech puts me in mind to recall how delightfully fun it always was when we switched clothes or horses to fool everyone… and I just might like to do that again. You know my deviously prankish mind… you know how I would like to play jokes on any men who might take an interest your way… so I just may surprise you, my dear sister, and begin wearing your clothes and pretending to be you…"

Cadence warned, "Dare not, sister… dare not… for we are far too old for such childish mischief… and there are enough idle tongues wagging against us as it is."

"You may think yourself too old, my sweet sister… but I am still full young for shenanigans and childish dreams." Florence laughed.

Cadence smiled and could not argue her sister's last point.

Florence flustered, "Well, if I cannot persuade you to choose a silk, at least pick a cotton fabric… what of that delicious brown you were mulling over? Would not that be a good summer choice? What of this lovely whitish cotton you were considering? Now that speaks of summer if anything does."

Cadence steadfastly resisted choosing anything, still remembering her father.

Florence turned to their mother for aid in the matter, "Mother, Cadence has picked the pale green cotton for her spring dress, but she could not decide between this brown and this creamy color for her summer fabric. What do you and Miss Tinsdale think?"

Mrs. Hudson looked over, considered seriously but fairly briefly and then turned to Miss Tinsdale, "Cadence will take creamy whitish cotton for her summer dress."

Cadence objected, "No, Mother... I would rather wait until later... you know... closer to summer... to settle on a summer choice."

"As you wish, then." Mrs. Hudson simply replied.

Florence's efforts were foiled and though she did not broach any level of anger in any way, she was truly somewhat diminutively frustrated and so she teased her sister, "Oh, Cadence! Why must you be so stubborn? How you vex me! Could you not settle on a second fabric for summer and be done with it? I know what you are doing and thinking. You are trying to please Father in this. But he does not and will not even know one jot of the matter... and what of pleasing mother and me?"

Cadence settled the matter firmly rather than settling on any fabric just now, "I will please you and Mother... and Father too, by choosing my summer fabric closer to summer."

Measurements were taken, styles were settled on and all relevant details were chosen as spoken to Miss Tinsdale, who was smiling broadly and none the less delighted that Cadence had only ordered one dress instead of two. As Mrs. Hudson and her daughters were about to leave Miss Tinsdale's shop, Mrs. Darby was entering. Proper happy salutations were offered all around before Mrs. Darby's attitude took a more serious tone.

Taking hold of Mrs. Hudson's arm and somewhat pulling her aside, Mrs. Darby advised, "My dear... we must stem the tide of malice against you and your girls... well, the hearsay and gossip is all the more so against Florence, but... there is a general tattle against you and your husband and even Cadence... oh, and your boys as well."

Mrs. Hudson was all fitful concern at her friend's news and thought that she might consider something towards fainting. As was oft per usual when she was around Mrs. Darby, Mrs. Hudson became un-customarily speechless and could not even gather the courage to look her esteemed friend in the eye. Her daughters saw the two women in close conference and upon hearing a little of Mrs. Darby's speech, suddenly decided to look at some lace with intense interest at great length. Miss Tinsdale chose to tidy some things nearby to also give some privacy to the two conferring ladies.

Mrs. Darby continued condoling with her friend, "I can imagine what you must be feeling... but worry not about my own good opinion of you, for I am your true friend and do believe in you and your daughters. I will help you in this... and truly... in every thing."

Mrs. Hudson was able to look to her friend with a budding comforted ease and the capability to firmly choose to gather her strength to remain standing and conscious, rather than to begin propelling herself towards the nearest chair for a faint.

More was communicated from Mrs. Darby to Mrs. Hudson, "When I arrived in town today not long ago, Mrs. Felter found me and was all agog with her news of having spoken to you here... so when I was quite finished with her, I instantly determined to come by and see any new fabrics and to think about ordering a new dress so that I might see you right away and speak to you. Mrs. Felter claimed to have warned you of sentiments against you... and she as much as told me that you are all ignorance and bliss... defending your Florence's actions with regards to Mr. Lawton... well, I told her that we all blame Mr. Lawton, wicked villain that he turned out to be... evil libertine that he is. We all mistakenly praised him to the heavens above at first and he proved himself a devil after all. I told her that your Florence is truly blameless and she should be disparaging Lawton instead of your beautiful daughter... indeed I did."

"Thank you, Mrs. Darby... you are a true friend complete."

Mrs. Darby was not yet finished with her friend on all that she felt to be pertinent matters of the moment, "Well, there is much more that perhaps I should tell you later on... at least I should save the bulk of my advice and the making of plans of repair together... though, perhaps there are one or two points I should mention *now*.

There has been much talk and many complaints against your boys for being so very rowdy… at the church picnic and then… well, you know… it seems that I just happened to miss out on the… well… entertainment, I suppose you could call it… but I did hear about your boys noisily chasing that dog all through town. Well, well… worry not too much about that… we women know that the bad behavior of boys is owing to their fathers' negligence… everyone generally blames your husband… not you, my dear. Are you supposed to go chasing through town after them… or anywhere else for that matter? No, no… I think not."

Mrs. Hudson braced herself for any more.

Mrs. Darby persisted, "Well, now… here's the most surprising point: there has been much speculation amongst townsfolk about Cadence having been leading young Stinham on or some such stuff and nonsense… though I do not believe any of it myself. Dear, dear, good Cadence. But, that is all such a lesser concern than the need to rein in and tame your wild and excessively rowdy boys… and though you are not as much faulted as your husband is… for leaving your boys to themselves far too much… of course many women do blame you for not rousing yourself to do… *something*. Boys must be disciplined by someone, you know."

Mrs. Hudson remained standing, steadying herself as she fought for calmness within herself whilst struggling for breaths of air from without.

As she continued, Mrs. Darby lowered her voice to shield against Miss Tinsdale hearing, "And about the boys… either scold your husband until he takes proper charge of his boys… or talk to your men about the place who can step in for your husband in his absence if need be… continuously… or intermittently… you know… when your husband is gone off on business… or even simply when he has no mind or strength to deal with the boys… you have and pay for hired hands… please do *use* them, my dear."

A speechless Mrs. Hudson had been feeling another more seriously real faint coming on and began looking at the nearest chair for relief. Her brow was all perspiration.

Mrs. Darby soothed, "Well, well… 'tis not the end of the world, my dear. Far worse scrapes than this have been smoothed over in no time at all when approached and handled properly. We will solve everything… I will solve everything. Leave all things to me. A few balls and parties, and everything will be set right for your daughters. Worry not. Wait and see. All will be well for you and yours… even speedily, I dare say. We will soon polish up your daughters' reputations and get them married off well… certainly long before Christmas is upon us."

Miss Tinsdale could not resist joining in a little and so moved over to lean in and try to help out, "Now, you know that I am not one to get involved, but, I did happen to overhear just a little of your speech just now, Mrs. Darby, and of course I picked up a few words of Mrs. Hudson's conversation with Mrs. Felter earlier, and I thought that perhaps I should tell you everything that I have happened to hear from all things recently mentioned here in my shop."

Mrs. Darby was all attention while Mrs. Hudson was secretly all dread and intently mooning over the nearby chair that would, in future, forever remain in her mind as Miss Tinsdale's fainting chair. Cadence and Florence's near distant ears perked up all the more as the two feigned playing with lace or anything else within their reach.

"Yes, yes… what news have you got that I do not know *already*?" Mrs. Darby was all impatience and looked to Miss Tinsdale for relief.

"Well… I suppose that Mrs. Felter has told you everything that she told me…" Miss Tinsdale began.

"Yes… *more*, I dare say… get on with it if you have anything new. Who else might there be? Who else has told you any news relating to Mrs. Hudson, her sons and daughters, and that horrid Mr. Lawton, or even that young Stinham fellow?" Mrs. Darby was all frustration.

Mrs. Hudson took refuge on the chair that she had been obsessing over, and then pulled out her fan to cool herself off with. She did not wish to listen any longer, but was compelled to keep her ears trained on every word that Mrs. Darby and Miss Tinsdale were saying.

"Well, Mrs. Stinham said…" Miss Tinsdale attempted.

"Yes… well, I am truly certain that I know all that you might know on that count, for I have had all from Mrs. Stinham myself! It should be terribly obvious that she is the first woman that I turned to for any information about Mr. Lawton or Vincent Stinham for that matter! Do you have anything new?"

"Mrs. Marsden told me that…" Miss Tinsdale tried once more.

"Mrs. Marsden came and told all to me *first*, to be sure… anything from anyone else?" Mrs. Darby corrected sharply.

"There was also Mrs. Bentley… she told me…"

Mrs. Darby interrupted again, "Of course you must know that Mrs. Bentley would have told *me* anything she knows… from the beginning…"

"Well… Mrs. Lennox said that…"

"You must know that Mrs. Lennox would have come to me first, I dare say and I have had the latest from her just today. I am quite certain that you can have nothing new to tell me… unless there might be somebody who would have spoken to you who hasn't already shared all with me. Could there be *anyone*?"

Feeling thoroughly flustered by Mrs. Darby's superior connections, Miss Tinsdale hesitated, "Well… I… I do not think so. No, I suppose not."

Turning first to Miss Tinsdale and then to Mrs. Hudson and even passing a glance over the Hudson daughters, Mrs. Darby settled everything for everyone there, "Well then, let us not waste any more time. Mrs. Hudson, Cadence, Florence, let us get to your house to iron out all these troubles of yours. I will order up dresses later."

9
Grand Plans

Mrs. Darby nibbled on her biscuit after heavily loading it with preserves, "I would not trouble my head about any such tattle, my dear."

"To own the truth, I dare say I have felt somewhat mortified." Mrs. Hudson settled into her favorite parlor chair more comfortably, before sipping her milk.

"Bother not that there are many heartless womenfolk around calling Cadence and Florence spinsters already."

"I *try* not to allow it to bother me, to be sure."

"Your daughters are full young and beautiful enough to bide their time in catching *just* the right man." Mrs. Darby sipped her own milk.

"Yes, truly, I do believe so myself."

"And your husband is rich enough to keep them, I dare say. You need not hurry them towards just any man for want of any *money.*"

"Certainly... certainly not."

"Waiting is sometimes the better thing to do, as we well know. Rushing into matrimony can bring the direst result."

"That is what I keep saying to myself... though it has brought me little comfort of late."

Mrs. Darby felt pressed to counsel, "Yes, well... even so... we do not wish to leave it any longer... you must do what you can do for them... you know... so that you will not miss any opportunity. They are ripe for the picking and you should not become complacent. You cannot afford to sit back and rest easy. You must strike while the iron is hot... and make hay while the sun shines... you know... all that sort of thing."

"Yes, surely I must try… I must do… something." Mrs. Hudson briefly glanced at her butter-laden biscuit and considered taking another taste of it, though due to lowered spirits her appetite had sorely waned since Mary had brought the tray in.

"Do not worry, my dear. As I have said before, I will help you. Let us begin planning some parties *now*." Mrs. Darby smiled, wishing to encourage her friend.

Mrs. Hudson perked up, "Yes… what first… a dinner party, a garden party… a ball?"

"A garden party must wait for more dependable weather. You do not wish to be rained out, my dear. Wait for the surer sunny days of summer."

"Yes, of course. You think of *everything*, my dear friend."

"A dinner party or a ball would be best, I do believe." Mrs. Darby counseled after another bite of her biscuit.

"I would like to *finally* give my daughters their coming-out ball."

"Oh dear… my dear… I fear it might be a *little* late for that. You should have done that when they were somewhat younger."

"Yes… I feared that I had missed that opportunity. My husband did not wish to pay for such an extravagance the few times I tried to begin to speak and plan of such a thing… and *now* it is all too late!" Mrs. Hudson was visibly distressed.

Mrs. Darby soothed, "We are not out east, you know… and so it does not truly matter… though… I dare say that I cannot understand why your husband is so very *tight* with his money. He is one of the richest men in these parts… though not as rich as my husband, to be sure… but still…"

Mrs. Hudson defended, if only a little, "My husband has his generous moods and his… other, well, less charitable moods. I cannot complain… truly, he is quite openhanded much of the time… if he *agrees* with the expense. I oft times must… convince him of the need or justification for the expense."

"Yes, and you *do* generally guide him so very well. Men do seem to need to be guided by us women. They do not always know what is best for us and our children. They are sometimes like little boys, I dare say."

Mrs. Hudson could not but nod, at least a little.

"Nevertheless, a ball is a ball. We need not call it a coming-out. That is neither here nor there. Your daughters have been enough out in *society*, already. Most folks around these parts do not think in those highbrow terms anyway, and thus it is of little import. A ball or a coming-out ball would be all the same to most folks in these parts."

"To be out *west* is my saving grace, I suppose." Mrs. Hudson smiled a relaxing smile of relief, and then took a little taste of her biscuit.

"Yes, we all get away with *murder* out here." Mrs. Darby chuckled and then her hostess laughed aloud with her.

Mrs. Darby was all seriousness again and continued her thoughts of import, "All *wild* frontier excuses aside, let us put our civil society heads together and set in motion our fervent efforts to show off your daughters so that you can get them married off before you begin regretting their desperate situations as spinsters."

Mrs. Hudson dug into the matter at hand, "As much as I would prefer a ball at once, I would think that my husband would be more amiable to a dinner party first. The expense would be less. No musicians would need to be hired for a dinner… and for a ball; there would be a dinner anyway."

"A very wise approach, my dear… talk your husband into a dinner party first and then work your way up to a ball a little later on in the summer sometime."

"Yes, yes… and I was thinking that Florence's paintings could be put up all over the place… to impress the young men, you know."

"Of course! She is a virtual *master*, I dare say! How did you bring her talents to such perfection of abilities on your own? One would think that she studied with the masters in Europe."

"Well, of course… *I* would have wished her to study with masters in Europe… but as you well know; my husband would not have gone for that… he would not even consider sending the girls to finishing schools out east to be polished. I was forced to do all myself for them. At least I was finished out east, though; I sometimes wish I could have fulfilled my own dreams to study art in Europe in my younger days."

"Well… I dare say that *none* would be the wiser… you have finished and polished them very well indeed, and their talents and abilities certainly do far exceed my own daughters' meager accomplishments."

"Do not disparage your *own* daughters! They are fully quite talented. I thought them truly accomplished."

"They never applied themselves like *your* daughters have done. My daughters were all about seeking husbands."

"Florence is quite like that as well."

"Though she manages to paint as if that is all that she does… no one would know that she did not paint all day long. Who would imagine that she spent any time on anything else?"

"Painting has always come to her naturally. When the girls were small, I put paints and piano in front of them both, and Florence took to the *paints* right away, while Cadence was *all* piano from the start."

"And it is a very good thing that you were so accomplished in both that you could teach your daughters yourself… to paint and to play so excessively well."

"While young I could not decide between the two disciplines and so I was taught and tried to learn both well. I thought that someday I would know which way to go, and dreamt of studying with masters of both music and art, or at least either, but… then I was married… you know, while still young… and my dreams for my own talents and abilities were… well… I was happy to put all my energies towards teaching my girls all that I knew."

"You have done very well by your girls… better than any other mother in *these* parts, to be sure." Mrs. Darby was most generous in her compliment.

"I only wish that their talents will aid them in catching better men."

"They have *beauty* enough to do the trick, I assure you."

"While most men are drawn to beauty... perhaps... *better* men appreciate ability and virtues."

"And your daughters have *all* such in abundance."

Mrs. Hudson all but blushed for the compliment, and paused to compose herself a little before continuing with party plans, "Thank you very kindly... you are too kind, as always... yes... and this all puts me to mind... I think that I might force Cadence to *play* for everyone. What do you think?"

"Yes, of course."

"She is loath to play for company... is always reluctant to give in to my requests for her to entertain guests... though she has overcome much shyness over some years and will play before even strangers now. Of course she will refuse to accompany her superior piano playing with her own beautiful voice, but Florence will be happy to sing like a bird, for she has as much a lovely voice as her sister. In fact, Cadence prefers to have Florence sing whilst she herself plays; that all attention will be drawn away from herself and onto her sister's singing. Florence loves the attention she receives when she sings. It is her only mode of performance, I suppose."

"That is a capital idea. Showcase both daughters at once with one performance!"

"Yes, it is an irony that Florence loves to perform, but does not love to play piano... she does not play nearly as well as Cadence, you see... well, at least she can sing equally well... but Florence loves to place her paintings all over the house, gives them as gifts and even paints in the fields... I do think that she secretly wishes to be seen by young men and that is why she goes *out* to paint sometimes."

Mrs. Darby laughed, "I do like that Florence of yours. She is a girl after my own heart! So much like my own daughters... wishes to be *seen* painting, indeed! I could see my own daughters having done that to seek out young men... though their paintings would have been nothing to look at, to be sure! At least *they* were each worth looking at!"

Both ladies chuckled together, took bites of their ailing biscuits and genteel sips of their ever warming milks and then settled in for more talk.

Mrs. Hudson took first fresh opportunity, "So, a dinner party it will be. You must help me plan the decorations."

"There will be ample spring flowers to choose from, I dare say."

"To be sure."

"Oh… and… you must have some garlands of leaves here and there." Mrs. Darby commandingly suggested.

"Oh, yes! What a genius you are!" Mrs. Hudson amazed.

The two ladies continued chattering animatedly about their grand plans for a dinner party at the Hudson home, while they each finished off their biscuits and milk. When their minds were fatiguing from as much the afternoon sun and resultant heat, as they were their important business, and their tongues were becoming somewhat exhausted for the visit, Mrs. Darby took her leave and was off to her own home.

Mrs. Hudson sought out her girls (who had disappeared somewhere or other) to share some of what she had discussed, since her husband was not due to arrive home for quite some time. A woman always enjoys repeating a conversation to another friendly ear, and so Mrs. Hudson wished for her daughters or husband to speak to, for Mary would not be the one to discuss such matters with, though she might be the only captive audience to be found any time soon.

As mother searched the halls of the sizeable Hudson house for any sign of her fair daughters, she mulled over many past months and even some recent years. When the first hint of a rumor of hearsay about gossip had been pressed upon Mrs. Hudson's ear that her own daughters were in exceedingly grave danger of fast becoming spinsters (by her dear trusted friend Mrs. Darby, the most dependable bearer of local news of all kinds), Mrs. Hudson had determined right that very instant, to throw some kind of party for her daughters. It was not as if she had not already considered the need for parties to put her daughters forward before, and indeed, long since. Mr. Hudson had not been so very cooperative where a coming-out ball or any such societal thing was concerned. He saw no need for throwing his girls out to be considered for marriage as yet and so society balls or any such thing were not important enough to him to warrant his putting down the necessary money. Well, now the girls were fully past old enough to deserve their day in society; and the general town and regional chatter and tattle against them was becoming so terribly severe, that Mr. Hudson could not refuse the expense of at least *one* dinner party. He had a heart, and he cared for his daughters' well being, to be sure.

The precious twins' mother determined that every possible eligible male about the town and within multitudinous miles around it, would be sure to be enticed by tempting invitation, to feast upon every culinary delight and the very great beauty, talents and abilities of the magnificent Hudson daughters. The best of Florence's many paintings would be prominently displayed throughout the front foyer and elsewhere, while Cadence would be cajoled into polishing up her most impressive piano pieces through constant practice prior to the ball, to free her nimble fingers to energetically and impressively perform those songs in public in the most glorious way possible at various appropriate times that auspicious evening. And of course, Florence would sing whilst Cadence played.

Mrs. Hudson did not wish to allow it to be said, or even considered in thought or speculated in prattle, that she had not done her full duty by her girls. Every opportunity for marriage would henceforth be allowed and offered. Though the girls were merely nineteen, Mrs. Hudson would set the stage for them to make good marriages as soon as may be. First a dinner party, then perhaps a garden party and finally a grand ball. By the time Mrs. Hudson would have her husband talked into a ball, luckily, the vegetable gardens and fruit trees round about would have reached their full splendor and thus a cornucopia of tastes would be available for all oral senses of everyone at the ball.

Numerous other marriages of late had likely sparked the chatter against her own daughters, Mrs. Hudson surmised. Of course

Florence's quick, short and failed engagement with the odious Mr. Lawton had surely added fuel to any prior fire. Then there were the silly speculations about Cadence's teasing of Stinham, who seemed head over heals in love with her (though the stupid and horridly rich frumpish young man was known for his falling in love with women of all kinds, all over the place). Perhaps somehow, Cadence's so recent rejection of Worthington was also thrown into the mix of things. Such was surely a possibility. Mrs. Hudson wondered who might have told anything pertaining, for it was a very great secret, or so she thought. Neither her husband nor her daughters would have possibly breathed a word to anyone, to be sure. Could Mary have overheard something and then run about telling everyone she knew? It was true that Mrs. Hudson had confided in her dear and trusted friend Mrs. Darby, about poor rebuffed Worthington, but, of course Mrs. Darby would not have told anyone about Cadence having refused him. If any word had gotten out, it must have been the responsibility of Mary's loose lips. Cadence would be entirely mortified if she suspected as much. Poor dear Worthington did not deserve any public humiliations, surely.

Mrs. Hudson soon got to thinking happily that since so many other girls had been recently married; such would be to her and her daughters' benefit, for fewer females would be attending their parties as rivals. Mrs. Hudson possessed full confidence in her daughters' abilities and attractions, and as a goodly mother, she would guide her feminine progeny towards the best suitors, for they were fully as lovely as any young lady in all surrounding parts of the territory. Mrs. Hudson also took comfort in the assurance that her husband would spare no necessary expense, if she could convince him of all the pertaining justifiable requirements. Mrs. Hudson realized that she could aid in reminding her husband of his true husbandly and fatherly duties, and to prick his pride so that allowing to reasons of shame on his part, Mr. Hudson could be wheedled into paying all contiguous needed expenses. His business ventures had paid off handsomely of late and he adored his daughters as much as any father, and thus he could be coaxed into paying any truly warranted sums, or be made to feel thoroughly guilty for not so doing.

Before Mrs. Hudson had the luck of finding her daughters or having her husband come home to talk to, Mary found and told her that a certain Mrs. Bruhor had stopped by for a visit. Mrs. Hudson happened to be near the upper back parts of the house when Mary found her.

"I have let Mrs. Bruhor into your Parlor, Ma'am. She is sitting there waiting on you." Mary announced.

Mrs. Hudson was openly mortified and annoyed, "Oh, dash it all! What is *that* woman doing coming to visit me? What is she doing in my own parlor? What a woman at what a time!"

"I am very sorry for it, Ma'am. I did not know that you would not wish to see her or I would have sent her away. I would have told her that you were not available." Mary apologized emphatically.

Mrs. Hudson promptly thought through any escape plans she might have available at her fingertips. Perhaps she could pretend to be out, or perchance she could feign sudden sickness or a fierce headache? Could Mary be thoroughly convincing with the revolting Mrs. Bruhor? Would Mrs. Bruhor believe whatever Mary might tell and explain to her, at the house mistress's request? Mrs. Hudson feared not. Would Mrs. Bruhor suspect that said house mistress was hiding out from her and any other cruelly key gossips of the town and countryside? Mrs. Hudson feared so. No, the woman of the house would simply have to face the consequences of not having completely and entirely forewarned her maid as to any and all such busybodies that she did not wish to speak with at present. Most unfortunately, Mrs. Bruhor would have to be reckoned with by Mrs. Hudson. The poor lady of the house made her way to her fair parlor (usually her very own treasured sanctuary, now turned against her as if a torture chamber), like a lamb to the slaughter.

Putting on her happiest of false faces, and straightening her attire, Mrs. Hudson showed up at the velvet curtains of her precious parlor doorway, "Mrs. *Bruhor*! I am most delighted to *see* you! What a joyous *surprise*! What have I done to deserve such a *pleasant* surprise as to be treated to your most *esteemed* company? Would you like some tea or something of the sort?"

Thankfully for Mrs. Hudson, Mrs. Bruhor was not the brightest candle on the cake, and did not truly notice Mrs. Hudson's overdone artificial glee at being subjected to her uninvited presence.

Mrs. Bruhor falsely smiled back, "Thank you, no, for I was just filled with tea by Mrs. Stinham at *their* place."

Mrs. Hudson sat down primly, straightened her silk skirt and ruffles about her and then looked at her unattractive, uninvited and most unwelcome surprise guest; *still* smiling, though straining somewhat to keep such a broad counterfeit grin firmly painted upon her face as she spoke, "And how are *you* this fine day, my *dear* friend?"

"Oh, quite well, as always." Mrs. Bruhor's own false smile was just commencing to begin to fade somewhat slightly.

"Good, good… *very* good." Mrs. Hudson still managed to keep up the smiling fakery.

"As I said, I was just over visiting Mrs. Stinham."

"Yes?"

Mrs. Bruhor's face became all serious somberness, "And Mrs. Stinham is *very* perturbed with you, I must say."

Mrs. Hudson's smile drooped perceptibly as she smelled a morsel of what might be coming due to the former hint from Mrs. Darby, though she tried to appear all innocent ignorance on the possible matter, "Oh dear, no… *why*?"

"Her *dear*, poor son has been all but jilted by your Cadence. Surely you must be *aware*?"

Mrs. Hudson near leapt to her feet to instinctively verbally thrash her disgusting visitor for her insolence but held herself back and down, and somehow found enough civil calm to say just the appropriate words whilst still sitting instead, "I have not the *foggiest* notion of what you are speaking. What could Mrs. Stinham and her son be thinking and speaking about, pray tell? Cadence has but barely spoken to the fellow here and there… and only to be polite, I can tell you *that* much for certain."

"No, no… Mrs. Stinham tells *quite* another story, I assure you, for her son as much as made your daughter an offer, and then was as much as refused. He was put to such pain after Cadence had *led* him on, as if down a romantic garden path, until he was *hopelessly* in love with her. They are calling her a *jilter*, you know."

Mrs. Hudson was past becoming furious. How dare she? How dare they? Well, she would keep her outward calm until later on, "Oh heaven's *no*, my dear... I know my Cadence, and she would have told me of *any* such offer or any such thing for that matter. I say again, she has only *rarely* spoken to the Stinham boy in order to be *polite*. She is a very *dear* girl and... takes pity on *all* sorts, you understand."

Mrs. Bruhor was becoming irritatingly adamant, "No... no... Mrs. Stinham was *certain*. Her son was certain. Your Cadence made him to love her and then jilted him when he offered. They say... that Cadence is the kind to play those sorts of injurious games with young men."

Mrs. Hudson violently wished Mrs. Bruhor from her parlor and from her house. There was no use in talking to the woman. She would not be reasoned with. She did not wish to find the truth, but only wished to pain her hostess with manufactured gossip from the neighboring house of the Stinhams. Mrs. Hudson determined to find a quick and easy way out of this laboriously hideous conversation.

Mrs. Hudson leaned forward as if to get up, as a symbolic gesture or sign and blatant hint for her loathsome visitor to observe and hopefully mind her manners in keeping with the desire of the hostess for the visit to be near done, as she herself said, "Well... I have my *own* informed opinion on the subject, but I will seek out the entire truth from my daughter... just to be certain. You and I need not hash the matter over any longer at present. I hope you will forgive me, but, I have *suddenly* realized that I need to speak with my maid about this evening's meal, that *all* will be prepared properly before my husband's arrival home. You know how our men can become so very *irritable* if they are not served a proper meal shortly after arriving home, after a long day's work."

Mrs. Hudson stood up, that there would be no doubt in Mrs. Bruhor's mind as to their brief and unpleasant visit being all but over and done with. Mrs. Bruhor was astute enough the take the blatant hint from her hostess and got up herself. Mrs. Hudson politely but firmly guided Mrs. Bruhor to the front door and could not scurry the woman out the door fast enough. Indeed, Mrs. Hudson knew that she had fairly committed a massive social blunder that Mrs. Bruhor would delight in spreading about the town and beyond. All ears would hear of how rude Mrs. Hudson had been the day that Mrs. Bruhor had openly accused Cadence of being a jilter of the poor Stinham fellow.

No sooner was Mrs. Bruhor gone out the front of the Hudson house than Cadence came in the back way. When Mrs. Hudson soon found her daughter, she could not contain herself in any measure, and suddenly spouted, "The *nerve* of that gad-about woman! Hideous! To think that she should come into my *parlor* to advise me in such a fashion! She came *uninvited*, mind you! She popped by, put herself on one of my beloved chairs, and began to speak in such a way against you… *you*, my dear child! You: a *jilter*! A jilter of that Stinham fellow! Can you believe that? It is the talk of the town! Common manufactured gossip! And it seems that Mrs. Stinham is spreading the lies around about the entire region. Young Stinham claims you charmed him and that he made you an offer that you rejected! What lies! What infamy!"

"Calm yourself, Mother. Sit down here if you must. Do not trouble yourself with such ridiculous nonsense."

Mrs. Hudson sat herself down on the bench that Cadence had motioned towards, and there in the hallway where she had found her daughter, she began to continue, "Perchance they could accuse you of jilting our poor, dear Worthington, though I would not call that jilting in the least… but *Stinham*?! You charmed and then jilted Stinham? How dare they even couple his name with yours in the same sentence! He is a buffoon! You are an angel! Even with all his money, he is not *worthy* of your bootlaces!"

Cadence stroked her mother's shoulder, "Calm yourself… truly… I do not care one whit. Surely the entire thing will blow over. It is such silliness. Who will believe it? At any rate, who of any worth could be convinced that I would do such a thing pertaining to Stinham?"

"I only hope that your treatment of *Worthington* is not out."

"How could that *be*? He would not have... we have not... *Mother*, you have not spoken of it to anyone, have you?"

Mrs. Hudson looked up at Cadence sheepishly.

"Oh, Mother! Who have you *told*? What have you said?"

Repentantly though defensively, Mrs. Hudson confessed, "I... *just* told Mrs. Darby... but I have not breathed a *word* to anyone else."

"Mrs. *Darby*?! Oh, no!" Cadence leaned against the wall for support.

"But she is my trusted friend."

"She is a *busybody*, Mother... loveable, yes, but still a busybody."

"Do not say such a thing about my dearest friend."

Cadence breathed long and hard, "I dare say the word about my spurning Worthington is *all* over the countryside by now."

"No... truly... Mrs. Darby promised not to..."

"Oh, Mother... how *could* you..."

"She came calling when I was in a weak moment... I sought comfort..."

Cadence sighed, "Well, what will be, will be. Feathers cannot be contained when scattered to the wind."

Florence came dashing in, "Mother... I saw that horrid old baggage Mrs. Bruhor driving away... what did she want with you?"

"Only to gossip against Cadence... for the word *is* that Cadence jilted Stinham." Mrs. Hudson explained.

"Cadence jilted Stinham?! *Ridiculous*!" Florence half laughed.

"Mrs. Bruhor had it from Mrs. Stinham herself... and she says that everyone is talking of it." Mrs. Hudson lamented.

Florence as much as brushed the gossip off, "Oh, who *cares* what they say or think? Anybody who has half a mind will know such could not be true. Stinham is next to mad in love for *most* of the girls in the town and around it. Who would expect Cadence to accept him even if he did offer? Who would accuse Cadence of flirting with *anyone*? More particularly… with *Stinham*… I shudder at the very thought, I tell you!"

Cadence smiled. Mrs. Hudson chose not to mention Worthington again.

Florence added, "Mrs. Bruhor is likely envious that the odiously rich Stinham did not offer matrimony to one of her *own* daughters, though they throw themselves at him enough! That woman should be hiding in shame for the way they carry on in public places! They were in the saloon t'other week when I went in, and if I had not known who they were, I would not have thought them of *any* proper society by the way they were behaving! I told you all about it, did I not?"

Mrs. Hudson sank, "You were in the salon again?"

Florence corrected, "Oh, no… that day… before… the only time that I have ever set foot in the place… you remember."

Mrs. Hudson chose not to acknowledge Lawton and his having taken Florence into the saloon, but then attempted to begin a lengthy speech, "Mrs. Bruhor is one to think it very fine to teach one's daughters to *improperly* push themselves forward in attempts to snatch men for marriage… but I am a woman of *propriety* and decency…"

Florence jumped in with a chuckle, "With her daughters being such *floozies*, how dare she speak a single word against Cadence!"

Her mother continued with her speech, "Yes, she teaches her daughters to do worse than she is accusing my own daughter of. I would say, that to throw oneself into the path of a certain man, that he may take notice of you, is one thing; but to behave like a barroom, saloon or dancehall hussy is another matter. Cadence and Florence… do not ever let me hear of such conduct from *either* of you!"

The girls simply laughed at their mother's metaphorical warning to them. The subject of trollops soon waned as they began to forget Mrs. Bruhor, to settle in towards the evening meal, though all such discussion was rekindled by Mrs. Hudson once her husband arrived home, and she promptly complained to him about the unpleasant visitor she had briefly though painfully suffered through that day. The girls helped their father calm Mrs. Hudson, in order that she may once again enjoy thinking and talking about her grand plans for jolly parties, spring through autumn, all designed to show off her wonderful daughters to deserving young men.

In that one evening, perchance through having fed her man so well (a carefully planned delectable selection of some of his most favored foods), Mrs. Hudson was successful in getting her husband to agree to pay for a dinner party in honor of their girls very soon, and even to promise to *consider* paying for either a garden party or perhaps a ball later in the summer months. Mrs. Hudson's sore distress caused by Mrs. Bruhor's idle tongue that afternoon was greatly alleviated by Mr. Hudson's grand husbandly and fatherly generosity that evening. Thus, the lady of the house did go to her bed very much pleased; and under the moon and stars that shone on her house that night, while she slept did she dream of grand plans and parties to come, all due to the fact that her wondrously generous husband spared no expense to bring her matchmaking plans to fruition. Her dear Cadence and Florence did find worthy young men that they might marry well, and her darling Jake and Hank did nothing to distress anyone, not even herself, for they were as good as gold in her pleasant night's slumbering vision.

10
Family Table

Mrs. Hudson frowned at her twins, "You should really try to come down earlier, girls. The boys were done breakfast at least half an hour ago."

The girls chimed in together, as they were oft inclined, "Sorry! Yes, Mother."

"You both seem to make a habit of being late to family table in the mornings."

Mr. Hudson could not resist adding to his wife's scolding, "Jake and Hank are off and away, gone to whom knows where and it is anyone's guess as to when they will be back again. If you two persist in arriving to meals after your brothers have scurried off, they will begin to forget of your existence. Do remind them now and then that they have living sisters, if you please."

"Indeed." Mrs. Hudson could not help smiling at her husband's jest.

Florence thoughtfully put in, "Yes, well… if we came down to breakfast when the boys did, I doubt that we would even have our hair fairly underway… and you know perfectly well that we young ladies must be allotted more time to ready ourselves than young lads, for we have a great many layers to fidget ourselves into in the morning."

Cadence chuckled at her sister's precociousness.

Florence continued, "The boys hardly need spend a half an hour or more at their dressing tables brushing their hair and pinching their cheeks like we are expected to and therefore *must* do."

Mr. Hudson smiled, "The boys' cheeks are naturally quite pink enough… likely from all that running around that they do. Pray, do not teach them to pinch their cheeks as you do yours."

The girls laughed. Mrs. Hudson smiled but quickly composed herself to seriously clarify, "You well know that they don't have dressing tables, anyway… and why would a boy need to spend all that time brushing his hair, I ask you?"

Florence half jested, "Perhaps they should?"

"Should what?"

"Have a dressing table and brush their hair more."

"No, no… all a boy needs is a washbasin and perhaps a looking glass." Mother answered daughter emphatically.

Mr. Hudson could not resist helping his wife, "Little is expected of boys when it comes to appearances, and their hair is short to be sure."

His wife agreed, "Yes, my dear. Indeed."

Florence defended, "Then you must allow us a little more time for making ourselves presentable each morning, Mother… for our hair is so very long and more is expected of us as to appearances, being that we are girls… and in point of fact, young women… and of marriageable age… though not yet married off… to your dismay, I must say. Therefore, you must grant us young ladies the many moments necessary to make ourselves fit to be seen."

"Yes, I suppose so… though perhaps you could try rising a half an hour earlier each day."

Florence jestingly protested rather loudly and in the harshest terms, "I object to that! Yes, I emphatically *refuse*! We sleep late even as fine ladies were always meant to do. All the time you are telling Cadence and me to be as fine European ladies and *now* you wish us to rise with the maids and menservants? Get up with the sun? You know that all the country gentry way over there eastward someplace, sleep in 'til noon or thereabouts… or even *later*, I dare say! Sleeping in late is behaving just as fine English ladies. And add to all that… you wish us to catch husbands as soon as may be as well! What of our beauty rest? No, I say that the boys can do without seeing us some mornings… and if they wish to have audience with their sisters before luncheon, they can stay in bed a little longer themselves... or stay at the family table or at least somewhere round about it until us fine ladies have come down to breakfast."

Cadence laughed along with especially Mr. Hudson, whilst Florence smiled and subtly bowed her head just infinitesimally enough to be noticed by only the most naturally skilled or highly trained eye.

Mrs. Hudson lost out on the laughter herself, for her mind had been briefly resting upon what to do to achieve the best dinner party that would offer her daughters the best choices in men and then, "Well, do try to make it to luncheon in time today to see the boys before they run off somewhere."

Her husband assisted, "To be sure. The boys need to be reminded this very day that they *do* have older sisters... and very beautiful ones at that."

Cadence quipped, "Father, you know that Jake and Hank would no sooner recognize beauty in a young lady than warts on a frog."

Her father answered her, smiling for the entertainment of it all, "To be sure... and they would prefer the natural beauties of frogs or toads... and lizards... to fine ladies such as yourselves, I dare say."

Mr. Hudson was soon off to his work, Cadence to her piano for some long-appointed and neglected practice, Florence to her paints and canvas to finish up a painting that she had started days past, and Mrs. Hudson took an opportunity to tire Mary's ears regarding plans for the upcoming dinner party. By the time luncheon was put on the table, Mr. Hudson had obediently arrived on time though the twins had barely found sense enough to get away from their paints and piano and come to table a little less than purely punctually.

"Girls, girls! Come break bread with us... and listen... your father and I are in the midst of having a conversation about your coming-out ball!" Mrs. Hudson delighted.

Mr. Hudson teased, "There is no *conversation* about it. As always, your mother does all the talking and I cannot put a word in for trying."

"And your general silence is why you are able to eat so very fast,

I presume?" wife observed to husband.

"And your overwhelming lack of silence is why you eat so very little whilst taking such great lengths of time to do it." husband observed to wife.

Cadence kissed her parents before sitting down with them at the table. Florence promptly dove after toast and preserves as she was seating herself.

Mother advised her daughters, "Do not forget to try the cold ham. We have some very fine ham today."

"Yes, this cold ham is a very fine ham… not so like the bad ham your mother has had served to us in previous days." husband teased wife.

Mrs. Hudson half lamented to her husband, "Why must you tease me so? It can become so very tiresome, my dear."

Mr. Hudson decisively answered, "Why, it is the duty of every husband to tease his wife."

"Stuff and nonsense! Oh, bother with you." Mrs. Hudson temporarily finished with her husband as he finished off his very fine cold ham.

Mother then continued to her daughters, "Girls! Your father has agreed to purchase extra flowers for your summer ball. The event will be the envy of everyone in the summer season!"

"I'll spend us into poverty, for the envy of others!" Mr. Hudson chuckled.

"Ridiculous! You could easily afford twice as many bouquets as we will be displaying." Mrs. Hudson defended in slight frustration.

"I beg you will not torture me with any more flowers. I will be sneezing enough as it is, my dear."

"Oh, tish! Do not *speak* such silliness!"

"I am only doing my duty. I *must* tease you."

"You take such *delight* in teasing."

"With you, it can be *true* joy."

"Now, you begin to vex me."

"Oh, no! Not that! And I only *begin* to vex you! Perchance I should make more efforts in the future!" he laughed.

Ignoring her husband's game, Mrs. Hudson tried to continue sharing her happy thoughts with her daughters, "Girls, your father has agreed on silk… and the lace I spoke of before… you know, for our dresses for the summer ball!"

Mr. Hudson broke in, "Now, I *really* must be done with luncheon, for silk and lace have appeared on the menu! I thought flowers were too much. I must away on matters of business."

"Where are the boys?! They are so excessively late to luncheon!" mother thought of her lost sons.

"I will find and send them." He kissed his wife quickly and was off and away.

As Cadence and Florence munched on their toast, tried the very fine cold ham and sampled other delights upon the family table, Mrs. Hudson continued chattering away to her daughters about the upcoming dinner party and the eventual summer ball in their honor. Mrs. Hudson needed no verbal responses from her table companions, for her conversation *towards* them was more a rambling thinking-out-loud sort of speech. The girls smiled their silent responses as they ate their lunches. Their mother was so very delighted that she had convinced their father to pay up for a dinner party right away and then also to fund her grand plan of a summer ball, likely to be held late summer when the many harvest seasons would amply supply all that she could hope to ask for. Mrs. Hudson confessed to her daughters that she had not yet pressed their father for a garden party nor broached the subject of any other party that she was hoping and planning to host for her girls, in-between the dinner party and ball that he had already agreed to; but she was very sure that if she played her cards right and asked him at the proper times, she would be able to bring him to her side on those plans as well. Mrs. Hudson was truly giddy with excitement. Planning parties seemed *everything* to her of late.

By the time Mr. Hudson found Jake and Hank and then subsequently brought them to the table to eat their midday meal, the girls had almost gone from the room and luncheon was nearly ready to be removed. Mr. Hudson did not stay long for family conversation for he was required to attend to his business matters off and away, but sisters reunited with brothers and joined in with their mother with many a scolding to the boys for having been late to luncheon after and despite all that had been said and done to get them to the table on time. All the more was warned about coming to the dinner table in time for the blessing on the food and all the expected pleasant family evening meal conversation that would be enjoyed by all there.

Later that night, Jake and Hank miraculously arrived to the family dinner punctually enough, but needed to be sent up and away to their washbasin to clean themselves up enough to be vaguely presentable and equal to the table setting. Mrs. Hudson would not allow for any wild behavior at her table, though they did all live out in the west. She liked to try to keep some semblance of civility and society in their household. Out-of-doors, the boys could run rampant, but, within doors, there would be peace, calmness and decent behavior. The lady of the house insisted upon such and the man of the house enacted any necessary laws and consequences to make his wife happy on the matter. Thus, the Hudson boys preferred to run about out in the wilds of the Hudson family properties, rather than to behave calmly within the Hudson house. And so it was that, rain or shine, snow or heat, Jake and Hank tended to remain *around* rather than *in* their family home, though with lovely spring weather after a long winter, the boys preferred to be as their mother wished: outside instead of in and underfoot. Indeed, with many roosts to choose from, Jake and Hank could camp out in multitudinously favored spots, though their favorite place to roost recently was a special secret hiding place above the summer kitchen, which currently put even their exceptional tree-house to shame on all counts in their minds.

Once everyone was seated for dinner, Father having offered the blessing on the food, family chatter began in earnest, though Jake and Hank gulped their food down far more than offering any opinion or thought, for they two wished to return to the outdoors while there was still enough evening and light for them to be able to get their fill of whatever mysterious energetic activities boys of their budding age tended to do on an expansive ranch. Though they were intermittently scolded by their mother for having bad manners for this or that offense, both boys, who's ages and heights were fast threatening to begin to turn them towards becoming young men, turned their full attention onto their plates and rarely looked up to see who was saying what. Mrs. Hudson had begun to speak of parties again, hinting of the need for at least a garden party and other such parties, though more particularly, focusing on the soon-to-be upcoming dinner party as well as the late summer ball. She talked much of decorations, foods, gowns and all such pertaining female delights, but most particularly she spoke of who to invite, or more precisely, which eligible men she might be able to get her hands on for her daughters to choose from.

"Mother, do you intend to marry us off in haste then, rather than taking the time to make the best matches for us?" inquired Cadence, half in jest.

"Of course not… indeed, though, if we tarry *too* long on the course of finding you both husbands, the choices will be very thin on the ground and you may be forced into a lesser match." Mrs. Hudson answered in all seriousness.

"But, could we not win better if we better ourselves a little longer?" Cadence stalled for time, not wishing to think of marriage any time soon.

Perceptibly shocked, Mrs. Hudson answered, "Mercy me! What more in beauty and ability could a man *want* for, than what you and your sister possess?!"

Mr. Hudson happily nodded obedient agreement towards his wife whilst Florence smiled widely at seeing the exchange.

Cadence softly smiled, "Thank you for your compliments, Mother, but neither of us cook."

Mrs. Hudson gasped, "That is what *cooks* are for!"

"But, what if we marry men who are too *poor* to pay for cooks?" Cadence half teased.

Her mother scolded, "Well, we will *not* be choosing from among poor men for my daughters."

"But, if I fall in *love* with a poor man…" Cadence began.

Her mother commanded, "Take care that you do *not* do that!"

"But, we cannot *sew* either." Cadence questioned.

Mother argued, "Stuff and nonsense! I taught you *many* stitches myself."

"But, neither of us has ever even *made* a dress." Cadence added.

Increasingly exasperated, Mrs. Hudson answered, "That is what *dressmakers* are for!"

"What if we marry adventurers who take us afar off onto a wild frontier where there are no dressmakers and we must sew our *own* dresses?" Cadence quipped.

Mrs. Hudson put her best effort forward, "Thank you for the advice and fair warning. No poor *or* adventuring frontiersman will be welcome to court my daughters… and *now*… your worries over all these things pertaining to marrying earlier are for naught."

"But what if I marry a rich man and then he *loses* all his money?" Cadence teased.

Mr. Hudson and Florence laughed. Jake and Hank looked up and then back down at their almost cleaned plates.

All exasperation now, Mrs. Hudson vented, "Learn to sew dresses, then! Learn to cook! I dare say you girls would learn all there is to know on either subject in a matter of days *anyway*! You are both clever enough, I dare say. Surely you could spend a day or so in the kitchen and then pay attention when we are next at the dressmakers for a fitting. *All* will be known to you and *then* you can marry."

Mr. Hudson was smiling between chuckles. Florence was vastly happy to be enjoying the entertainment as well. The boys were somewhat oblivious to the clever conversing circling above their heads, although, with desserts in front of them, it would not be long before they were begging their parents for release into the out-of-doors.

Cadence tried to continue teasing her mother, "But, what if…"

Mrs. Hudson turned to her husband in desperation, "Oh, Mr. Hudson! *Help*! Say something of assistance!"

He smilingly offered, "Cadence is doing so very well *without* my assistance."

"Oh, Mr. Hudson! What *good* are you to me?!" wife complained bitterly to husband.

Husband defended in jest, "I dare say that I pay for our cook, at least one dressmaker and not to mention many other…"

Wife defended with her own line, "And why ever *not*! I have born and raised your *children*!"

Husband agreed, "You are surely in the right, my dear. You have given me strong lively sons and lovely talented daughters."

Wife pleaded, "And will you help me find husbands for our daughters? You must help me to convince them to marry!"

Mr. Hudson complied, "Right you are, my dear. Worry not, for I will help in the case. Our daughters will surely receive offers from rich men, two of whom will take them off my hands and pay their cooks and dressmakers and…"

Jake interrupted, "Mother? Father? Can Hank and I go out now? We finished off everything on our plates."

Mrs. Hudson corrected, "*May* Hank and I."

Jake tried again, "*May* Hank and I?"

Mother quickly glanced over her sons and their plates and then nodded; whilst Father nodded an agreement to his wife's bestowing command. Jake and Hank were off and running, though both parents instantly called to their sons to slow down until they got themselves completely outside.

It was well into darkness before Mr. Hudson rounded up his sons and got them in to be scolded by his wife for not having come in far earlier and on time on their own. The entire family then enjoyed a little time by a small evening fire in the candle-lit parlor, where Mary brought them warm drinks to go with a little bread and cheese. Jake and Hank were reminded not to be messy by both their parents, in-between general conversation of all. Soon the Hudson sons were readied for bed and sent to their slumbers for the night, Mr. Hudson took his wife to his library to show her a new and very interesting book that he had acquired that very day, and the daughters stayed in the parlor for some sisterly conversation before each retiring to her own room for the night.

The next day, morning birds had been chirping and singing their many varieties of songs and arguments long before Cadence and Florence showed up for breakfast.

After Mrs. Hudson waved her daughters to the table, her face demonstrated slight consternation at Florence's elbow on the table and Cadence's napkin left beside her fork rather than promptly being placed upon her lap after her having sat down, "Girls, girls… please *do* show some pretext of culture! Florence, your elbow! Cadence, your napkin!"

"Yes, my dear girls, I married your mother for that very purpose." Mr. Hudson smiled.

Mrs. Hudson looked over at her husband, "What is that you say, my dear? What do you mean?"

"Well, my fine wife… merely that a man needs to be shown how to *appear* to have culture, and his wife can teach him just how to do it."

"Oh, tosh! Sometimes you are prone to say the silliest things." was her reply.

With a smiling wink, he responded, "I'm generally prone to leave that to *you*, my dear."

Florence and Cadence giggled and smiled.

Jake interjected as he was half standing up from the table to leave, "Mother, Mother… can I… I mean… *may* I… go to the stables to feed oats to my new horse?"

"Sit back down and finish your eggs first, dear." Mother calmly counseled.

"I *hate* eggs, Mother. You know that I do." Jake protested, somewhat whiningly.

"Do not say *hate*, dear, I beg you. That seems to me to be vulgar… and expressly extreme as well." Mrs. Hudson stated, still calmly, and then turned her attention to straightening out the napkin on her lap.

Jake turned for manly counsel, "Father? Must I eat up *all* my eggs? You know that I detest them."

"Eat only just half your eggs, perhaps? That might be just the bargain. What do you say to *that* compromise, my dear Mrs. Hudson? Let the boy stomach only *half* of his eggs, since he detests them so very much, eh?" Mr. Hudson suggested to both his son and wife.

Mrs. Hudson gave in, "Oh, all right then… but go get Hank from wherever he's already gone off to. Perchance Mary has some sugar, candy, or old leftover fruit or vegetables from the cellar such as carrots or apples to spare? Go to the kitchen and fetch something that you may treat all the horses in the stables to more than just oats. What do you say to that?"

Jake agreed with a hoot, was given a stern look to stay calm by his mother, and then was gone off to the kitchen to acquire treats for the horses. Soon Mr. Hudson had to be off and away himself, to his own work. Luncheon that day was to be a scattered affair for the family. Mr. Hudson was attending a business luncheon. Jake and Hank were taking sandwiches into the trees or fields, or some such other place of their own choosing. The girls were to go to town with their mother to begin to find any necessaries for the dinner party that was soon to be thrown in the Hudson home, and so, the ladies would take their own luncheon in town. It was a fine day to drive in to town and the Hudson women were a chattering delight all the way, somewhat simply in anticipation of eating out together.

Soon after the Hudson women had settled into their dining hall chairs, Cadence leaned over in a whisper, "Sometimes I prefer to keep to my room just that I do not need put on my corset. They are such binding contraptions."

Mrs. Hudson stopped eating, her mouth agape with shock and then came to her senses in a forced whisper, "Hush, child! Corsets are no subject for *public* consumption!"

Florence joined in on the leaning in and whispering and speaking of corsets in public, "That is why Cadence whispered, Mama… nobody will hear us if we lean close and whisper… anyway, too true, for I know not why we must wear them at all."

Mrs. Hudson recovered herself and continued whispering, leaning further forwards towards her daughters over the table with a grand smile, "For *beauty*, of course."

Florence whisperingly giggled, "Yes, *all* for the sake of beauty we must be bound up in our binding contraptions."

Mrs. Hudson whisperingly concurred, "Well... yes."

Florence put in, still whispering, of course, "As much as I detest the things, I do admit that in order to seem more beautiful, I will accept some discomfort... or even a little pain."

Mrs. Hudson concurred in a whisper again, "To be sure."

Cadence countered, also still whispering, "But, I have heard that in wilder places than here, women do not even wear corsets at all."

Mrs. Hudson was all astonishment, though still maintaining a reasonable whisper, "What? Heathens? Savages? Harlots?"

Both sisters giggled and then Cadence recovered enough to give her whispered corrective opinion on the matter, "No... simply women who are thrust into far more rustic conditions... women who must work so very hard and long days that it is not *practical* in any way to bind oneself, in that sort of wilderness circumstance of life."

The whispered womanly conversation gradually moved towards more acceptably public topics and thus the women's voices each cascaded into more audibly vocal tones once again. Mrs. Hudson sighed, "It is so *relaxing* to take a meal without having the boys to contend with."

Florence laughed, "What *ever* do you mean, Mother?"

Her mother answered her in all seriousness, "I can truly enjoy my meal in a *tranquil* manner for I do not have to reprimand and scold incessantly... you know how I must always ask the boys to quiet or calm down, to stop this or that, to please behave, and so forth."

Cadence smiled, "But still you must remind Florence and I to remember *our* manners from time to time as well."

Mrs. Hudson nodded smilingly, "From time to time, yes... but with your brothers, it seems that I must *always* be on guard."

Her daughters nodded and then Cadence offered, "Though Father is nearly always there to help you reproach them."

Mrs. Hudson let out a lengthy sigh, "Yes, once our sons were somewhat grown, I as much as handed them off to your father's care."

Cadence reminded, "Though a woman's gentle counsel is oft needed by both father and sons?"

She answered her daughter, "Oh, yes… of course. And oftentimes I wonder if I am derelict in my duty towards my sons by leaving so much of their instruction to their Father."

Cadence tried to help, "Though Father does so much more than scold them… he does teach them of many things… and of becoming men."

Mother answered daughter again, "Oh, yes… for, what does a *woman* know of a man's world… and a father is better prepared to raise his sons to be ready for the world of men."

Florence interjected a happy thought, "And Father also does so very well at providing the family feasts and every *other* good thing for us."

Mother responded to her other daughter with a grand smile, "Yes, and I do tend to think that the main providence of a man is to bring home the money… and the duty of his wife is to spend such funds on his behalf. What does a woman know of business matters, numbers and making money, but she must make it her business to gather things in number with her husband's money."

They all chuckled and then continued sampling the fare that they had ordered to their table.

Soon Mother complimented her daughters, "You both look so very lovely today."

Florence took the fine opportunity to tease her sister, "Yes, Cadence, you do look very lovely… though I do wish you would follow my sense of style more. Sometimes I must complain bitterly that you, who look so very much like me due to heaven and nature, must insist on going against *everything* that seems natural and divine to me, by choosing your dresses and doing your hair so… so plainly compared to mine. Indeed, I far too often times feel like I am staring at my looking-glass when I look at you, for you seem to me to be a reflection of my very self on a dowdy day. I am very sorry and ashamed of you to have to say this, but, I dearly hope that nobody ever mistakes you for me, for they would think me very dull that day… very dull indeed."

Mrs. Hudson sat betwixt her two beautiful daughters, not knowing quite what to say. She was reeling a little and feeling quite shocked at Florence's speech, herself most assuredly not having intended the conversation to go in that direction at all, for she was about to bring up the hopes of her lovely daughters meeting prospective husbands that day.

Cadence took her sisters jibe very good-naturedly, "Dear, sweet and stylish sister of mine, worry not for I very much doubt that anyone would ever mistake you for me… at least certainly not since we grew up and came to dress so very differently. Even if you *did* your hair so plainly as mine and put on one of my simple dresses, I am quite certain that folks round about would soon recognize you, for your lively behavior would give you away."

Mrs. Hudson smiled with relief and decided to forge ahead, "Enough of that sort of teasing, my girls, for I will not allow it. I was about to say that since you are both looking so very beautiful today, I truly hoped that we might run into some eligible young men for you to meet with."

Florence playfully turned to her twin, "Our dear mother loves us, I dare say, for she is *always* thinking of marrying us off!"

Mrs. Hudson did not quite know what to say to that, and chose to say nothing, being not in a mood to banter teasingly, for she did not know whether Florence meant her words as a compliment about a mother's efforts for her daughters' happiness, or a jibe in her trying to be rid of her girls.

Without falling into the good luck of finding marital prospects for the girls, even with all the running in to all sorts of folks that they knew, and despite running up against a few unpleasant gossips who discomfited Mrs. Hudson greatly; the Hudson women were soon done their searching in town and Cadence drove them home by their favorite new little buggy. By the time the family convened again together at the dinner table, Mrs. Hudson was full of her terrible news and shared it with her husband as soon as the mealtime prayer had been offered and done. As all promptly heard, though the girls already knew all, she had been subjected to sour gossip against her fair daughters from the likes of Mrs. Bruhor, Mrs. Felter, Mrs. Marsden and even Mrs. Stinham.

Perceptibly outraged, Mr. Hudson swiftly jumped in before his wife was even quite done, "Oh, balderdash and hang them all! Why are mountains made out of anthills by these ridiculous women round about? Florence was engaged and it was ended. Cadence gently declined an offer. That is all. Have these bitter old rumor-mongers nothing better to do than to attempt to besmirch the pure reputations of two innocent young females? They ought to be horsewhipped for their insolence!"

All around the table were silent at Mr. Hudson's uncommon seriousness of temper, until Mrs. Hudson tried, "Well… horsewhipping might be going just a *little* too far."

Father and daughters burst into laughter. Mrs. Hudson smiled at having created such a reaction.

11
Being Seen

Mrs. Hudson was well into a flurry of activity pertaining to planning first a dinner party and then at least a ball later on, though her mind was still very much engaged on a garden party and other in-between parties as well. Her grand plans encompassed all possibilities. Merchants in town were beginning to find optimistic delight in their own monetary possibilities as well, as Mrs. Hudson's plans magnified. Her thoughts included ways of gradually convincing her husband to pay for all she desired. She wished her daughters somewhat involved in her very great efforts, though she only truly needed them to nod their heads and say yes a great deal to whatever she had decided upon doing or buying. This involvement did not offer her daughters a great deal of enjoyment, to be sure. In fact, such was fast becoming fairly vexing to them.

Florence wished to be away. Indeed, the more their mother was trying to bring her girls in to her own dizzying plans and efforts of showcasing them towards worthy matrimonial matches, the more Florence decided to find ways out of such commitments.

Florence decided to bring Cadence into her own suddenly growing plans, "Would it not be a comical diversion if we found ourselves husbands *before* Mother could throw her first party designed to put us on display in front of all the young men that she will invite for us to choose from?"

Cadence looked up from her book inquiringly, as she relaxed on her settee.

Florence continued, "Allow me to begin dragging you away from Mother's daily party planning adventures, to take you into town and indeed, to any town social or dance that is happening this fine spring season, for I have young men on my mind."

Cadence was all agog at the suddenness of it all.

Florence spoke more of the matter on her mind, "I have been tossed in love, the town gossips are full of it, and I wish to traverse forwards towards a far better love than I have known. You cannot rebuff me in this, my dear sister. You know how I have been broken-hearted. You know my embarrassment. You understand the pains of planning parties with Mother. You must go out with me… for I wish to be *gone*… and to be seen by all eligible young men in these parts… and you would not have me do anything beyond the bounds of propriety on my own, would you?"

Cadence was only a little flabbergasted, sincerely trying to find a timely pertinent answer.

Florence continued in her pleading, "I wish to go to a few socials where I can mingle with some young men on my own and in my own way, before Mother throws her first party for us. Mother wishes to throw balls and parties in our home so that she can entirely control the list of guests, the activities and all introductions to work in our favor. I fear it will all be too tiresome… and perhaps even an embarrassment to us."

Cadence was about to open her mouth with her own thoughts when Florence sighed, "I know I did not do well with Lawton… and you could help me… prevent me… in such a blunder again. You know I have always been inclined to marry early rather than later. You know how I have secretly sought the man of my dreams… when I go out riding… and painting… I feel a certain sense of rushing, finding, hurrying along towards my truest love. You have long known that I do."

Cadence swiftly responded, "I do know you… and your passions… and you know how I think… that I think it best to wait a while, for with age comes wisdom and a better choice is likely when one is a little older."

Florence could not but counsel, "But sister… my dear, sweet sister… you must learn to follow your feelings more… you think,

think, think... but you must also allow yourself to feel."

Cadence offered her own counsel, "My own dear, sweet sister... you should temper your passions by thinking first... you know... before leaping into attempts at love."

Florence lit up when suggesting, "Well then... you will help me think more and I will help you to feel more... and we will go to town together... and seek to be seen... by handsome young eligible men... as we seek them out for ourselves!"

Cadence sighed, "You know that I would prefer a book to... to being seen."

"But you cannot leave me to my own devices in this. You must protect me from even myself... for you know that my passions will lead me somewhat astray. Perhaps you must think *for* me?"

Cadence was long in thought and Florence was all impatience, "Indulge me... though you would infinitely prefer sitting at home at your piano or in your books... please do indulge your poor, poor, heartbroken sister. Give me *diversion*! Get me away from Mother! I beg you! Take me to where the young men are, and then *protect* me from them!"

Cadence started up laughing and soon the two of them were laughing uproariously together.

To town they went, that very day. Cadence made Florence promise a number of things, in order to give her own promise of tirelessly going to many places and events with her sister (though Cadence knew that she would find most of such exceedingly tiresome to herself). Among such things as protecting Cadence from the likes of young Stinham, Florence was made to promise that under no circumstances would she and Cadence enter the saloon. No matter how dashingly handsome or strikingly rich any young man entering therein may be, the girls were not to follow. No, Cadence decreed that if need be they could conjure up ways to make the young men follow them into more appropriate places. Propriety was of the utmost concern to Cadence in this matter and she would hold Florence to it, in spite of herself, if need be. Besides, as she explained to Florence, the weather was generally very fine, and they could sit or stand out-of-doors in town here and there and be seen all the more; as well as spend a great deal of time in this or that shop, if rainy weather sent them indoors. Cadence convinced Florence that the right sort of man would happily follow them into any proper place.

Florence was giddy with excitement that she was away from their mother (and all the grand party planning drudgery), as well as seeking out diverting activities of their own. Her heart was bounding with the hopes of finding her own true love in the face of some sudden new acquaintance any day. She knew that perhaps such hopes were somewhat far-flung and silly, but she also knew that staying at home was not the place to find and meet new young men (nor was Mother all too entertaining).

Cadence was all patience with her sister. She wondered if she needed to support this adventurous fling to help Florence either towards finding her beloved fellow for marriage, or to teach her to settle down in to a more comfortable kind of attitude such as she, herself, possessed regarding young men and marriage in general, moreover. At any rate, Cadence did not mind getting away from their mother and all the generally tiresome party plans. It was a truly personal relief to her as well, to divert to elsewhere.

Once in town, the girls began their adventure in seeking out new young men, by sitting on a bench in the shade in front of the bank. Florence had concocted a scheme thinking that perchance rich young men heretofore unknown to them might visit the bank, and therefore the Hudson young ladies would be seen sitting prettily in front of said financial premises as the men came and went relative to their dealings with all their money. Cadence did not admire the scheme nor think it likely to be fruitful, though she supported such a proposal in order to humor her sister. What would it hurt anyway? To sit together anywhere in town, at least anywhere not close to or downwind of the livery stables, would be a pleasant enough time. They could pass the time chatting happily, regardless of who may or may not see or speak with them. It was a handsomely beautiful day and the air was fresh where they sat.

Cadence remarked candidly, "I did not think you so very

mercenary before."

Florence glanced back to her sister from scanning the street, for she had been seeking out pleasant looking young men, "Mercenary... me?"

"Yes, of course, you... mercenary... for to sit in front of the bank hoping to meet a rich man to marry... you do not think this a mercenary scheme?"

"Oh, 'tis not truly a well thought out scheme at all, to be sure... more a momentary passing whim... for... to sit here is as good a place as any in town... and if it were ever to work... 'twould surely please Mother... for you know how she depends upon our marrying wealthy men."

"Well, I dare say that Mother will fully approve of the plan. Tell her about it when we return home this evening and I would suspect that she will offer you a piece of cake or some other delight as a rich reward for your worthy efforts to find a rich fellow." Cadence teased.

"I dare say that you are right. You have given me a right pleasant idea. I will be spoiled with some extra dessert or other tonight, for my good deed today!" Florence grinned.

"I will grant you that out of a dozen pleasant spots to sit in town; this one is as good as or better than any of them. I approve of your choice to start out today, in our adventures in being seen. And may you find yourself a rich young pleasant fellow today, for your trouble."

"What of *you?* You are far more practical than me... do you wish to marry rich?"

"I cannot say that I have given it much thought, truly. You know that I have given marriage very little thought in general, to date."

"Well, you know that I am the kind to marry for love... I have never wished for a rich man... but I would never say no to one with piles of money, if I really liked him."

"What folly it would be to say no to money, for the *sake* of saying no to money." Cadence smiled.

Florence laughed, "I dare say that would surely be folly. No... it is truly stupidity. Say no to money simply on some sort of principled snobbery against money itself? Insanity!"

"To be sure." Cadence agreed thoroughly.

Florence near jumped in her seat, "Oh dear me! There is Mrs. *Bruhor*! Heaven help us!"

"Look the other way… *quickly*. Pretend that you did not see her."

"Oh my and mercy me… I do not wish to talk to that gossiping baggage. If she spots us, she may come over." Florence was all dread.

"Pray that she has no business in the bank today… and that the sun stays in her eyes to keep her squinting so badly that she cannot spot us after all."

"Oh, what will we say if she comes over to chaw with us?"

"We'll think of something, I dare say… or we could choose to let her do all the talking."

"Yes, well… she likes to do all the talking, to be sure." Florence giggled.

"The more she talks, the more we'll have to tell Mother when we arrive home tonight." Cadence grinned.

"Too true… and Mother always finds Mrs. Bruhor *highly* entertaining." Florence sneered.

"Your attempt at sarcasm succeeded." Cadence smiled at her sister, as she patted her on the back rewardingly.

Florence whispered, as if there was a likely possibility of being overheard from across and down the street, "Oh look… now Bruhor has found *Felter*!"

"And what a pair they make, I'm sure." Cadence rolled her eyes a little.

"Yes, look at them go at it together." Florence disgusted.

"To be sure, I am certain that they have *highly* important matters of rumor mongering to discuss."

"Oh my heavens! They are gabbing and looking this way." Florence lamented.

Cadence whispered in a highly cautionary tone, "Let us appear deeper in conversation than they appear to be, and do not look over at them."

"To be sure." Florence seemed almost fearful.

"Ah... if only we could shut out the likes of them from our thoughts... and enjoy the lovely day. Drink in the day, my dear sister... drink in the day."

"You are quite right. Why do I care what they think and say... when I know that it is all balderdash and gibberish?"

"They will think and say whatever they will... and those who are *wise* will not tend to believe any of what women of that ilk tend to say." Cadence mused.

Just then a handsome stranger passed by them, going into the bank. Florence all but swooned openly. Cadence could not help but smile at her amusing sister.

Cadence whispered, though the young man was now well inside of the bank, and they were out front and at one side of its doors, "Do not swoon *openly*, my dear sister... you do not wish to appear desperate, do you?"

"Oh no... yes, of course... I must play aloof and as if I do not care one whit."

"That is surely the way to go about it. I know little of these matters, but I *do* know that to appear not to care makes one the most attractive of all."

"Yes... but... was he not fairly handsome?" Florence was all curiosity.

"I do think so."

"I wonder who he is."

"Truly." Cadence did not really care, but wished to care at least a little for her sister's sake.

"Do you think he looked at me? Did you see?"

"I did not really notice... but I will watch him when he comes out."

"Yes, watch and tell me if he glances my way at all." Florence thrilled.

"I promise I will."

"Do you ever wonder who you will marry? What he will be like? What he will look like?"

"Not as yet, I suppose." Cadence sighed, took a quick glance at Bruhor and Felter out of the corner of her eye. They were still busy nattering, though not looking towards the Hudson girls at present.

"Oh, I have wondered since I was young." Florence thrilled.

"I know."

"Yes, I suppose you do." Florence smiled in remembrance.

"My mind has been engaged on other things, I suppose."

"I do not understand you."

"I know." Cadence smiled.

Florenced blurted, "Oh for... look! It's Mrs. *Marsden* now! She has joined the two other biddies!"

"I dare say that she will be filled in on... whatever they have stirred up between them thus far."

"Surely. Are they looking our way?"

"Let us not look. Let us not care." Cadence counseled.

The handsome stranger came out of the bank, glanced over at the girls, and tipped his hat to Florence in particular, for she was all blatantly coy smiles his way. He carried on to cross the street. The three gossips were watching from afar, and their eyes stayed on the stranger as he eventually passed by them.

"Did you *see* that?" Florence delighted.

"To be certain... I did. I saw that I need not tell you whether or not he glanced at you, for he fairly *stared* your way."

"Yes, he did, didn't he?"

"Yes, truly he did... and I happened to see our dear three friends staring as well. I wonder what they might conjure up to say to their prattling cohorts about anything they *thought* they saw." Cadence chuckled.

"Indeed... but... why did he not stop and *speak* with us?"

"I dare say he will inquire about town... you are easy enough to describe."

"Yes... he will spy around about me... perhaps?"

"I surely would if *I* were he." Cadence smiled as she patted her sister's knee.

"Oh… I will not sleep tonight for thinking and wondering about him!" Florence all but fainted away.

"Perchance not… but I would advise you to *try*… for a sleepless night oft brings a headache by morning." Cadenced teased dryly.

"Perchance he will come back later on to converse with me… us?"

"Perchance."

"Do you think he will?" Florence was tremendously hopeful.

"Perchance."

The girls chatted about various things as well as the handsome stranger. Florence looked about and then, "Oh merciful heavens! Now Mrs. *Stinham* has joined the group of three. What in heaven's name could keep them all so occupied?"

"Gossip."

"I dare say. Are we not to see but one handsome stranger and now four gossips? Who next? Mrs. Darby?"

"Perhaps." Cadence closed her eyes in budding boredom.

"Oh, this is rapidly growing *dull*. My own grand plan has all been but for naught!" Florence lamented.

"You *did* smile at one handsome stranger… and more to the point; *he* smiled and tipped his hat at you." Cadence reminded.

"Yes, that is *something*, to be certain."

"You will have *that* to tell Mother. She may even be thrilled."

"Too true." Florence laughed.

Florence tired of waiting for her new handsome stranger's return, or the appearance of any other young men, whilst many an older uninteresting or married fellow went in and out of the bank. Indeed, the twins could survey the main town street and there was truly no person of import to them, to be seen. Thus, Florence chose to change their plans of staying in town at length to getting their buggy and riding home earlier than she had previously planned, thinking that taking some scenic side roads on the way home might heighten their chances of seeing and being seen by more handsome strangers. Once aboard, Cadence took the reins while Florence took charge of looking out for dashing young men. To Florence's dismay, there happened to be no handsome strangers to be found this day, all the way home.

The following day, Florence convinced Cadence to go riding for a good portion of the afternoon, and miracle of miracles, Cadence convinced Florence to ride sidesaddle (for Cadence did not intend to gallop and did not wish to be left in Florence's dust if the habitual galloper might choose to gallop away from her walking horse sister). Florence had promised not to gallop and to only walk her walking horse, alongside Cadence who would be walking her walking horse as usual. The girls made certain that their mother was aware that Florence's sidesaddle was being dusted off for use that day, and that her walking horse would be walking only, though to their surprise and infinitesimal dismay, Mrs. Hudson was so preoccupied with her dinner party planning that she was only briefly *fairly* thrilled to know that Florence would ride just as a fine English lady alongside her fine lady sister for the afternoon. The twins enjoyed their ride immensely that day, though they only were privileged enough along their way to see and wave, smile or nod to a few young men whom they already knew. Florence thought the afternoon an abysmal failure, though Cadence reminded her sister that they had most certainly enjoyed a lovely ride on a lovely day, and more especially that Florence had not forgotten her sidesaddle riding lessons after all. Another point of thanks, Cadence reminded Florence, was that they each were not boringly encumbered at home by their mother's party planning.

The very next day, by Florence's decree, painting out-of-doors was the order of the day. Cadence would be forced to pose as model for Florence, who would paint, or at least begin to paint, a large portrait of her sister. Florence labored for much time and with more thought as to where would be the best place to be seen by young men as she was painting. She finally came up with a fairly busy crossroad of sorts as the perfect place to see and be seen by fine young dashing strangers. The chosen crossroads was a far-flung place in Cadence's estimations, and she was not so sure that such a place was an idyllic setting for a portrait to be done of herself by her sister. Florence could not be reasoned with, for she had firmly decided upon the outdoor portraiture substitute-studio location, so the Hudson daughters set off in their buggy towards the place to see and be seen whilst painting and being painted. Not a very long time after the planned event was well underway, Cadence was beginning to complain of the dust that was whirling about due to the many buggies, horses and such stirring up the dirt, going to and fro and back and forth. Adding to this difficulty, Florence was lamenting that not one single handsome stranger had been seen amongst all the travelers passing by. To be certain, the girls had been waved and smiled at and even spoken to by many a person driving or riding by, most of whom they knew; but this was not the grand day of meeting dashing strangers that Florence had hoped and planned for. Even the portrait of Cadence was not working out well at all, for with all the interruptions of greeters, and the need for shielding themselves from the near continual dust, very little proper posing nor productive painting had occurred. The twins rode home all disappointment. Florence was so very saddened. Cadence was not much up to the task of consoling her. Both were quite happy to arrive home to clean up and then eat and rest throughout the evening.

In some following days, Florence came up with this or that thing, most of which resulted in going to Church (which they most usually did every Sunday anyway), dropping in to visit this or that neighbor (which did not end up helping them towards meeting any new young men), and going to town again a few times (which did not have even the success of their first try in town, no matter what bench they sat on in front of this or that shop). Cadence began to tire of the exercise while Florence began to complain bitterly of the sore and entire lacking of social functions to go to. What had happened to the spring season social calendar of these parts, after all?! Was all to be left to their own mother? Were all the gossips in collusion against them? Why were there no parties or dances as yet with spring nearing over? Surely the weather was *more* than permitting! Mrs. Darby had promised Mrs. Hudson to host something at her place but had not got around to such as yet. When Florence tried to lament to her mother about the stark deficiency of parties or social functions to go to, Mrs. Hudson could not find patience for such, due to all her energies being spent on preparing for their own upcoming party. To Florence, all seemed lost. The Hudson girls would *never* get husbands!

12
Dinner Party

The day had finally come. Oh happy day for Mrs. Hudson! That is to say, oh happy night: for the poor soul's day was still full of last minute preparations and she was near to entirely exhausted before the afternoon was beginning to wind towards her party dinnertime. Mrs. Hudson had been so busy bustling about that her hair was in tatters, her dress all a mess (even though she had donned an expansive apron for the day to help Mary and the other maids that had been borrowed or near bought and brought there) to prepare for the night's event. Mrs. Hudson was so horridly frantic with final details that even her very own husband was required to shoo her away from the kitchen and send her up the stairs to finally get dressed for the evening. For all her frenzied behavior, one would have thought that she was fighting a house fire, and Mr. Hudson had to laugh at her hysteria even as he pushed her towards readying herself for her famous dinner party. Indeed, he had to solicit the aid of their daughters to get his wife to her room to prepare herself, with promises that he and the girls could manage instructing the hired helpers to finish any little thing that might be left undone while the woman of the house finally cleaned up and changed for her own truly auspicious evening event.

When all things seemed in order for Mrs. Hudson's party, Cadence and Florence went up to help their mother with her dress, her hair or anything that she might be in need of, even if it was only to calm and soothe her. When they arrived at her door to offer their assistance, their mother was expressing her thankfulness at having planned a more European country kind of affair that would begin later in the evening than might normally be expected by the kind of people who ran ranches and had lived out in the west at great length. Her daughters agreed that an earlier party would not have done, given the frenetic state that they had seen their mother work herself up to. Between the two of them, the twins soon had their mother settled down to a relatively tranquil state of temper and thus she was able to join them in going down the stairs in high style and steadiness, in a ready attitude to greet their soon-to-arrive guests. Very light refreshments were available for arriving guests to partake of as they each awaited all invitees to gradually and finally appear, and thus for the late evening dinner to be eventually served.

Having just set eyes on young Mr. Stinham, Florence swiftly whispered to her sister, "What is *he* doing here?! And his *mother*! Of all the…"

Cadence knew of whom her twin was speaking about in such harsh terms but quieted tones, and thus she was ready to answer, "Father insisted on the Stinham family being invited… since he does some business with old Mr. Stinham."

"Mother must have been *mortified*!"

"To be sure, though, Father was required to put up plenty of cash for this little affair, and so Mother was required to put up with his altering of the guest list to some degree."

"Must we speak with the odious mother or son?"

"I understand that our paying them any special attention is not requisite."

"Thank the merciful heavens above!"

Cadence noticed young Mr. Stinham staring at them out of the corner of her eye and so turned to generously give him the slightest smile and nod, for forgiveness sake, particularly as she did not know if young Stinham had played any part in the sowing of any seeds of slander against herself. Forgiving the mother and her circle of cohorts would be an entirely different matter and a more difficult and lengthy venture to be certain. On so slight an encouragement, Mr. Vincent Stinham dashed over to her side in instantaneous delight.

Young Stinham gushed, "Miss Cadence! You are looking *ever* so lovely tonight! Indeed, you are *perfection* itself!"

Cadence could but, "Thank you."

Despite wishing to appear continually and completely cordial to all, Florence could not help but roll her eyes, if only just a little.

Stinham continued lavishing his praises toward his object of affection in the fair pianist twin, "Your gown is... *exquisite*, if I may so say."

"Thank you." Cadence repeated.

Stinham then turned his attention to Florence, which initially mortified her beyond even *her* supremely vivid imagination, "And of course, *you* are looking lovely as well... but forgive me... may I take this opportunity to personally apologize for any part that I played with respect to... that blackguard Mr. Lawton. You *poor* innocent creature... I have such *regrets* in the case."

Florence felt compelled to reply, "Well... *that* is done and past. I haven't given it a second thought in quite some time. Thank you though, for your kind sentiments."

Stinham continued towards Florence, "Well, I wish you *every* happiness... towards a worthy match in matrimony."

Florence again exerted herself in replying, "Thank you... and you as well."

Stinham nodded at Florence and then turned back to Cadence, "Indeed, I also wish *you* every happiness in marriage."

Cadence feared any further conversational movement in the direction of matters of marriage where Stinham was concerned with respect to herself, and only managed to get out with a nod, "Thank you."

Though Jake and Hank had not been primed with instructions to harass young Stinham the evening through (perhaps an oversight by Mr. Hudson, or a decision by Mrs. Hudson towards heightened peace for all, publicly proper appearances, and lowered personal embarrassment to herself throughout the entire evening), the two Hudson boys were soon right there (in a sort of previously conditioned rote memorized training), verbally assaulting young Stinham by pummeling him with silly or otherwise humiliating questions. Florence and more especially Cadence, each breathed lengthy sighs of relief at the signs of the lively and most foreboding reinforcements in the form of very young opponents up against Stinham. The Hudson brothers were so very formidable and effective, that Cadence and Florence were able to silently and gracefully slip away from the severely disappointed and dejected, assaulted Stinham.

Cadence and Florence were able to traverse about the rooms, visiting this or that person. Florence was on the lookout for the handsome stranger who had tipped his hat at her while she coyly smiled in front of the bank on that certain day in town, though she had received no assurance from her mother as to any handsome strangers having been invited. Sadly for Mrs. Hudson, there was no regional book of handsome strangers to apply to for guidance. Where did one find young men that one did not know as yet? How could new young men be invited if they could not be found? Mrs. Hudson had invited all folks that she knew whom she wished to invite, plus all those that Mr. Hudson insisted she invite, and then there were additional invitations that had been extended to those unknown to her (who would be brought by friends and neighbors). Invites to unknown persons were what Mrs. Hudson pinned all her hopes on, for any handsome stranger could only be found amongst such. She prayed that there would be some eligible young men brought to her dinner party. The evening would eventually tell all.

Doors had been opened up between the dining hall and a ball room, where enough in the way of tables and chairs had been perfectly placed and readied for the dinner party. Cards with invited guests' names had been placed at each table setting, that each guest might be guided to where he or she was expected to sit during the dinner, though there were some scattered seats left available for tentative unknown accompanying guests of guests (and the twins' mother surely hoped that many a rich handsome young man would be among such said guests). Mrs. Hudson had not wanted seating to end up in a wild willy-nilly arrangement by any means (this was not a barn yard picnic, after all!), for she did not wish for certain folks to sit by other folks, and more precisely, she wished for particular folks to sit near her and her family. The dinner went off splendidly, more to Mrs. Hudson's surprise than anyone else's.

By the time all had eaten, the lady of the house truly wished that this party was already the end of summer ball she was truly looking forward to, because with the tables and chairs quickly cleared to the sides of the rooms, ample space for dancing would have been provided. However, there was no band of musicians in sight. Well, it was a goodly trial run, at any rate, she thought to herself. Thus, Mrs. Hudson would simply have to settle for the planned events already scheduled for her dinner party. The highlight of the night was to be when Cadence would play and Florence would sing, but this had been staged for somewhat later on, as more of a culminating conclusion of the evening's ending. For now, there was to be men off in the sitting room and women sitting in the parlor for a very short while, to aid in initial digestion, and then mutual visiting once again of all who had come. Soon all were to move about to converse and laugh at will in relaxed fashion.

As the womenfolk sat chatting in the parlor, Florence was disappointed for having not seen any arrival or sign of her handsome stranger from in front of the bank, though another handsome stranger had caught her eye and indeed, she was quite certain that she had been so fortunate as to have caught his own eye as well. When all parties came together again for casual conversing, Florence forced Cadence to accompany her for some semblance of a kind of support, whilst she made her way near to where the new handsome stranger was in the midst of a lively discussion with some older gentlemen. Florence had made sure that she and her sister had sauntered oh so very slowly, closer and closer to the new handsome stranger, so as not to draw attention to what she was about. Florence felt so especially clever in her clandestine movements to progress gradually more closely towards the man she wished to meet. By the time Florence and Cadence were standing fairly near to Florence's new handsome stranger, the stranger himself had noticed the fair Florence and then made his own efforts to be introduced to her. The thing was accomplished. Florence was finally introduced to the new Mr. Turner Gilson.

Mr. Gilson was everything charming and while Florence was being captivated by the handsome young man, Mrs. Hudson was delighted to be hearing from her many friends and neighborhood acquaintances, that Mr. Gilson was fairly wealthy and very single, never ever having been married at all. As Florence put herself forward towards the very willing Gilson, Cadence did her best to hide in the shadows, having no desire to converse with anyone, and especially wishing to avoid young Stinham for the remainder of the evening.

The Hudson boys did their part to keep Stinham away from their dear sister. Indeed, the lads were so actively successful in diverting Stinham that Mrs. Darby began to take full notice of the lads, and soon was correcting, chiding and even criticizing poor Mrs. Hudson, after sitting down beside her.

Mrs. Darby rebuked her hostess for the evening, "Your boys are running quite wild and truly wreaking havoc tonight, my dear. This seems to me to point to follies and foibles in you and your husband's rearing of your boys, I fear."

Mrs. Hudson tried to explain in a whisper, "Please do not tell a soul, but my boys were likely let loose on young Stinham by my husband, to *defend* Cadence from the upstart fellow's advances."

Mrs. Darby good-naturedly chuckled, "Ah... I do understand and comprehend *all* now, my dear friend... but did you know that your boys have been using vile creatures against the young man?"

Mrs. Hudson raised her brow quizzically.

"Frogs and lizards in his pockets, and spiders and snakes on his head and such, I tell you."

"I did not know... I assure you. In fact, I do not think they were asked to work on young Stinham tonight, after all. They were acting on their own I fancy, based on a former dinner that he came to here."

"Yes... they are quite independently precocious."

"I dare say that perhaps I should not have handed them off to my husband so soon."

"Yes, perchance you should have tried to hold them back, slow them down and discipline them just a little longer."

"I suppose it is owing to the fact that my husband saw them as hardly mine and his very own, to a great degree... from the time they were near babes, you see. Indeed, though we named them Jacob and Henry, and I wished to call them by their true formal names, with Mr. Hudson, they were Jake and Hank from the start. I confess that I had not full power over them from the *beginning*, for they were so much my husband's sons."

"Hmm..."

"Well, I do have my *daughters*. I deferred and gave in to my husband in his western ways and names for the boys, but he gave in to my eastern ways with our girls names... in his own opinion."

"And their beauty and accomplishments do you credit, to be sure."

"Thank you."

"And you will show them off tonight?"

"Cadence agreed to play and Florence is to sing."

"I cannot *wait* for their riveting performance."

Mrs. Darby and Mrs. Hudson continued speaking about Cadence and Florence whilst each sought them out with their eyes. Florence was found still to be busy with the most eligible Gilson. Cadence was busy hiding from Stinham, though the occasional other silly or stupid fellow who thought himself a likely suitor for the beautiful pianist kept cornering Cadence for brief periods of torture to her, here and there, now and then. Due to such persistent pursuers, Cadence found escape and respite in finally being called upon by her mother to play piano for everyone. Florence was torn between wishing to stay close by Gilson's side and being pleased to show him how well she could sing.

13
Mr. Gilson

Someone was at the front door. Of course, Mary roused herself from somewhere between the kitchen and elsewhere to go and see who it might be. Mrs. Hudson promptly wiped her mouth with her napkin in preparation for company, having just finished off the last morsels of her breakfast. The poor woman had ended up sitting alone for the last moments and cold bite or few of her morning meal, since she had been talking so much about her previous night's party and even a little of Gilson, that she was eating very little during the meal itself and thus she had finally been abandoned by all her family, each one of them having left in cascading fashion to run off to do their own important matters of business, practice, play or otherwise. Mrs. Hudson met Mary leading Mrs. Darby into the Parlor. Before Mrs. Hudson could offer the appropriate greeting as hostess, Mrs. Darby, near out of breath, proceeded to interrupt whatever the lady of the house might have been about to say.

"I had hoped I had not come over too early. I am relieved that you seem to be done your breakfast, for when I was not nearly done my own, Mrs. Lennox… you know… she brought that new Mr. Gilson to your party last night… well, she came over to my house first thing this morning to… well, to tell me of how Mr. Gilson was all on and on about your Florence. He wanted to know everything about her and your family… and as much as asked about… well, pretty much declared… well, Mrs. Lennox said that it seemed as if Gilson is thinking seriously about…well, you know… getting to know Florence much better. Mrs. Lennox thinks a marriage between the two might be soon in the offing… for Mr. Turner Gilson apparently does not wish to waste any time in choosing his bride. He is ripe for the picking, my dear!" Mrs. Darby was on the edge of her seat with giddy excitement.

Mrs. Hudson quickly answered, to make sure of getting something in edgewise, "Well… that is most interesting news."

"Yes, yes… most interesting, to be sure." Mrs. Darby sat back, calming herself a little… taking a healthy pause for breath's sake.

Mrs. Hudson took further opportunity to be a proper hostess to her current guest and constant friend, "Would you like anything? A cup of something… biscuits… or cookies, perhaps? I dare say we have some leftover cake and all sorts of *other* wonderful things to choose from…"

"Oh no, dear me, no… I near had my fill during breakfast and then I had a little more with Mrs. Lennox… no… I am stuffed to the gills and could not possibly put in another thing to save my life!"

Mrs. Hudson went back to speaking of Gilson, for she was truly interested to know more of him, "He's tall and handsome, I dare say…"

"Yes… oh, yes… he is so very tall and terribly handsome.'"

Mrs. Hudson took a sudden wise and serious turn, feeling pricked a little with the memory of Lawton as well as recent reminders from her husband to be protectively guarded for her daughter's sake, "How well does Mrs. Lennox know this Mr. Gilson?"

"Oh, very well… very well, I would say."

"I do not know Mrs. Lennox all that well. Do you trust her judgment?"

"Oh, yes… very much. She is a very great friend of mine and I would say that I trust her implicitly."

"And she thinks that Mr. Gilson would be worthy of my Florence?"

"Oh, yes… indeed, I would say so… yes, I would."

Mrs. Hudson smiled. Mrs. Darby inquired, "Well? What does your Florence think of the dashing Gilson then?"

Mrs. Hudson momentarily considered and then shared, "Well… I did not know whether or not I should say as yet… or if I should encourage Florence in his direction, but now that you give me your report from Mrs. Lennox and you tell me that you trust that Gilson must be a worthy kind of fellow… I suppose I can divulge secrets to you… and only you, my dear trusted friend… *please* do not divulge a thing I say on the matter… well… Florence is certainly enraptured with the fellow thus far."

Mrs. Darby thrilled, "Ooh… that is very great news *indeed*! Of course I would not tell a *single* soul!"

Mrs. Hudson continued, "Of course… you know… they have not truly been alone together or had much in the way of private moments. Their time spent together last night might as well have been watched and listened in on by everyone."

"Indeed, yes… you will have to get them alone together… well… not truly alone, of course… nothing improper… but off to themselves to some degree… so that you can move… or hurry… things along."

"Yes… I suppose…"

"Yes, of course! You do not want to let him get *away*, do you?!" Mrs. Darby was incredulous.

"Well… perhaps I have learned a little to be… *cautious*…"

"Oh, yes, well… I know what you are saying… you are thinking of Lawton… but, Gilson is not Lawton, I can *assure* you."

"You feel certain, then?"

"Oh, yes. Mrs. Lennox thinks the world of him. He is all things charming."

Mrs. Hudson hesitated briefly and then expressed what was on her mind, "Perhaps I would feel fully confident in hurrying things along if you checked with Mrs. Lennox a little more for me. Could you inquire of her somewhat… find out everything about Gilson… before…"

"Yes… very wise… very wise to be sure… I will inquire further for you."

"I do not wish to lead Florence astray in any way… I do not wish to be scolded by my husband… we do not wish to have Florence's heart broken yet again…"

"Did your husband scold you pertaining to Lawton?"

"Not really… no… certainly, he did not fault me in the least in that case… but last night after the party was over and even a little this morning at breakfast, he did give me cautionary words about Gilson. My husband feels especially protective over Florence's tender passionate heart."

"Oh yes… what a good father he is to his children."

"He is especially fond of Florence. He understands her… well, he certainly appreciates… her free and wild spirit more than I do, I suppose."

"Oh, yes… to be sure."

Mrs. Darby's uncharacteristic pause caused Mrs. Hudson to stop and think what she might or should say next.

Mrs. Darby diverted, "Well… what a party that was! You would hardly know that you had all those people and everything the way it was last night to look at the place today. Your Mary must have been up all night cleaning!"

"I do confess that Mary had her work cut out for her, but, we did bring in those extra maids and then… would you believe that my daughters and sons helped clean up a little last night and also this morning before breakfast?"

"Oh… how did you accomplish *that*? Get any work done… out of your *children*? I am quite certain that I never was able to do such, even *once* in my entire life!"

The ladies continued in their visit in Mrs. Hudson's parlor. They spoke of many things, though mostly of Turner Gilson and his Florence, and how wonderful such a match would be.

All the while upstairs, Florence had been hiding in Cadence's room. To be certain of not being overheard by Mary or even her mother, the painter sister was whispering (or at least trying to whisper, often at least speaking in lower tones for the most part) this and that thing of Mr. Gilson to her pianist sister. Florence could not but seem to be all aflutter and dissenting confusion. Cadence was trying to be the sage sister, full of proper wise counsel.

Florence debated within herself whilst consulting without to her sister, "He is full handsome and so very tall, to be sure. Though what has *that* to do with anything? What do I care about him… or any other man for that matter? Why should I suddenly rush into love again? I do confess that I am strongly drawn to Gilson and believe that I could surely fall in love with him if he loved me first, but… then again, I am all affright to allow myself to feel anything akin to love for any man… at least as yet… I am truly all confusion. Though, after what happened to me with Lawton, perchance I should be altogether done with men!"

"Done with men? Surely not… after only *one* mishap… surely you should allow yourself to try again with someone else? It is neither fair nor just to hold the sins of one man against another. Let each man prove himself by his own actions." Cadence countered.

"To own the truth, I fear to tread there… if only just a little."

"But Lawton was… he was not *typical*."

"Likely true, though…"

"Simply be more cautious in your next attempt."

"You see! That is something I do not wish to do again! I do not wish to *attempt*! I wish to wait for the right man… I would so much like to do it all right, rather than attempt… and have it go badly again. It is so… mortifyingly… embarrassing."

"Though nobody faulted you… Lawton fooled *everyone*."

"*Some* did fault me."

"A gaggle of gossips? Nobody of *consequence* faulted you."

"Rather than running about being silly chasing after men, I wonder if I should instead apply myself to steady study… more like you do."

"We are very different. I do not think… that I need a man… as you do."

"If *you* are born to spinsterhood, then perhaps, so am I. We are two sides of the same coin, as you have said yourself." Florence mulled.

"Think, Florence. You will resign yourself to spinsterhood because of one blackguard of a man? Simply because you believed in Mr. Lawton you will give up on *all* men entirely? Surely not!"

Cadence showed irregular passion.

"I have realized that I should try to learn a little from you. Father's speeches to mother earlier caused me to pause. Perhaps I should be a little more cautious."

"And let the pendulum swing the *other* way for fear of your heart being hurt once more?"

"*You* are a fine one to talk. Your caution caused you to decline Worthington's offer."

"Perhaps I should follow your example a little and learn to listen to my heart more." Cadence reflected.

"I see what you are feeling. You are rethinking your refusal of Worthington, I think."

"I admire him greatly. I still feel terribly for wounding him."

"Do you love him?"

"I do not think so… unless I could say that I love him like a brother. He is… or at least he… was… a dear friend. Now, enough of me… and Worthington. What of you? Tell me about Gilson. Do you think him creditable of… at least a friendship?"

"Yes, perhaps he is… though, who am I to judge *any* man, for I have proven myself abominable at recognizing man from beast."

"Well, that messy affair is all past and nobody in their right mind faults you for it one jot. Anyone of sense blames that blackguard. He was the deceiver… not you. What did you do but to fall in love with him and to say yes to his proposal?"

"That should be enough. I cannot choose a man rightly and so I should *refrain* from choosing at all." Florence was all somberness.

Cadence became very playful, "Oh, tosh, as our dear mother would say! And as she would also say, besides being so very tall and handsome, Gilson is also very rich. Everyone says he has a good deal of money. What *more* could a girl want than that?"

Florence giggled and then turned serious once more, "Well, Mr. Lawton was said to have been rich, and it all turned out to be his dead wife's money… which he squandered and gambled near all away… and then it seemed that he came west to seek out more money in much the same sort of way."

"Well, Mr. Turner Gilson has his *own* money, I dare say… and he seems to have his sights firmly set upon you, Florence. He was most particularly attentive to you last night… indeed… right from the start, after he first arrived and set eyes on you, he had eyes for no other. They say he is anxious to find a wife as soon as may be."

"Again, you really do begin to sound like Mother. Please *stop!*" Florence looked all false shock and horror, and then the girls both erupted into laughter.

There was a knock at Cadence's door, the girls both instantly looked to the door in surprised astonishment, and then Mrs. Hudson walked in, "I wondered where you girls had gone off to. I was walking about the halls of our house looking for you when I heard you laughing in here. I must say that it brings a mother joy to hear the laughter of her daughters."

Both girls smiled outwardly, feeling a particle of guilt within for leaning towards any mockery of their mother. Mrs. Hudson proceeded to tell her daughters everything that Mrs. Darby had told her and also of her own request of finding out more about the man Gilson. The girls were both glad of the new information. With all her cautious talk, Florence was from her heart more desirous towards Gilson than away from him. Cadence, though cautious through to her heart, still thought that Florence should give Gilson a chance and was truly happy to see her mother exercising vigilant prudence at the behest of her father. Perhaps with all the diligent watchfulness all around, things would turn out well after all. Perhaps Turner Gilson was truly the man for her sister.

In the coming days and weeks, in her efforts to exercise due caution, whenever Gilson was to be around, Florence made a habit of taking Cadence with her as another and very trusted mind over the situation. Mrs. Darby hosted a little impromptu party at her house and Florence uncharacteristically held Cadence close to her in all her associations with Gilson there. That evening brought Florence and Gilson one lengthy step closer together. They each seemed to have eyes only for each other, and all eyes upon them could see the match being made.

Florence was on Gilson's arm at church and in the town. The two were seen together round about near daily. Though Cadence was usually nearby (for Florence wished her still to be so), Florence was quite lost in her own small world where only Gilson existed to her. She was all alight with love for her own Turner Gilson and could not hide any of it from the world around her, even if she had wished to try to do so.

Gilson and Florence were fast becoming the talk of the town and beyond, for all the women were full of the ever increasingly delightful news. When pressed to the point, Mrs. Hudson could not deny that a match must be imminent. Many female folks wondered if such was already done and being kept a secret for some unknown reason. Mr. Hudson had not yet found a thing against his prospective son-in-law, though he was exercising all his powers to find something. Mrs. Darby was so very excited for her friend and for the part she felt that she herself had personally played in bringing the thing about so perfectly. Cadence thought that perhaps she was to lose her sister and gain a brother very soon.

Appearances surely were that Gilson loved Florence and would ask her to be his bride any day, but especially suddenly, there was shock all around. Mr. Gilson was abruptly absent from town and word soon came in from outside of it that he was very unexpectedly engaged to an excessively rich, somewhat older, fairly unattractive widow in a neighboring town! Further word was that Gilson had been friendly with such said widow for quite some time, though none seriously considered that anything of a nuptial kind could be in the offing, being that Gilson was so young and handsome and rich enough himself not to need to lean in any mercenary direction when it came to a matrimonial choice.

Speculations fired up. All believed round about the town that it was blatantly obvious that Gilson must love money more than anyone or any thing. Why and how could he choose to marry such as he was doing, when the likes of Florence Hudson was before him? Had he been tossed between love of Florence and the widow's money? Were his actions accidental or deliberately calculated? Did he not have enough cash and properties himself? Did Mr. Turner Gilson falsely set his cap for Florence, flirting with her and thus using her to make his rich widow jealous? Did he intend to use Florence as a cat's paw from the moment he met her? Did he orchestrate such a romance with the young beautiful Florence to make himself seem more attractive to the older woman that he secretly wished to marry? Did Gilson use Florence to speed up his attempts at becoming engaged to the rich widow?

When reliable news of Gilson's engagement reached the Hudson home by way of Mrs. Darby into Mrs. Hudson's own ear (and then to be passed on to her own family), Florence took to her room in tears, and wished to be left alone. She remained there quite solitarily for some days. Cadence could not gain admittance though she wished with all her heart to console her sister and condole with her. Mrs. Hudson was all mortification and took to her own room in tears and woefulness. Mr. Hudson felt real outrage when he learned of the news. If not for Cadence holding him back, he might have done something regrettable towards the contemptible scoundrel, though he would have had to ride many miles to do it.

The tide of the town gossips generally turned the Hudson way, and much in the way of hateful detestations was sent into the wind to become a whirlwind towards the town where Gilson was soon to live with his older rich bride, after a European honeymoon tour. There was plenty of pity for poor Mrs. Hudson and her daughter Florence. Mr. Gilson was publicly spurned in his absence (verbal floggings regarding him flying all around), for using the young beauty so abominably. His name was coupled with the title of 'jilter' and would ever remain so in all the women's minds. Gilson the jilter dare not ever come to *this* town again. He would receive daggers for stares every moment he was there.

14
Off of Men

Folks through the town and round about it did not blame Florence Hudson to any degree in the matter relating to her having failed to catch Mr. Turner Gilson. It was more than plain for all to see that money was his heart's desire complete, when he suddenly engaged himself to a wealthy older widow instead. Florence was nevertheless, all mortification.

There may have been a few seasoned sour gossips who conjured up some stories that hinted against Florence's character, suspected improprieties on her part or some such other alleged female follies in her person, but all folks with any sense in their heads at all, entirely faulted Gilson for everything. While quite generally redeemed publicly, Florence continued to feel humiliated inwardly. Though wholly vindicated throughout the horrid turn of events, she was still entirely embarrassed for having fallen in love so fast and thoroughly for such an unworthy pretender.

In a comparatively short space of time, Florence began to realize that her pride remained far more wounded than her heart, for that heart did begin to mend fairly quickly. Aided by instant and severe injury, Florence's love for Gilson fast faded towards a dying ember, soon to be ashes alongside her deeply buried past affections for Lawton.

Florence gradually decided that she might be destined or doomed to fail with men. She soon determined to devote herself to an honorable spinsterhood and locked Cadence's arm in hers in the process, even as she followed her sister's noble example. Florence would dedicate herself to her paints even as Cadence had long been committed to her piano. Serious study was the painter's sure defense against falling for a man again. Such did seem to work for Cadence and thus Florence intended that it would work for her as well.

"I will be like *you*, my dear wise sister. You have shown me the way." Florence sighed as she reclined with more repose on her chaise.

"Oh, please do not call *me* wise, for I might truly be as lost as you feel." Cadence smiled from Florence's chair nearby.

"How could you be lost? No, I think that I should forget all about men even as I remember to paint daily. I have been disloyal to my talents and must forevermore be constant to my art."

"It would certainly do you no injury to paint more."

"Yes, yes… that is just what I am feeling… *you* have been spared heartbreak due to your diligence to the piano and singing and reading. I must do likewise with my paints and singing and reading, to protect my heart from men." Florence was all firm assuredness.

"That is surely one way to look at the matter."

"Yes, we two sisters will be happy spinsters, throwing ourselves most passionately into our arts and study that we will fall to *no* temptation where men are concerned."

"Are *all* men a temptation?" Cadence wondered aloud.

"Oh, yes… I do think so."

Cadence thoughtfully queried, "Was Father a temptation to Mother?"

"Well, I suppose in a way he was…"

"Do not let them hear you speak so…" Cadence began to caution.

"Well, of course, Father is a good man…"

"But?"

"Perhaps mother could have married… a little later. She has always lamented her lost dream to study painting or music with masters in Europe. Her father offered her *all* that… and she turned it down for our father. Just think what she missed." Florence sighed.

"And this was folly on her part in your own opinion?" Cadence seriously posed.

"Not folly… though… she does sometimes seem to regret… a little."

"A little… sometimes… though, I doubt that she *truly* has deep regrets."

"I suppose not." Florence played with a ribbon.

"Perchance she is happier in the life she has chosen than she might have been otherwise?" Cadence offered.

"That is hard to say. No one can be certain." Florence doubted.

"I suppose."

"Well, Mother's choice in Father was a good one for her, for he is a good man. But, I have been tossed in love *twice* now. I am determined to repent of my flirtatious follies. I will be a painter spinster and embrace becoming an old maid. I must dedicate my life to becoming a great painter *instead* of handing my heart over to a man again. Let the gossips chide, for I will revel in it!"

"You will propel the pendulum in the *opposite* direction by swearing off of men forever?"

"*Yes*, I will be just like you. I declare that I *swear* off of men forever!" Florence proclaimed with delight.

"Though, I cannot say that I have sworn off of men, especially forever. I am hesitant… I have been mulling the matter over… I do not know as yet. I think that perhaps the right offer, just the right offer… at the right time… I *might* be convinced to say yes."

"*No*! Do not speak so! You and I must be spinsters together forever! Promise me you will!" Florence was all vivacity, half serious, half playing.

"I cannot honestly promise." Cadence smiled.

For a good deal longer, Florence playfully tried to exact promises and oaths from Cadence that they would remain serious but joyful spinster sisters together all their days. Cadence was firm in her indecision about ever marrying, and counseled Florence to remain at least likewise. The twins finally left Florence's room and went down to join their family. After the blessing on the food at the dinner table, they were most suddenly accosted with their mother's newest plans.

"*Girls*! I have convinced your father to allow me to go ahead with even grander plans for your ball later this summer!" Mrs. Hudson delighted.

Mr. Hudson smiled as he surveyed food before him. Jake and Hank were each already busy eating. Cadence and Florence looked at each other, neither knowing what to offer quite yet.

Mrs. Hudson continued sharing her latest plan, "I will invite more people this time... more young men. We will bring the *best* young men from the farthest regions around here... that I might put you forward... that you will..."

Florence countered vehemently, "I am so sorry, Mother... but I cannot acquiesce to your plan. I have *no* wish to meet young men."

Cadence tried to gently assist, "We have no wish for another party as yet, Mother."

Mrs. Hudson insisted, "Oh tish tosh! We will have the ball that I have been planning, after all!"

Florence was adamant, "If you host a ball, I will not come... I will sit up in my room if I must... for there will be none but silly suitors and gabbing gossips in our house... and you know how Father detests tedious company."

Cadence tried to soften her sister's message, "We do not wish to waste Father's time nor money."

Mrs. Hudson lamented, "But, your father has already offered up his money and told me to name the night. He has agreed to allow me to throw a grand ball. How will you two get husbands if I do not..."

Florence interrupted, "I do not want a husband. I have learned of late that I was meant to be none but a painter. I will not speak for Cadence, for she may or may not follow me in this, but I am determined to become a spinster."

Mrs. Hudson dropped her knife and fork simultaneously, "Oh, Saints above! Do not be *ridiculous*, my dear! Your recent tragedy with that... that rogue, has all but blown over already... just like your engagement to that what's-his-name did. Likely as not, not one single soul blames you one particle for any of either disastrous situation."

"No, Mother... I am determined to make a true artist of myself.

I was born to *paint*, as you well know, for I can do nothing else anywhere near as well and…"

"Nonsense! You are quite as accomplished as anyone at *many* things!"

"Well, it is high time then, that I put all my passions and energies into paint and canvas that I might begin to excel at the one art…"

"But to *never* marry?! Florence! That… the thought is… unconscionable! Cadence? Mr. Hudson? Talk some sense into the girl!"

Mr. Hudson sat still, waiting and watching the eventful show unfold before him, choosing to stay out of the fray and leave all to his wife and Florence for the time being. Cadence was not certain that she could be of any help to either party, feeling particularly that she was sitting somewhere in-between. Jake and Hank continued eating.

Florence was quite firm, "No… there is no talking me into anything when it comes to marriage. I have behaved abominably foolishly with my flirtatious ways and I must repent of them… I am humiliated beyond ever overcoming the horrid feeling that has come upon me… twice. I have been talked of alongside scandal enough for more than one lifetime and I truly have no taste for men anymore anyway. I do not seem capable of discerning the best of men for I am only able to pick but libertines and mercenaries. Besides, most men are idiots, bores, rascals and beasts. No… it is done… I am *done* with men."

"But to never marry? To never have children of your own? Saints preserve us! What would the angels above think of you, for choosing to turn your back on your divine destiny?!"

"Oh, Mother… not everyone is meant for marriage. It seems clear that I am not. Heaven will understand this decision… more than my past follies where men are concerned, I assure you."

"I do not think that true… but… how will you be provided for? You need a man to care for you…"

"Father will provide for me, I am certain. And then there are my darling brothers as well. I am loved and guarded by men enough in our family."

Mrs. Hudson could not argue the fact that her husband would never forget either of his daughters where his money was concerned and that her brothers adored their sisters and always should continue to do so, "Well, yes, but..."

"And besides, if I throw myself into my work, I will attain enough skill and ability to make a living for myself. I will paint for my food and lodgings if I must."

Mrs. Hudson looked at her husband in desperation. He loved his wife too much to leave her to struggle so exasperatedly with her own devices any longer, and so he proclaimed, "I fear and dread to speak such, but I must warn you my dear daughter, that all but the most vigorously promoted artists are notoriously poor... and the world does not as yet... entirely appreciate... the female painter. You must not trust in your paints and canvases to keep you in luxurious comforts all your days."

"Yes, well, I will succeed where others have failed! Besides, how could marrying a poor man be any better? How could we possibly feed all our children? I am better off alone."

Cadence tried to assist, "You know this is your current passing whim, my sweet impassioned sister. You will love again, you will want to marry, and you will desire children."

"Perhaps you will marry and have children and I will be their beloved aunt."

Mrs. Hudson energetically put in, "Yet, you have always intended to marry. You will heal from these injuries. Truly you will."

Florence willfully objected, "No... these mistaken paths with men have led me to realize that I was born and meant to paint... men have only been my distraction and mistaken road in life. Why did Heaven give me talents but to magnify them? Everyone knows that if a woman marries, woe be unto any talent she may possess, for she must throw it all away to sacrifice herself on the altar of marriage to be a wife and mother. To be a great painter, or pianist, or writer, a woman must forgo matrimony altogether. Look at *you*, mother? Your abilities and accomplishments are far behind you."

Seeing the injured look on his wife's face, Mr. Hudson could not let this sophistry of philosophy pass without sharing a little kindly, sincere and most serious fatherly wisdom, "But, in becoming and continuing to be my wife and your mother, Mrs. Hudson has accomplished more than all the artists of the world put together. Her motherly arts and work has been of the divine. Heaven smiles upon all her successes. How can you diminish them with such a speech? I would not allow her to trade any of her angelic mothering for all the earthly glory she could have attained in Europe alongside any of the masters who would have gloried in her talents. I am a most fortunate man that she chose to marry me instead of traipsing off to Europe to study with the masters. Their great loss was my great gain. You girls and your brothers cannot be compared with any painting, work of literature or musical composition. Children are a gift and a challenge to parents from God. No earthly accomplishment is near so divine as nurturing and raising one's children. Do not try to argue with me on this point. I will not relent in the least."

Florence did not dare to counter and was repentantly humbled as she felt a little twinge of regret for having caused her father to have felt the need to speak so, to comfort her mother. She hoped that she had not pained her mother with any true regrets about leaving her arts far behind her in such a sacrifice that had given life and happiness to their family.

15
Mr. Bentley

In the front hall foyer, Mrs. Hudson watched with keen interest out of the corner of her eye as Cadence seemed all aflutter attempting to quickly open the letter that had just arrived to her from Jonathan Bentley. After having read at least the introduction, the twin smiled, sighed, and continued to read some more. Mrs. Hudson sat fixated and breathless as if on the edge of her seat, waiting for any news.

"Well?" Mother inquired of daughter.

Cadence glanced over briefly to communicate, "Well, what? Oh… yes… Jonathan does very well… yes, our dear young Mr. Bentley's focused study and studious efforts have paid off handsomely. He does very well in his schooling."

"Good, good… very good." Mrs. Hudson smiled broadly.

Cadence returned her attention to the letter as she finished perusing through it. Her face fell a little in a slight frown.

Having been watching her daughter most intently, Mrs. Hudson was now all concern, "What? What is the matter, my dear? Is something wrong? You look so very *grave* all of a sudden."

"Oh, it is nothing… really. It is just that I had hoped that he could come home for a visit before going off to Europe to finish his studies… but he will be going to Italy straight away."

"Oh, dear, how very sad for you."

"It seems that there is not the time for him to make a visit home before going abroad."

"Well, does that not mean that he will be finished all his schooling all the *sooner* and then be coming home for good more speedily?"

Mrs. Hudson offered to make the sad news more comforting and cheerful.

"Yes… I suppose so… yes, you are right. We will surely see him soon enough to be sure."

Mrs. Hudson thought that Cadence held onto the letter as if some sort of keepsake. Seeing her daughter in such a state in such circumstances, mother thrilled over a mind full of happy imaginings and could scarce keep her lips sealed as she went about the rest of her day's business, containing such excitement as if trying to hold a very large bubble of air under water. Oh, if only she had time to go over to see Mrs. Darby to consult with, but, nevertheless, she wished to speak to her husband first and he would soon be home. As soon as she was able after dinner, she found her husband off in solitary retreat with his books, and thus she pounced upon him in his lair of a library, where she would be sure to find ample private moments to express her speculations and the best luck at forcing her man to listen to her every word. As is typical with many a husband, at first, Mr. Hudson thought that he could continue reading even whilst giving his wife a little of her due by paying her a semblance of whit of attention (or at least attempting a partial appearance of it), for she had sat down near him and it was clear to him that she desired full audience to whatever was on her mind.

"*That* is a match in the making, my dear!" Mrs. Hudson speculated in an excited whisper of sorts to her distracted husband as he relaxed with his book by his small warming fire, trying to concentrate on the most interesting text before him (rather than truly lending a sincere and attentive ear towards his wife).

He offered some curiosity to appease her as he continued reading, "What? Who?"

"Bentley, of course! Were not you *listening*?" wife demanded in query.

"Bentley?" husband questioned half-heartedly.

"Jonathan Bentley and Cadence!"

"Bentley? Jonathan and Cadence?"

"*Yes*!" expired an exasperated wife to most vexing husband.

"What?" he questioned again.

"I told you! Stop reading this instant! Listen to me. I do not wish to *repeat* myself again and again. Lend your ear and I will tell you once more."

Mr. Hudson looked up from his engrossing book and over to his wife, "Bentley and Cadence?"

Mrs. Hudson lowered her voice again, "Yes. Cadence received a letter from Bentley today and she was most pleasured to receive it."

"Cadence and Bentley have been corresponding like brother and sister for years. Cadence would no sooner consider Bentley than… well… than any of her cousins or… or poor Worthington, for that matter. A girl does not fall passionately in love for someone she thinks of as a brother."

"What do *you* know of these things?!"

"A great deal more than you give me credit for, my love, I assure you."

"Well, you did not see Cadence with her letter from Bentley *today*. She was… all flushed… and… well… most attentive to his news… and very distressed to read that he will be going to Europe straight away to finish his studies instead of coming home first. She would not part with that letter for anything, I am sure of it. She is most assuredly in *love* with him."

"No. You are wrong. You must be wrong. I cannot believe it."

"You *will* believe it when you see them together."

"That will not be for quite some time I suppose."

"Yes, as much as a year or more."

"So much can happen in a year… especially at their ages."

"Well, I suppose she could meet someone else."

"Or *he* could meet someone else. He will be in Europe, after all… all those *romantic* Italian and French ladies throwing themselves at the rich American, I dare say."

"Do not even *say* that!"

"Well, he may be there to finish his schooling, but I fear he will learn more than…"

"Hush! Tush! Jonathan Bentley will save himself for Cadence.

They have been the best of friends since they were children and I do now believe that they have secretly loved each other all along. Jonathan has not fallen for anyone else in *all* this time that he has been away out east and he will hold out a little longer throughout his European tour. He has been as constant to Cadence as any man ever has been to his beloved, *or* betrothed for that matter... I wonder if... they are *already* engaged... perhaps I should ask Cadence."

"*Ask* her then... and end all this speculation. May I read my book now?" Mr. Hudson requested with a smile.

Fairly exasperated, Mrs. Hudson returned, "Go back to your book reading, then. At least our girls have a *mother* who cares enough to consider these things in earnest."

The next day, Mrs. Hudson was as if a spy as she was exceedingly attentive to Cadence's comings and goings, and did, as a very good mother might, happened to notice that Cadence had already prepared a letter in response to Bentley's. Oh, happy day! This was a *sure* sign of true love, to be sure! A marriage was up and coming! Cadence could easily wait a year for Bentley, and since Bentley had been *so* true to Cadence all these years (writing faithfully as her dearest friend from childhood), not even European young ladies would turn his head to make him forget his dear Cadence! Why had this mother not realized before that there had been budding love between her daughter and Bentley?! It should have been so obvious to her! Was she half blind?! No wonder Cadence rejected poor Worthington! She was in love with Bentley all the time! Mrs. Hudson wished to sit down (for the excitement of this sudden discovery was near too much for her to contain still standing), though she must stand regardless, for she felt that she must find out something from Cadence about the coming match with Bentley.

Mrs. Hudson was thinking what she might say to or ask of Cadence, and the consternating in her mind was so outwardly obvious that Cadence ended up asking her what was the matter.

Mrs. Hudson tried her utmost to hide her true and full feelings and thoughts regarding her hopeful speculations about Cadence and Bentley, and so managed in a most awkwardly casual way, "Oh... I...

just happened to notice that you have written a letter… could that be in answer to our dear Bentley?"

Cadence did notice her mother's strange behavior and tone, but did not hesitate long in curiosity over such, deciding rather to carry on normally, "Yes. I have written a return letter to him. I thought I should be prompt that it will be sure to reach him before he sets sail to Italy."

In a strangely masked manner, Mrs. Hudson inquired, "And… what might you have… *said*… to our dear Jonathan?"

Cadence paused, truly beginning to wonder what strange oddities might be bouncing around in her mother's brain at the moment, though she continued in a usual manner despite, "Well… I told him of how we all are… and any recent happy news of the neighborhood that I could recall… and expressed to him that I wished he could return home for at least a brief visit before setting off for his European tour of studies."

Mrs. Hudson was all alight, "Oh yes! It would be so very good if he were to come home *first*! He has been away for so horribly long."

"Yes, though… I do not think it is quite convenient for him to come home first…"

"Though you as much as requested such?"

"Not an entreaty… more of a sentiment."

Mrs. Hudson was ever so slightly hesitant, "You have… missed him… I think?"

"Yes, of course. He is and always has been a very dear friend. Florence and I both missed him greatly from the time he went away to school out east."

"Yes, but I think that… *you* especially have missed him?"

"I suppose he and I were *more* like brother and sister… and we have corresponded a great deal since he went away."

"You write to him fairly often I notice… though Florence does not write at all…"

"She is not the kind of person to be diligent in writing letters, as I think you well know."

"And yet you are… truly diligent… where *your* Jonathan is concerned?"

Cadence suddenly realized what her mother was about, "*My* Jonathan? Mother, do not imagine…"

"No, no… I understand. Do not say anything. I do not require it."

"Mother? You are not speculating about a secret match between Mr. Bentley and me, are you?"

Mrs. Hudson tried to hide her guilty feelings and swayed from the truth of what she believed, "No… no… of course not…. most certainly *not*, my dear."

Mrs. Hudson got herself away and to Mrs. Darby's house as soon as she possibly could. Anxious to share her speculation about Cadence and Bentley with her friend, though not wishing to be overheard by anyone in the Hudson household, she thought it best to visit Mrs. Darby before Mrs. Darby visited her. Cadence had so flatly put down the idea of a match between herself and her Bentley that Mrs. Hudson knew it would not be a good idea to be pondering the possibility where Cadence or even Florence or Mary might overhear some of her own musings, and Mrs. Hudson truly did wish to be able to muse entirely freely over the matter.

"*Yes!* I do believe that I can look forward to an imminent match between my Cadence and that wonderful Jonathan Bentley!" Mrs. Hudson thrilled in Mrs. Darby's grand parlor.

Mrs. Darby leaned forward attentively, "Cadence and Bentley?! *Bentley*?! But he has been gone off to school out east for *years*!"

"Yes, but they have been *corresponding*… Cadence has been writing letters *faithfully* to her dear Bentley and he has been doing likewise in return, the *entire* time he has been gone. The proposal and acceptance may happen in letters, but happen it likely will."

"Oh… Oh, I see!" Mrs. Darby drank the news all in.

"Yes, they were like brother and sister when he went away… but now… well… if you could *see* the way that Cadence lights up when one of Bentley's letters arrive… of course Bentley writes to our entire family, you understand… and Cadence writes to him on

190

behalf of all of us... entirely in keeping with *propriety* you know... though Cadence hoards Bentley's letters like treasures of her very own. I had not noticed what was going on until just yesterday."

Mrs. Darby queried, "Yet you say that he is going off to Europe for a year or *more* to finish his studies? So much could happen in a year, I fear to mention as warning, my dear."

"That is *precisely* what my husband was saying... that Cadence may find love with someone here... or that Bentley will find himself a pretty French or Italian wife."

"Well... that is too true my dear... too possible and *quite* likely. A year is such an especially long time when one is young and prone to falling in love."

"Though... Cadence has written to beg Bentley's return home here, before he sets sail for Europe."

"Do you think that he will come then?"

"I do not know... but if he *does* soon return... we will know that Bentley changed all his grand plans at Cadence's whim and thus we will know that an engagement in the offing is *certain*."

"Though a *lengthy* one, to be sure."

"Well... yes... but they are both steady enough in character and temperament... it will not seem so much of a hardship for them as it would be for some."

"Very true. I can picture Cadence at her piano and books whilst Bentley is at his studies abroad. A year could pass more quickly for the two of them compared to many others who are less constant. And though long engagements are likely as not to end, as to end in marriage, with the likes of Cadence and her Bentley... well... yes... I can certainly picture them married at the end of it all... and very happily so." Mrs. Darby was obviously satisfied with the match.

Mrs. Hudson smiled satisfactorily. She was happy that her friend approved of Bentley for Cadence in marriage, and overjoyed with the possibility herself. She and her friend talked further on the happy subject for quite some time, and then before Mrs. Hudson left Mrs. Darby's parlor for her own home, she had a firm promise of secrecy from her friend.

For days afterwards, it was all Mrs. Hudson could do to refrain from talking constantly and telling everyone she met or knew, of her firm belief in Cadence's forthcoming betrothal to the wonderful young and most eligible Mr. Jonathan Bentley. Indeed, though she restrained herself in a way many might not have believed an openly lively woman like her capable of; she could not but succumb to going over for an uncommon visit with her dear retiring neighbor, Mrs. Bentley. A fairly quiet woman who tended to keep to herself and indoors, Mrs. Bentley was more than surprised to see her more gregarious neighbor, Mrs. Hudson, bearing a basketful of flowers surrounding some lovely baked goods and preserves, standing at her door for an impromptu visit.

Mrs. Hudson was on a mission of at least two things. She desired to gather information regarding Bentley (and any proclamations he might have made to his family about Cadence or his possible fast approaching homecoming). Mrs. Hudson also wished to begin to form a lasting friendship with Mrs. Bentley (that she finally now realized had been long overdue). In all the years that their children had played together, Mrs. Hudson had not made much effort to become fast friends with Mrs. Bentley. Mrs. Hudson supposed that perhaps she had been too busy with many things and ever busier with other friends, to make worthy efforts making friendly with Mrs. Bentley. But now that they were so very likely to join families, Mrs. Hudson did believe that she should repent of her own former follies and make especial efforts to befriend the mother of her own future son-in-law.

To her great disappointment, Mrs. Hudson could not find anything out about Bentley's plans to marry Cadence, or to come home for a visit before going off on his European study tour. She wondered if Mrs. Bentley wished to remain secretive about anything that she might know of, for after all, they were not (nor had they ever been) bosom friends. Well, no matter, Mrs. Hudson would work on Cadence at home to see what could be found out, and also continue to pay visits to make friendly with Mrs. Bentley until she knew all. Mrs. Hudson consoled herself to at least know that she had begun to work towards a dear friendship between her and Mrs. Bentley. This closeness of friendship would surely help future matters in speeding things along (or at least securing things) between her Cadence and Jonathan Bentley.

After arriving home, still feeling disenchanted frustration over not having wheedled anything out of Mrs. Bentley about her son being passionately in love with her own daughter, Mrs. Hudson was accosted by Mary with news of the affair! But how could Mary know of what was building between Cadence and Bentley? Who had told her anything? Mrs. Hudson did her utmost, as a loving and devoted mother, to find out from Mary what she knew and who she had gotten the information from. It seemed that there was a growing rumor in the wind and nobody knew the source of any of it. A little bird had told them all! Could Mrs. Bentley have told somebody something? That was not very likely, though the Bentley maid may have overheard something in the household and then spread it about. Mrs. Hudson did worry greatly for Cadence, for she knew that her daughter would not like being talked about in this way, particularly if she did not have a firm offer from her beau as yet. Mrs. Hudson extracted a near oath sworn promise from Mary that she would not breathe a word to anyone, inside or outside of the Hudson household. The lady of the house impressed upon her maid the very great danger of any prattle reaching the ears of her dear daughter Cadence, nor into her sister's ears either, for if Florence got any wind of it she would most surely tell Cadence all. This was an extremely delicate matter and Mrs. Hudson did not wish the prospective proposal to be hampered in any way.

Luckily for Mrs. Hudson (in reference to her girls finding out any of the latest countryside news), Cadence and especially Florence seemed to be staying true to their supposed efforts of staying spinsters, for they were both focused on daily steady study at home. Florence was painting with a grand passion and Cadence was ever more at her piano. The Hudson girls spent hours on end reading in their rooms or in the parlor together. They spent many hours in conversations of many things. The long hot days of summer were driving the twins indoors or into the shade, and there was nothing pulling them to town or even anywhere else. Indeed, their determination or perhaps more to the point: Florence's determination to remain unmarried, to become a spinster and to dedicate her life to her paints; were keeping the sisters only to themselves, to each other and to their intimate family members. Florence was so faithful to her plan not to meet young men, that she only rode her horse on the Hudson properties, declined offers to dinners and parties, and passed on invitations to dances and socials. Florence and therefore Cadence along with her had become true recluses. Thus, with Mary's cooperation (upon threat of certain pains or even outright deadly dismissal) Mrs. Hudson was most amazingly more than able to keep the town tattle away from the ears and minds of her two fair daughters.

Some weeks passed with the news of Cadence and Bentley flying round about the town and surrounding territory, but never entering the Hudson home. Mrs. Hudson was a true grizzly bear mother on this most particular point, in the protection of her little female cubs. All the while, she, herself, was shocked, grieved, frustrated and flustered: every time she heard anything from anybody relating to speculations of an engagement between the fair Cadence and the rich Bentley. Mrs. Hudson was also especially guarded when she and her family all went to church together each Sunday, she being suddenly uncharacteristically unwilling to arrive early or to leave in a tardy manner (for visitation's sake of any friend: near, dear or otherwise; or indeed, beholding to any other reason at all); for mother and wife whisked her entire family in and out of the church so briskly (as if she were now a whirlwind of unsociability), that all her acquaintances and friends (who were not *in* on her secret complete) wondered what the woman was about.

Most fortunately, Florence and Cadence had not caught even a wisp of a wind of any hints of the tattle about any of it, as yet. Besides erecting a grand wall as a fortress around about her house, Mrs. Hudson was running about, trying to gather flying and floating feathers of gossip that she might attempt to bag all rumors up to prevent Cadence any distress, or moreover, to cause Mrs. Bentley to hear of and then wish to end the affair before it had wholly begun. While Mrs. Hudson was all success in keeping prattle from Cadence, she felt as if she could do little to keep any of it from Mrs. Bentley. Mrs. Hudson gave thanks many a time that Mrs. Bentley was most oft in her home and not the kind of woman to engage in prattling around or listening to any common gossip around the town. Just to be certain of how things were with Mrs. Bentley, Mrs. Hudson went over bearing gifts to visit her often. All seemed well, although even Mrs. Hudson could see that Mrs. Bentley was all curiosity as to the sudden transformation of her neighbor towards her in such very great efforts to become happily intimate friends.

Suddenly, any female tongue that was ever in the habit of spreading any word to anyone, was wagging with the most exciting news! Bentley was come home! Bentley must be home for Cadence's sake! The word that the little countryside birds told round about was that Bentley temporarily paused or even forsook his European tour of study to come back to secure his most virtuous Cadence for matrimony. When Mrs. Hudson heard the news, she was all agog to her husband about it and determined that the Hudson family must invite the Bentley family over post-haste! Mary was sent into high gear to prepare everything. Mr. Hudson was required to say yes to every little or extravagant expense that his wife deemed a necessity. Indeed, Mrs. Hudson was so very ecstatically beside herself with a frenzied joy about young Jonathan Bentley's return home to his family and their general neighborhood that she could not even bring herself to mention the fact to Cadence for fear of gushing over the matter so passionately that everything that mother suspected would instantaneously be revealed to daughter.

Just as Mrs. Hudson was about to have her husband invite the Bentley family over, an invitation to dinner came to the Hudson home from the Bentley house! Mrs. Hudson begged her husband to announce the event to his daughters, for she still feared to give all her secret thoughts away to her astutely perceptive Cadence. Cadence was overjoyed. Seeing this reaction in her daughter made Mrs. Hudson all the more jubilant. Oh, but, all needed to happen soon, for Mrs.

Hudson feared that she would have a fit of a seizure just over the excitement of the anticipative waiting for everything to come out! How much more of such could a loving mother endure?!

Though Mrs. Hudson was most expectant of a grand dinner party including a generous guest list, she was most pleasantly surprised to see that only *they*, the Hudson family, had been invited to a very intimate dinner at the Bentley home. Mrs. Hudson had made certain to have her husband give lengthy lectures of instruction to their sons as to demanded behavior for that most auspicious evening. Jake and Hank were to be all that they could be in the way of manners and etiquette. Mrs. Hudson even took to calling them Jacob and Henry for the evening, in part to constantly impress upon the boy's minds the necessary formality of the occasion (by using their formal names), but also to lift her sons esteems up in the minds of Mr. and Mrs. Bentley.

The evening was a grand success in Mrs. Hudson's mind. Her boys were on their very best behavior and so did not cause any distraction, displeasure or discomfort whatsoever to anyone of the party. Indeed, Jake and Hank were as quiet as mice and as still as rocks, behaving entirely befitting of their formal names: Jacob and Henry. Cadence and young Bentley were both perceptibly joyful in each other's company. Mrs. Hudson's fair Cadence and the wonderful Jonathan Bentley were deep in conversation about the east and Europe, and a great many other things all the evening through. Indeed, the two lovebirds could not seem to be separated for a moment, for they were obviously fast and faithful friends, and oh so much more. Florence joined in on their conversations much of the time, and this did not seem to displease the young Bentley in the least way, whatsoever. What an agreeable young man he had become. To be sure, he had always been an agreeable lad. What a perfect son-in-law he would make. What a perfect brother to Florence, Jake and Hank.

In the midst of the evening, Bentley even admitted that it was Cadence's letter to him, urging him to come home for a visit before his departure, which convinced him that he so thoroughly missed his home, family and friends and thus he must (and had managed to) rearrange his plans to come home for an extended visit. An *extended* visit, mind you! Mrs. Hudson was filled with great joy to an unexplainably immeasurable degree.

By the end of the evening, Mrs. Hudson had proffered an invitation to the entire Bentley family to come to the Hudson home for dinner especially soon and had procured a happy acceptance. Dinner with the Bentley family at the Hudson home turned out much like their first dinner together in the Bentley home. All was pleasant bliss. Cadence and young Bentley continued their seeming courtship. Florence, Jake and Hank joined in on the pleasant conversations. Jonathan Bentley seemed in the clouds joyful over his renewed acceptance by all the Hudson family. Even Mr. Hudson enjoyed getting to know young Bentley better. It was also excessively apparent to Mrs. Hudson that Mr. and Mrs. Bentley approved of them all and most particularly of Cadence.

Mr. Hudson was fast becoming convinced by his wife that perhaps Bentley *was* for Cadence after all and that she would feel in kind towards him. Mr. Hudson advised his wife to wait patiently, though she wished to interfere to hurry things along. Mrs. Hudson became so anxious to have an engagement done and announced publicly, that she began to add such a wish to her nightly prayers. She begged the heavens above to secure all things between her Cadence and that superb Bentley boy. Surely it had become high time for their betrothal! What could keep them apart now?

16
Other Offers

After Jonathan Bentley had returned to the neighborhood, the tongues of womenfolk all around were wagging about the impending engagement of young Bentley and his Cadence all the more. Much frustration was felt and expressed round about due to neither Bentley nor Cadence being seen much in public. Folks wished to see the two together. What were they about? Were they colluding in a sort of rendezvous kind of hiding? However, the little that Bentley was out and about *without* Cadence did happen to cause some hopeful women to throw their daughters at him as bait for a different option of marriage than what was so widely speculated to be so nearly settled. Some mothers felt that until the thing was done, there was still a chance for one of their own girls to secure the worthy young Bentley.

Generally unaware of other mothers' labors to try to snag Bentley for their daughters, Mrs. Hudson worked her own motherly machinations in efforts to secure Bentley for Cadence. Mrs. Hudson near continually invited the entire Bentley family (and also young Jonathan Bentley by himself) over to dinner many, many times. The two families were getting along famously. The Hudson boys were looking up to their older friend Jonathan in an increasingly vast measure and holding him and his character in higher and loftier esteem by the day. Jake and Hank were required to be on their very best behaviors so very often, that such practicing was bringing about somewhat of a change in the boys and thus, as they approached the earliest stages of young manhood, they were being aptly prepared to stand up as worthy male citizens in and around the town. Both mother and father were becoming prodigiously proud of their young upstanding sons.

The ever budding and glowing rapport between Cadence and Bentley was a thing at least reported through town by the means of Mary, who was always observing and listening (as any attentive housemaid would tend to do), and also by way of Mrs. Darby's knowledge due to Mrs. Hudson keeping her friend up to date on every tiny event or thrill from her own motherly perspective. At least the town prattlers were somewhat satisfied to have these bits and pieces of news emanating from the Hudson household, though any self-respecting busybody knows that when two people are on the verge of an engagement towards matrimony, the least that they can do is to be seen courting a little in full public view, that all eyes may have a chance at getting the slightest glimpse towards their fill of the affair. A diminutive peek now and then seemed a minimal requirement.

Though there was no solid or proper source for the report, even still, speculative news *was* that young Mr. Jonathan Bentley would engage himself to his beloved Cadence, continue on to Europe to finish off his studies, and then return to marry his betrothed in a year's time before beginning work for his father's business. Cadence was to play piano and read while she waited the year or so. All seemed fixed and planned for their future.

Unexpectedly, the bees began to buzz all the more and fast into a frenzied wild commotion when a certain person arrived back on the scene. Worthington was returned! The entire territory became agog with the news! Little birds were flitting about with this conjecture and that. Rumors had it that Worthington had come back to rescue his own prior claimed damsel from the other prince who was now vying for her affections. There was even some succulent speculation that there might end up being a duel between Worthington and Bentley, for it was feared that passions might flare up greatly between the two competing suitors, since it was not quite decided whether or not Cadence might still be considering Worthington after all. If Cadence could not decide which man to choose, perhaps the young men would choose between themselves in a fight to the death as such contests may indeed end in. Who would be the last man standing? Who would win Cadence for marriage?

Mrs. Hudson was all distressed as she was brought bits, pieces and snippets from Mary and Mrs. Darby, and with Worthington now on the scene, Cadence's mother was all confusion. Because of his frequent business with Mr. Hudson, Worthington was many times over at the house and though there was no sign that Cadence liked him any more than before (and it still seemed quite clear that she liked Bentley far more), Mrs. Hudson could plainly see how heartbroken Worthington still was over Cadence, and thus said mother was fairly worried that Worthington could upset the entire match between Bentley and Cadence. Bentley was of such a gentle nature that perhaps he might be frightened off by Worthington. If Bentley got wind of Worthington's former proposal to Cadence (for it had been in the air for quite some time), or if Bentley suspected any attachment for Cadence on Worthington's side, perhaps Bentley might walk away from Cadence altogether; out of honor, fear or otherwise. Mrs. Hudson speedily worked herself into a frenzied state as she lamented to her husband about her enormous and assorted anxieties. What was a mother to do in such an event and quandary? She tended to assume that there was nothing that she should do that could guarantee other than to complicate matters and perhaps speed the demise of the almost match she had become so dependent on.

As a dotingly good husband often is wont to do, Mr. Hudson did offer to solve everything for his poor distressed wife by taking all matters into his own hands. He told his dear wife that he could talk to both Bentley and Worthington separately, and then also to Cadence, to see what was what and what may be. As a father, he could set things to right. He could get Cadence married off to one of the lads and be done with the mess. Yes, one young man's heart must be temporarily broken in the midst of the arrangements, but such was life and Cadence must choose only one husband, even if perchance she now loved two young men. Mrs. Hudson was beside herself distressed all the more. Her definitive answer was an absolute and resounding *no*. Mr. Hudson dare not interfere and must refrain from so doing, just as she must. They must wait and see what would be.

Now, Florence had been observing her fair sister with Bentley all the while before Worthington had returned, and no sooner was Florence thoroughly convinced of a coming match between her twin and their childhood friend Bentley than Worthington came and threw hints of doubts into her mind. Florence had bit her tongue on the matter long enough. It was high time for her to ask her sister where her heart resided.

"Have you anything to tell me, my dear sister?"

Cadence looked up from her near sitting though lounging position on her bed, for the two sisters were visiting late at night in the pianist's room, "I... do not know... what you mean?"

"Oh... merciful heavens, I have held my tongue long enough! I cannot wait any longer for you to decide to open the discussion or divulge to me on your own accord... I must ask you... are you and Bentley to be engaged towards marriage?"

"Bentley and me?!" Cadence was astoundingly surprised.

"You are *not* to marry Bentley, then? You do not love him?" Florence was quizzically astonished.

"Bentley and I are... fast friends. I... do not think that we could ever be anything more to each other."

Florence forcefully corrected, "No! I am sure you are wrong... at least in the way things are on Bentley's side. He is *passionately* in love with you. It is clear for all to see!"

Cadence was perplexed and shocked, "*No*... that could not be... I have not felt any sign... no... we are only like brother and sister... surely you see more than what is there between us."

"I was certain that you loved him and he you. Perhaps he only loves you, then. Oh, my dear sister... you may be about to break *another* heart! You should not have encouraged him so."

"It cannot be... I cannot believe that Bentley loves me... we are truly only good friends... indeed, I say again... we are only like brother and sister... as we have long been."

"My dear sweet sister… I fear that he has been led *by* you to love you… far beyond something brotherly." Florence shook her head very slowly.

Cadence was all concern. She had not thought of such a thing before. She had seen no sign that Bentley loved her. Her mind filled with lamenting for having been so friendly and unguarded with her dear childhood friend. Oh, that she might not break another heart! She still could not wash Worthington's sad looks from her mind. She hoped in her heart and soul that Bentley did not love her in that way.

Florence warned, "You will need to amend your ways… or Bentley will offer you marriage. So, he has not asked you as yet then?"

"No! Nothing of that nature, to be sure… we have never talked of anything relating at all to…" Cadence worried further. She had seen no signs with Worthington either. His proposal had come at her blindly and she had been entirely unprepared to answer him properly, save for her sister's prior hint of a warning.

Florence pressed, "Cadence… think… or should I say… feel… are you certain that you do not love Bentley?"

"I am certain." Cadence's face displayed true sadness as she near bewailed, for her soul was aching with the question of whether or not Bentley loved her, as well as other related questions.

Florence saw her sister's pain and was quick to her side to comfort her with the fondest of sisterly embraces. Cadence began to weep. Florence did not quite know what to do. It was usually herself who was weeping and being consoled by Cadence. Why should her steady sister be crying? Florence risked, "What is it? What is the matter, dearest Cadence?"

Cadence cried all the more at feeling her sister's compassion for her own heartbreak. Florence held Cadence as she wept for a time. Fairly soon, Cadence was able to fully compose herself to begin to explain, though with a few attendant tears and occasional sobs, "Oh, Florence… what am I to do… no… I do not love Bentley any more or in any other way, than the way I love our brothers… though…

though... I must finally confess to you that... that I have been long since realizing that... that I *do* love... Worthington."

Florence was all astonishment, "Worthington! *Worthington*? You love Worthington?"

Having at long last declared her suppressed feelings to her sister, Cadence suddenly felt a joy surge through her and thus her tears turned happy, "*Yes*! I love Worthington! I do love him... ever so dearly! I do wish so much now to marry him! I deeply regret... that I did not realize my true feelings for him before... before I rejected him."

"And now he is come back! You must *tell* him!" Florence was thrilled at such news, her thoughts being on Cadence and Worthington's future happiness together, though having forgotten poor Bentley for the moment.

Cadence turned broken-hearted once more, "*How*?! How can I tell him? What if he has... stopped loving me? I... I can scarce look at him. I cannot seem to speak to him. I do not know what he is feeling now. He barely looks at me and does not speak to me either. Does he despise me now? Does he still have any loving feelings for me? Do I have any chance with him now? Would he... could he possibly offer marriage to me again? I feel such a passionate love for him now, but..."

Florence strongly desired to know all, "When did this all come about... and how? Please tell me all, Cadence! You must explain all to me! I cannot sit *still* here wondering over every detail!"

"I think it was... *after* Worthington's declaration of love to me... at first I felt such a compassion for him... for his heartbreak... because of me... because of my rejection of his love. Compassion began to turn into other feelings... and he had gone away... as if forever. My regrets for him became my own regrets for me as well. The more I thought about him, the more I began to feel a love for him. Perhaps to *be* loved... is to begin to love. Knowing that he loved me enough to offer marriage to me, made me begin to think... to think about our fast friendship... our many moments of pleasant conversation... our mutual interests... I began to thoroughly feel how dear he had grown to me in all the time I had known him."

Florence seemed to comprehend all, "Ah... I see what you have been feeling and thinking. After feeling so very badly about declining his offer, you thought about him such a great deal that your worry over his injured heart, opened up your *own* heart towards him."

"Yes... that seems to explain it all."

Florence simply smiled. Cadence continued, "I was confused at first, but somehow my thoughts... any wariness about marriage in general... my thoughts that Worthington was only a mere friend to me... it all became entangled with my feelings... my thoughts seemed to fade towards... or begin to turn in to feelings, *instead*... and then I began to feel a love for Worthington... beyond the kind of love one feels for a friend or a brother. I now love Worthington... enough to marry him. I truly do love him."

Florence became all quizzical, "It all seems so strange to me now. You were all friendly-like with Worthington until he declared his love for you. You have been, and continue to be so very friendly with Bentley... and now... you *know* that you love Worthington... and yet, you do not approach any sign of friendliness with him. How will Worthington ever know that you finally love him if you do not show it?"

Cadence was all worry, "I *know*! I cannot seem to force myself in that direction. It is all ease for me to speak openly with Bentley, though I cannot bring that conversational friendliness back with Worthington. It is all my fears, and my feelings, of course. If I knew that Worthington still loved me, perhaps I could speak with him as we did before. But, try as I might... and believe me... I know that it has not shown... but I have tried... I have tried to be myself again with Worthington... but I cannot manage it! I so fear... his rejecting me... his rejection of my love for him! What will I do?!"

Florence pondered. Cadence furthered, "I do not know how to let him know that I love him now. I fear to truly try, for I could not bear his spurning of my own love towards him."

"Perchance you should put it all in Father's hands, for he may be able to settle everything for you." Florence suggested in earnest.

Cadence recoiled, "No... no, I cannot... I do not dare... I fear to try that... what if... oh... I feel so very mortified for having rejected Worthington's first, best offer. I cannot imagine Father wishing to be connected to the case again, for he was so sadly disappointed... I do not think that I have ever seen him quite like that before. He truly felt deeply for the broken heart of his young friend and associate... and did not understand what I was about in passing on such an offer... particularly being that Worthington and I were such dear friends. Mother was most unhappy as well."

"Father and Mother knew? Why have you not told me of this before?"

"Worthington asked Father's permission for my hand before offering his to me, and Father near instantly knew that I had declined the worthy offer. Mother quickly became aware of the matter. I was taken in to Father's library to be chided and scolded most severely. Forgive me for not having told you... but, I simply wished to forget the entire business and carry on as usual."

Florence paused and then lit up with a sincere offer, "I will tell Worthington! Leave it all to me!"

Cadence considered. She truly considered at some length whilst Florence sat on edge with baited breath. Cadence's first answer was her final one, "No. No... I could not bear even that. I do not wish for you to intervene for me where I cannot work something out for myself. I must let the fates decide or the angels interfere *for* me. I cannot take matters into my own hands nor allow you to do such for me. No. You must abstain from doing anything for me in this."

Florence considered suggesting and protesting this or that thing to convince her sister of other wisdom in the matter, but, she could see that Cadence was thoroughly determined to stand by her decision and thus Florence remained mute on the point. They both sat silent for a length of time before speaking of other things. Cadence seemed wishing to speak of any other thing. It was clear to Florence that Cadence's heart was truly breaking, though her feelings were so well hidden from the world.

When Florence finally retired to her own room, sitting by her candle pondering in the still darkness of that night, she firmly decided that she must secretly handle and fix everything for her dear beloved angelic sister. She must save her sister from herself. Cadence was in no frame of mind to think clearly. Her heart was heavy and her mind was muddled. Her judgment could not be trusted. Yes, Florence determined that she would first speak to Worthington about Cadence to determine if his heart was still safely true to the pianist. Once knowing such, Florence would confess to him of Cadence's love for him, and could then press and encourage poor Worthington to try again with Cadence. If Worthington still loved Cadence enough to marry her, and was assured of her love in return for him, he would surely find the courage to risk his heart one more time, since, knowing his heart was truly safe with Cadence, it would be no risk to his heart at all!

Completely contented with her decision to save her sister, Florence's still active though sleepy mind drifted to suddenly find the poor forgotten Bentley! Oh, dear, poor Bentley! She would have to take care of poor Bentley as well. Who else could do it in time?! He must be let down as gently as could be, in keeping with the situation. Poor, poor Bentley's dear and kind heart! Yes, Florence must try to save Bentley's heart as much as could be. Once it was determined by painter that Worthington would again ask Cadence to join him in matrimony, Florence would have to swiftly take Bentley aside to let him know that Worthington and Cadence loved each other, before any engagement between them could be announced to all the world!

Florence could not allow Bentley to discover from bees, little birds, the wind, innocuous busybodies or more especially, vicious gossips: that Cadence was to be married to Worthington. No, Florence must kindly break the difficult news to him, to ease his pain. Florence realized that she should also tell all to Bentley. He should know of Worthington's former declined offer to Cadence and Cadence's subsequent falling for him. Perhaps if he knew that Worthington was so much there before him (that Worthington had come to know so well and then had declared his loved to Cadence while Bentley had been away for so very long), then Bentley would not take the news so terribly hard. Florence truly did not wish for Bentley to be terribly hurt. Indeed, she did not wish for Bentley's heart to be harmed in any way, but if his heart must be injured, she would do all she could to ease its wound and to restore his heart as much as she could do as his childhood friend. She knew that Bentley had always been so much more friend to Cadence, though she also knew herself as his dear sister. She would be his sister, a sister and friend that he could lean on when his heart was aching, for his heart would be broken *because* of Cadence, and Cadence would have no power to mend Bentley's heart in any way. Florence must and surely could be up to that task. Florence would lovingly mend Bentley's broken heart.

As a few days progressed, Florence went about her chosen sincerely important tasks, and because she truly believed that she could not leave anything to fate (and so could not wait for chance meetings with either young man), she unfortunately was compelled to risk reaching beyond propriety somewhat by seeking out and thereby forcing meetings with both Worthington and Bentley. In the light of day, Florence was seen with each young man, here and there, by busy bees and squawking birds. And thus, scandalously delicious rumors began to fly about the countryside. It was speculated and then carried on the wind that Florence was trying to steal either Bentley or Worthington from Cadence to keep for herself. What kind of sister was this?! To orchestrate two improper clandestine meetings with each of Cadence's beaux?! How could Florence do such a thing? She must have no heart! Florence must surely be purely mercenary or entirely jealous of her poor twin sister to be doing such a horrid thing! Who would Florence marry?! Would Worthington or Bentley be manipulated by such a young woman? Could Florence possibly convince either young man to turn from Cadence and spurn her, to then marry Florence?!

The furious fiery gossip swiftly reached poor Mrs. Hudson's ear, for Mary and Mrs. Darby were always at the ready to deliver her any morsel, or especially such flaming feasts. Though she would not believe that Florence could possibly do such a thing against dearest Cadence, the poor woman's ears were burning just the same, and she was beside herself distressed over the matter. Mrs. Hudson was found pacing the halls of her house (all the while hiding from her daughters, for fear of saying the wrong thing or even anything of the matter) by her husband when he came home early that evening. After discussing all such as husband and wife in Mr. Hudson's private library, Mrs. Hudson was convinced to bide her time waiting patiently, bite her tongue and say absolutely nothing, and let the thing play out to see what would be. Mr. Hudson assured her that things were not what they seemed, gossips were most usually very wrong and that all would likely turn out well. Mrs. Hudson did not do nor sleep well that night and kept to her room the next day.

Mrs. Hudson did not see Worthington take Cadence into the garden for an audience with him. He did not speak first. Cadence did not think that she could, but (after all her talk with Florence about leaving all to the fates and angels), she had quite suddenly realized that she must exert herself (now that she saw her chance to do something) and she did firmly believe that she must do her utmost to extend herself to let Worthington know that he should try for her hand once again.

Cadence leapt in, "Mr. Worthington... Connor... I must speak with you. I... since you... because you... well... I..."

Worthington nervously interjected, "Miss Hudson... Cadence... I must speak to you as well... I..."

Cadence was all anxiety, "I was over-cautious before... I was thinking too much... I did not allow myself to feel... and after you were gone away... I began to realize...well... tell me it is not all too late for me. Have you *changed* your mind... your heart... your opinion of me?"

Worthington's manner eased, "Cadence... when I returned... I did not know... I saw you and Bentley together..."

"It was not as you might have thought... we are only good friends... like brother and sister..."

Worthington smiled broadly, "Like brother and sister... such words of yours in reference to me, haunted me so much before…"

Cadence repented her words but could not take them back, "Oh… I am so very sorry… I did not mean… it is different now… with you… I…"

Still smiling, Worthington continued, "I will confess that I was heartbroken to see you with Bentley… your friendly rapport… your obvious high regard for one another… I thought that my broken heart would take quite some time longer to mend for it broke a good deal more at the thought of you and Bentley… at seeing you both… thinking that he had won your heart where I had lost…"

Cadence was on edge, "Connor…"

With a most confident smile, Worthington calmly posed, "Cadence, will you be my wife?"

Taken thoroughly aback at first but instantaneously shocked most happily, Cadence instinctively went against her steady nature and passionately threw herself into Mr. Connor Worthington's arms. After a brief ecstatically euphoric embrace on both their parts, Miss Cadence Hudson pulled herself away to compose herself towards propriety once more, stood back ever so slightly and spoke, though not all too calmly, "Oh Connor! I feared that I had passed over the only man I could ever truly love and be happy with!"

Also composing himself, Mr. Connor Worthington answered with a hearty chuckle, "I know… I *knew*."

Cadence looked up ever so quizzically at her now secured man, who swiftly attempted to clarify, "Florence explained…"

"Florence?" Cadence queried.

"Yes, Florence… she spoke with me about you and…"

"But I told her not to… I… oh, that *angel* sister of mine!"

Worthington and Cadence were as blissful as any newly attached couple ever could be. Though they both felt like shouting out from the rooftops to announce their fresh engagement, Cadence requested a little pause of secrecy before announcing their betrothal to the world. She explained that she wished to assure herself that all things were in entire order for propriety's sake. She was comforted to be promptly told by Worthington that he had once again sought approval from her father before asking her a second time, also having explained enough to Mr. Hudson to set his mind at rest that the outcome would be favorable this second attempt. Connor did not feel the need to ask if there were any specific reasons for Cadence's wish for a temporary secrecy and postponement to announcing their mutual joy to the world around them. He gladly gave his new fiancé her secret due.

Cadence did not find it necessary to go into any explanation (lengthy or otherwise) about not wishing to injure Bentley. She felt a need to compose herself to know what was best to be done about the poor fellow. She thought that perhaps tomorrow would tell her what she should do, although, the next day, Bentley asked Cadence to walk into the garden with him. Cadence was horrifyingly unprepared. What could she say to a proposal from Bentley without injuring his heart?! Oh, the disaster of it all. There was never any way to come out of such a situation bearing roses instead of thorns!

Bentley's inquiry was so tremendously sudden that it took Cadence's breath away, "I... wish to know... if... I have a chance... with... *Florence*."

"Florence!" Cadence near fell down, though she managed to steady herself to stay standing.

"Could she be convinced to someday love... me? I have loved *her* forever, you see."

Cadence's eyes were as wide as ever, "You... have *loved*... Florence?!"

"Yes. I love her. I have loved her since we were all children playing together... I have loved her. I always feared that she was beyond my reach... that she could never consider me... she is so very... effervescent... but perhaps you could ask her... tell her... for me. You see... after reading your letter to me, I decided that I could not go away for so terribly long without trying for... Florence. More than a year is such an eternity and I deeply feared that *another* man would surely secure her heart before I had even half a chance to. I dared not wait until my final return..."

Cadence smiled, shaking her head. Bentley continued, "I decided that as difficult a task as it seems to me... and though my heart may be dashed to pieces... I must at least let Florence know how I feel about her before going away. I had planned to write to her to tell her... but... your letter... well... I suddenly felt compelled to come home and try... *something.*"

Cadence was overjoyed that she did not need to worry over Bentley's heart because of herself and Worthington, and she thought that perhaps stranger things had happened than someone like Florence learning to love someone like Bentley.

Cadence attempted to comfort Bentley in his most interesting sort of distressing state, as she felt instant compassion for him, and also a sudden inspiration within, of a firmly powerful epiphany, "Bentley... I do believe that Florence loving you *might* be possible. Indeed, I do. I have seen no true sign as yet of her loving you beyond friend and brother, but...I do know that she *does* love you deeply in that brotherly friend way already... and I surely know of at least *one* solid happy case where a deep friendship and brotherly, sisterly kind of love quickly turned into a truly matrimonial kind and depth of love."

"*Truly*?!" Bentley was all suddenly, happily hopeful.

"Yes, truly... Bentley, let this be my solemn promise to you as your dear friend and as if a sister, that I will do *all* in my power to help Florence at least give you a chance at a love that will lead you both towards a happy marriage together."

Bentley sighed deeply, standing taller, gaining in faith and strength. With a grand smile, Cadence tried, "Bentley, my dear boy, leave all things to me for now. Allow me to speak with Florence... let me work on her... I may have to take things a little gradually, for your best bet... though I will let you know how things go. Worry not. I have a very good *feeling* about all this. I cannot think but that Florence very well may be convinced to love and marry you."

Pitifully though mostly happily, Bentley answered in a query, "Do you *really* think so?"

"I do believe so. She is so very fond of you... she thinks so very highly of you already... she loves you so much in every other way...

it seems to me that bringing her to love you *enough* to marry you will not be so very difficult a thing to manage, after all."

Bentley's eyes lit up as if candles flickering in the midst of a cheerful wind. Cadence sent him away with many happy thoughts and hopes. Cadence began her grand plans in regards to Florence. If she had not thought her thoughts and plans divinely inspired and truly providential, she would not have dared to attempt any such thing. Indeed, such machinations were generally so beyond her very nature. But, Cadence was full of confidence where her feelings, heart and soul were concerned this day, and she also felt a great debt of gratitude to her sister for intervening in the way that Florence had done to help heaven's efforts along in bringing herself and Worthington together.

That very night, Cadence took herself to Florence's room the moment family movements towards retiring for the evening began. She had previously thought that she would break the new interesting idea to her sister quite gradually (over a number of days at least), but, surprising near as much to herself as to her sister, she could not seem to help but plunge in.

"Florence! I must *tell* you of what happened today!"

Florence looked to her sister, smiling with a deeply great inward satisfaction, sensing that news of Worthington and a betrothal with her sister was about to unfold.

Cadence stepped back slightly in her thoughts to first say, "Oh, but… I near *forgot*! I must thank you from the bottom of my heart, my dearest angelic sister! It is a very great secret for a short time, but, Worthington and I are engaged, thanks be all to you and heaven above!"

Florence accepted the instantly offered hearty embrace thrown at her by her ecstatic sister. Before Florence could pause to enjoy some much awaited lengthy conversation (on her part) about Worthington and her sister, Cadence once again could not remain silent.

"Florence! You will not believe what *else* happened today!"

Florence's curiosity rose.

Cadence revealed, without thinking through what was best for her to say at all, "Bentley took me into the garden… I thought he was about to propose to me… I was all mortification… I did not know *how* I was going to be able to let him down gently… I did not wish to break his heart… but then… what do you know? He asked me about *you*?! He told me that he loved you! He said that he has loved you since we were all children playing together! His heart has remained constant to you *all* along! Can you believe it?! We feared that he loved me… but he has been in love with you all along! He returned home for you! He feared that you could never find interest in him, but he did not wish to risk losing you to another man while he was away. He pines for you to give him a chance… he hopes and prays that perhaps you could someday love him! I told him that I would speak to you. Are you not… shocked?! What do you think? Could you… consider… loving Bentley? Do you think that you could learn to love him… enough to marry him?"

Florence sat still, trying to absorb the stunning news. She began pondering deeply.

Cadence began trying with another kind of approach, "I'm sure this is all too sudden. I have shaken you. You appear truly dazed… you surely do. I should not have said so much all at once. Did I *assume* too much? Could you not ever love Bentley in that way? You only could ever love him as brother and friend as I do? Do please say something my dear sister. Do I need apologize profusely for telling him that I would try with you for him? I only wished to repay you for talking to Worthington for me. Oh, dear… have I overstepped my bounds enormously? Will Bentley's heart be broken after all? We can at least *forestall* such… if we are careful. Shall we let him think that perhaps he has a little chance with you… for a time… and then help him to gradually get used to the idea that you only love him like I do?"

Florence slowly turned her head, all seriousness, and took a very deep breath before she spoke, "You know… I was shocked… truly quite shocked… at first… but… suddenly… it seems to me that all such simply *fits*. It all makes great sense to my mind. I truly think that I am finally ready to settle down with a quiet, calm, gentle man…

you know… instead of the dashingly stylish, flirtatious flattering types that I have been pining over, wishing for and wasting my time with heretofore. Bentley is *exactly* the kind of man that I do need. To tell you truthfully, I am enamored to know that he has loved me all this time. How very *romantic* of him! I never suspected! I thought that he loved you! I truly did! When I spoke to him of you… Bentley never… I could not see what he was feeling about me!"

"You spoke to Bentley about me?"

"Yes… I could not allow Bentley to hear of your engagement with Worthington in a public way… after I knew that he would try again for you… and of course I knew that you would accept him… so, I knew that I must save Bentley from hurt and harm as much as could possibly be. I broke the news to him as gently as I could."

"You spoke to Bentley to try to soften the blow!"

"Yes… and he did not give himself away one jot! I did not suspect his heart was mine for even a fraction of moment! Oh, but he does hide his feelings so very well!"

"Well… you were looking in quite another direction… you were so diverted thinking that he loved me… that you did not have eyes to see clearly that it was *you* that he loved all the while!"

"To know that he has been so tremendously constant to me… to think that he has *always* loved me… that is… just so… excessively *attracting* to me. He feared I could not love him?! How darling! Could he be sweeter… than to love me so passionately all this long while… and yet to hide his feelings so guardedly? I have been his *secret* love all these years?! Oh, beautiful Bentley! I think maybe… I also have loved him… even unbeknownst to myself… in an inner hidden way… all along!"

Cadence was quite happily shocked, "Do you really think so? You could love him… you have loved him… you would… *marry* him?"

Florence gushed, "Oh yes… and you know… to marry a dearest friend… that must be the very *best* thing, after all!"

Cadence happily concurred, "To be sure… I do believe that to be best of friends with your own husband is the kind of thing that truly makes love last a lifetime and beyond."

Leaning back, Florence sighed with a joyful smile, "You know… Bentley suddenly seems to me to be all the more handsome and tall… you know… simply because he loves me so very much… and has always remained so excessively faithful… to me. He has loved me… and me alone… even when far away for so very long… and meeting many lovely young lasses, I am sure… to be sure… to be sure. Just think, my dear sweet sister… my beloved Bentley passed all those other females over, for his memory of me and our childhood days. And it is not as if I was cognizant of anything enough to give him any encouragement my way. I did not write an answer to any of his letters to our family! How very horrid of me… and yet he continued to love me! It is *you*, my dear sweet darling sister, who kept the fire burning brightly with your own letters back to him, as if for me in his heart! Oh, what a sister you have been to me. Oh, what a fool and a heartless idiotic baggage I have been! I could have lost him for my folly. If he had not been… if he was not such a tremendously good sort of person… such a magnificent young man… surely his head would have been turned to and fro and he would have forgotten me almost instantly! I am very certain that there were plenty of young women who threw themselves at him out east, you know! With him being so very tall and handsome… and rich as well… of course he must have been fairly accosted with beautiful young ladies. And he stayed constant and faithful to me through it all! It is truly quite amazing of him to save himself so fully for me.

And here I was… behaving so horridly stupidly with such… stupid horrid men… wasting my heart on such unworthy blackguards. I was flirting with rogues and we know what I got for it. Bentley loved me truly without any flirting or machinations on my side. All the while… there was Bentley… far, far away from home… confronted by temptation after temptation… and yet he stayed so steady in his heart towards me! What a man amongst men he surely is! Oh, thank my lucky stars and the heavens above that you wrote to him to beg his return home and that he had the sense and the heart to *comply*! I do believe that though he came back home hoping to begin to secure me… it is I who was saved… it was I who was able to secure *him* through lucky fate and divine providence… and angelic interference… for he did not go off to Europe to become bewitched by some foreign young woman over there! Those romantic and exotic French or Italian ladies could have forced him against his very will to forget me! Perchance a fine young noble English lady might have erased his memory of our sweet happy childhood days together! Oh! To think that I might have lost my beloved Bentley before I ever knew that he was mine and meant to be for me! I am his woman! I am a new woman! I have been changed from a lowly horrid caterpillar into a noble and beautiful butterfly! My Bentley *loves* me!"

Cadence finally put a word in edgewise, "May I tell him… to ask for your hand… tomorrow?"

"Oh, yes… I will surely say *yes* to him! I cannot believe my good fortune! My own Bentley!" Florence swooned.

"He will be beside himself in shock, I dare say!" Cadence happily announced.

"Yes! Happy, joyful, heavenly shock!" Florence continued in her heartfelt and passionate swooning.

"I dare say that mother will be shocked as well… and to think that she was thinking us fast becoming spinsters." Cadence chuckled.

Florence giggled, "Oh, yes! We must break it all to her gently, for if we do not take care, she may surely come down with a fainting spell, or even have a fit or a seizure!"

"Yet she will be so very happy to have secured both Bentley and Worthington for her sons. She could not possibly have done better, I dare say."

"Yes, yes, she will be complete joy!" Florence burst forth with a lengthy hug for her beloved sister.

No thought was given by the girls as to *when* their marriages would or could possibly take place. No exact dates were contemplated. For all the twins both knew, they would each marry tomorrow, or a year from now, for such did not seem to matter. They did not seem to grasp the capacity for the moment to worry about such infinitesimal details. They were each too busy feeling in love, speaking to each other of their loves, and drinking in the joy that they were sharing relating to their future separate days of married bliss. They would be spinsters no more, for they each would be wed!

All things were done properly and promptly. Cadence was able to speak to Bentley right away the following day. He was ecstatic shock, but composed himself enough to speak to and request permission from Mr. Hudson at the earliest moment possible. Mr. Hudson was surprised but most satisfied with the news of the assured match. In his suppressed giddiness, he said things such as *m'boy* more times than anyone would wish to recall, though only he and Bentley were any the wiser for it and could soon forget any such silliness from an elated father. Bentley easily stole Florence away to the garden, where, in her favorite purple dress as if the most stunningly gorgeous flower there, she said yes to him almost before he could get the question out to her. Once all such was secured, and Bentley took his joyfully shaken person home to tell his own parents his happy news, Mr. Hudson took Mrs. Hudson into his library where Cadence and Florence were awaiting in giddy splendor. Their mother near fainted at the news of an upcoming double wedding for her twins. She was as much agog with what preparations lay before her as she was to know that both her daughters had successfully accepted offers from most eligible and wonderful young men, whom she and her husband would happily call their own sons forevermore.

As some days progressed, plans were more firmly settled. The twins' wedding would be held almost as soon as possible. There was no need for Florence and Bentley to wait the year to marry since he firmly wished to combine a European wedding tour with finishing his studies abroad. Florence would paint with masters in Europe while her husband completed his own studies, and Mrs. Hudson could imagine herself painting with her daughter in spirit (or simply picture herself painting there in her younger days, with masters many years before). Worthington and Cadence did not care one whit whether they would complete any wedding tour out east or anywhere at all, for they were fixedly thinking of having their house built as soon as may be instead. Within the year or so, both daughters would surely be settled in their own grand homes nearby, for both Bentley and Worthington would be capable of exercising their business efforts and grand plans predominantly in the area, just as Mr. Hudson and old Mr. Bentley had been so very successful in so doing for many a year past.

On a day prior to any engagement announcements yet being made publicly, as Mrs. Hudson prepared to soon go over to beg Mrs. Darby's help in planning the grand wedding of the twins, she suddenly wondered in some distress regarding the most proper or best way to have the betrothals of her twins announced to the world, having just remembered recent unpleasant rumors against her fair daughters that had been soaring round about. She happened to see and then caught Cadence in the front hall and stole her away into her parlor for a discussion as to what might be best to be done.

"Cadence, my dear… I must speak with you on a most urgent matter."

Cadence looked to her mother with concerned inquiry.

"Cadence, I have not told you… well… I was trying to keep it all *from* you… from you and Florence… you see… there have been all manner of horrendous rumors flying about the countryside regarding you and Worthington and Bentley… and Florence and… well… now that all is settled so wonderfully… all the scurrilous gossip truly matters not one jot… but… I wonder what might be the best way to straighten out all the false reports that have been spread amongst the busybodies of our territory…"

"Reports? What reports?" Cadence wondered aloud to her mother.

"Well, the town tattlers… they have been so very busy speculating for weeks… about you and… well… whom you might marry and so forth… well… I need not recall or mention *every* silly or spurious detail… but there was much talk… I was so very distressed through it all… but I told Mary to stay mum… on pain of near death, you know… I did not wish to worry you and Florence… nor did I wish anything of your marriage in the offing to be interfered with… I was so very glad that you and Florence were playing spinsters so much within the house and our properties recently and were saved from it all... but I was *tortured* with everything... I heard it all...had it all from Mary and Mrs. Darby... at least... I could not go anywhere without being burdened with the prattle... I was so very discomfited."

Cadence was stunned to oblivion and back, but managed to shake off caring what might or might not have been said, and simply consoled her mother by patting her hand gently.

Mrs. Hudson continued, "Well... we must announce your engagements in some public way... but I dread the looks and what people might say... you know... everyone thought that you were for Bentley and he was for you... and wondered where or how Worthington might fit in or try to get you back for himself or... and some thought that Florence was trying to steal one or the other away from you... and now it is clear who is for who... and there is to be no duel over you after all and..."

Cadence was shocked to hear the silliness, "Florence stealing one or the other away from me? Duel... over me?"

"Yes, yes... there was no end to the ridiculous speculations... but all that is past now... well... it will... it must... be past... but I do not wish to explain away every stupid rumor one by one... point by point... that would tire me so exceedingly... over and over with *every* person who will ask me all about every little thing... I fear I will have to keep to my bed until just before your weddings simply to avoid all those women and their many questions... each excessively torrid jot... well... perhaps you can help to save me from all that nonsense and horror... I was wondering if there might be a way to straighten everyone out with the least bit of trouble to myself..."

Cadence nodded, understanding near most all and seeing a quick easy solution, "Mother... I would think that the best way to go about these sorts of things is to tell everything you wish to be known to perhaps *one* person whom you know will spread the word for you. Then you will not need worry about telling anything more than once, particularly if you stay home as much as possible initially... you know... until the word has traveled for a short time and the rumor dust has had a chance to settle somewhat... all whilst you begin happily planning our wedding events."

"Yes, yes... that is it... share all I want to be known with one person, who will then tell *all* to others and so forth."

"If you share your happy news about our engagements and some of the pertinent details as to how it all happily came about... you know... to one or maybe two persons... they will each tell a few of their friends and so on. All other false speculations will die away after a very short time... the truth will smother falsehoods... and then when you finally must go to town to order and buy up everything needed for our wedding gowns and dinner and such, all you will hear are *congratulations*."

"Yes... yes... I think that you are right... but, *who* should I tell?"

"Mrs. *Darby*, of course."

"Though she will not tell a soul unless I instruct her to do so." Mrs. Hudson pondered, naively.

Cadence smiled broadly at the thought of her mother's chatty friend being so quiet with such information, "Then give her *permission* to tell just a few trusted friends. That will set the fire in motion, I assure you."

"Why not simply *instruct* her to tell everyone?"

"But then... that would spoil all her fun... you know... to feel like she is keeping some secrets from many folks. No... let her think that you do not wish everyone to know everything."

Mrs. Hudson nodded, but did not entirely understand all that Cadence was implying or insinuating, for Cadence did truly believe that Mrs. Darby would be delighted to spread some sizzling news, and would be far more diligent in so doing if she thought such pertinently fresh news to be somewhat of a secret, rather than if she had been given leave (or worse, *instructions*) to tell everyone everything. If Mrs. Darby thought that she held no secrets whatsoever (that all was already or soon to become common knowledge to all), she might not tell anyone anything, after all. That would not do. No, it would be a far better thing if Mrs. Darby believed that she possessed the very latest buzz, that she held a bee under a hat, contained a bird on the wing, for then a bee would be buzzing furiously in her bonnet and thus she would must needs fly to share everything she now knew with everyone she barely knew. To further secure the spreading of the news, Cadence would tell Mary what she wished to be known, for Cadence *knew* that Mary would be entirely faithful to the task of telling everything that she knew, to every maid or anyone else that she was acquainted with, within many miles round about. And thus, the news would be rapidly spread throughout their territory, with the least degree of distress to the Hudson mother.

When Mrs. Hudson visited Mrs. Darby to share the news of the twins' engagements and how the matches truly came to be, she also relished with delight in planning some parties surrounding the coming weddings, and gaining Mrs. Darby's sage advice based on her many years of experience on all things relative to such events. Mrs. Darby tried to be attentive to her friend regarding planning parties, while she tried her utmost to hide that she truly could not wait to push Mrs. Hudson out of her door, so that she might begin telling all her many trusted friends every tiny detail that she had just found out about the twins and their coming marriages.

All town tattlers and busy gossips in the surrounding territory were very soon thrown into chattering confusion as they ran about, huffing and puffing, trying to set the new truths straight amongst themselves. Cadence was to marry Worthington and Florence to marry Bentley, after all (though some thought and got it the other way around, which truly and fully confused many on the actual crucial points of who was to marry whom)! There was to be no duel over Cadence and for her hand! Everyone was happy!

Most fortuitously, Mrs. Hudson was generally spared from the buzzing noise of all town and territory tattling, for she remained home during the initial blistering commotion, and more precisely, her mind was firmly set upon all such many things that she, as a goodly mother, must prepare for her daughters' weddings. When consulting her husband as to what he would be happy or at least willing to pay for, her grand plans were quickly made smaller and simpler by Mr. Hudson.

"Now that word is spreading regarding our twins' betrothals and the date is fixedly set for their weddings, I must quickly decide how many events we will be able to pull together and throw relating to the final grand event, my dear Mr. Hudson... oh, and also how many people we should invite." Mrs. Hudson began.

"We will have a wedding... and perhaps a dinner... and invite only the most immediate family... and perchance a few of the closest friends... and be done with it." Mr. Hudson thought (or at least hoped) the matter closed.

"No, my dear husband.... everyone expects *other* parties beyond the wedding and dinner." Mrs. Hudson held up her fingers to count off each necessary event, "There must be the engagement party (which I must pull off very soon so that people will not talk and blame me for not doing my duty by my girls), perhaps a rehearsal dinner party for the evening before the wedding ceremony (for we must rehearse everything the day or night before the wedding), of course the wedding (which will be an exceedingly grand event, my dear), the actual wedding dinner itself (which should of course have a band to play for a dance or perchance a grand ball of sorts), perhaps an after wedding party (such as a bon voyage party) for all of us to celebrate after the new grooms and brides are off and gone on their wedding journeys (or tours or whatever they have chosen) and... let me think... I will have to speak with Mrs. Darby further regarding what is expected out here... she was not very forthcoming with ideas when I first spoke to her... I suppose that she must have been suffering under some slight headache... shock at my news... or something..."

"No, my dear wife... I do not see the wisdom in having all these parties. The lads are already caught in our trap, my dear... there is certainly no need to throw party after party. I know that I must pay for a slightly lavish wedding and I understand that I must also pay for a wedding dinner in the form of an abundant feast so that people will not think ill of you... but all these other secondary parties are balderdash."

"But, my dear... I... well... Mrs. Darby reminded me that since the girls are being got off of your hands in one motion... and that you are killing two birds with one stone... or should I say that you are getting two grooms for the price of one... and marrying off two daughters for the trouble of only one... remember... it is a *double* wedding, my dear... well, you could certainly afford to pay for... for more parties than you might have otherwise been willing to pay for... if each daughter had married separately in different seasons or years. Think of what you are *saving!*" Mrs. Hudson tried.

"No... you know that it is in my nature to think of what you are *spending* and if I wish to be saving, I must pull back the reins on you, my dear wife. I count myself blessed to see two daughters married at once... and all without coming-out balls and the like... but, it would surely be folly on my part not to take advantage of the savings opportunity before me, by spending more for no apparently rational reason. No, there will be a wedding and a dinner and perhaps a band to play for some dancing. I do enjoy some dancing with my wife now and then... and if I must pay the piper myself, to hear and dance to the songs of my choosing, so be it." Mr. Hudson smiled.

"Mr. Hudson, you are thwarting my grand plans again." Mrs. Hudson smiled good-naturedly (especially at the thought of dancing together), even though her husband was not being terribly forthcoming with all his money.

"Well... it seems that all your grand plans were not necessary to find the girls worthy husbands after all." Mr. Hudson seemed almost a smidgen smug.

"I suppose so... though it would have been grand to fulfill all my plans by hosting all those parties." Mrs. Hudson sighed slightly.

"Oh, I do not think so, my dear... for in all your efforts to reach perfection as a hostess, you send yourself into a frazzle whenever you orchestrate such a thing." Mr. Hudson reminded.

"Well...you are right there... for 'tis terribly taxing on me to throw a party. I barely lived through the last one."

"And I must protect even my wife from herself. No, it will be few parties for you my dear. I wish to keep you alive a good while longer." Mr. Hudson chuckled.

"I suppose I should thank you then." Mrs. Hudson was truly quite jovial, despite feeling a little pinched for her husband's pennies.

Mr. Hudson became quite thoughtful, "And… I am loathe to take too much credit for my part, but, I did tell you that all these feminine traditions of yours are not necessarily the best or at least the only way to find husbands for one's daughters."

She teased in a correcting tone, "Well, it is not as if *you* rounded up the lads yourself."

"Still… the girls seemed to do fine on their own, I dare say… even after all their talk of becoming spinsters."

"Yes, they surely did find and will marry their young men anyway."

"I knew all along that the job could be done with little trouble or expense." Mr. Hudson seemed all knowing.

"Well… we do not know for certain that all was done with little trouble to our girls…" Mrs. Hudson counseled her man.

"What fuss and bother and trouble! Who needs all these parties, dinners and dances? Men should handle these things, I say. Keep it simple. Women spend far too much time and money on all these sorts of complicated events… and to *what* end? Can all these many social functions justify a man's cash and his wife's sanity, if such can be done better without any of the trouble and expense? I dare say that perhaps I should rein you in even further and refuse to pay for any wedding dinner and such at all. I am tending towards a beautifully simple wedding affair… everyone to the church and then to the train… and perchance that is *all* I will agree to pay for!"

"Oh, Mr. *Hudson*!"

6036643R00140

Made in the USA
San Bernardino, CA
29 November 2013